KEANE'S CHALLENGE

KEANE'S CHALLENGE

IAIN GALE

HERON
BOOKS

First published in Great Britain in 2014 by Heron Books

an imprint of

Quercus Editions Ltd
55 Baker Street
7th Floor, South Block
London W1U 8EW

A CIP catalogue record for this book is available
from the British Library

HB ISBN 978 1 78087 364 0
TPB ISBN 978 1 78206 092 5
EBOOK ISBN 978 1 78087 365 7

This book is a work of fiction. Names, characters,
places and events portrayed in it, while at times based on
historical figures and places, are the product
of the author's imagination.

10 9 8 7 6 5 4 3 2 1

Printed and bound in Great Britain by Clays Ltd, St Ives plc

Typeset by Ellipsis Digital Limited, Glasgow

For

Florence, Rosie and Issy

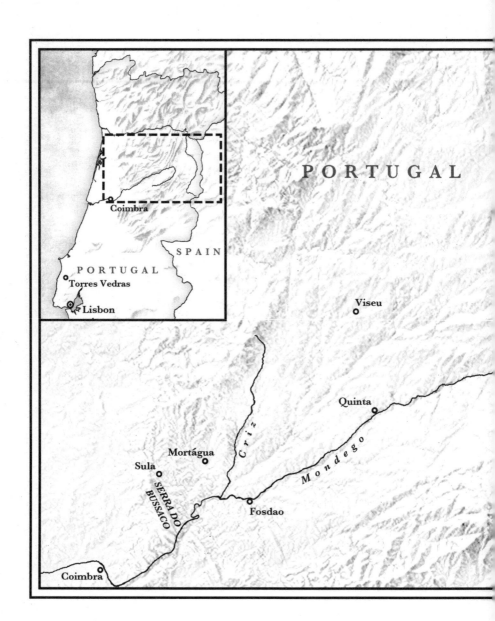

SPAIN

Côa

PLAINS OF LEON

Duas Casas

Pinhel

Alvesco

Barca

Almeida

Villa de la Mula

Fort Concepcion

ornos

Celorico

San Pedro

Alamada

Gallegos

Castello Mendo

Ciudad Rodrigo

Guarda

Richioso

Touronnes

Nava d'Aver

N

W   E

S

0   5   10

Miles

1

A dozen men sat low in their saddles amid the tall pines and stared at the road which wound about the hillside down below them. The sun shone through the trees and the air was heavy with the scent of pine, borne on a slight breeze, but otherwise the day was still. One of the men patted the neck of his horse, which had been startled by some movement close by: a snake perhaps. But not one of the horsemen spoke a word, and when a noise came to them at last it was that for which they had been waiting: the sound of iron-shod horses' hooves on the hard, baked earth of the road. The sound of cavalry. The sound of the French.

Captain James Keane stood up in his stirrups and rose slightly in the saddle, straining to listen, trying to estimate the numbers of the approaching horsemen. Not enough for a squadron. A troop certainly. A company at most. Sixty men. That would do, he thought.

They could hear the jingle of harness now and the whinnying of the fast-approaching horses. And with it the occasional word or two of command, called out in French.

And then they came into view, the sun glinting on the polished brass helmets of the leading troopers: a half-troop of green-coated French dragoons, trotting ahead in skirmish order. From the sweat-flecked flanks of their mounts Keane could see that they had been riding hard and fast for some time, and as he had predicted they would, had slowed down only when they had reached this part of the road where the climb would have made their pace impossible. A trot was the best they could manage now.

The leading party rode, well spaced out, on either side of the road, their carbines drawn, their eyes sweeping the track from side to side. Keane could sense the fear and apprehension in their minds. They were right to be afraid. Behind the scouts rode the main body of the dragoons and with them a solitary, blue-coated horseman. Anyone might have supposed that with an escort of such a size this man in blue must surely be a general or some dignitary. But closer observation revealed that his rank was that of a mere captain of infantry. Across his horse's sweating flanks were draped two leather saddle-bags and these were the reason for the escort. Keane knew he was a courier, carrying orders and messages from the French high command to officers in the field, and since the French had invaded Portugal the previous year the number of men in any such courier's escort had grown steadily as the attacks on them had escalated.

The mountains were teeming with guerrillas, a people's army of peasants and ex-soldiers that had risen up to drive off the invader, and over the past months their attacks had become bolder and more confident and the guerrillas ever more brutal in their treatment of their captives. Keane had seen the inhuman horror of it at first hand. He was under orders to find and intercept any French courier that he could, in particular before the guerrillas got their hands on them and tortured them to death. Quite apart from such barbaric treatment being meted out to a fellow officer, it was far better for intelligence purposes to retrieve any courier alive than merely be handed the bloodied papers that he had carried. Now he had that rare chance.

Keane knew that he and his men had not yet been seen and that timing was vital. He nodded to the man on his left, a wiry youth who, putting his hands to his mouth, gave the call of a wild bird. One of the dragoons looked up at the noise but did not see them and thought nothing of it. He looked away and then, perhaps thinking the better of it, glanced again towards where the sound had come from, thinking that he might have seen a flash of sunlight, reflected on steel. But by then it was too late for him to save his life.

The dragoons rounded the bend in the road and, sensing some-thing wrong, stopped in their tracks. The lead cavalryman shouted something. But it was only half finished before his head exploded, as a well-aimed bullet smashed into his temple. There were other shouts and Keane saw two of the dragoons raise their carbines to fire as the others went to draw their sabres, knowing sensibly that now that would be the only way to save their lives: with sword against sword. Then, from Keane's left, on the road below, with a great roar, a mass of cavalry swept towards the dragoons. Blue-coated and wearing the distinctive dark brown busby of the hussar, they swung their razor-edged, curved light cavalry sabres above their heads and yelled as they spurred towards the French.

But their war cry, though familiar to Keane, was not that of Spain or Britain. It was the guttural roar of '*Gott Mit Uns*' that rose above the trees, as King George's loyal Hanoverians took death to the French.

Keane did not wait to watch the fighting but, turning to his right, sought out his sergeant.

'Sarn't Ross?'

'Sir?'

'Down the hill. With me.'

Pulling hard against the reins to turn his mount's head, Keane spurred his horse, pacing, down the slope and, sabre in hand, led his men out of the trees. Most of the dragoons had ridden to the front, to face the oncoming German attack, and only a skeleton guard now remained with the courier. Now Keane and his men came down hard upon them, yelling like the banshee. Keane careered into a green-coated cavalryman, knocking him back as his horse, used to the fury of battle and as keen as her master, kicked and butted hard into the other man's mount. The dragoon was pushed off balance and struggled to stay in the saddle then, swinging wildly, he drove his long, straight Klingenthal blade towards Keane. It missed him entirely and, without bothering to parry, Keane cut to the left with his own weapon and connected with the man's arm, nearly severing it close to the shoulder. The dragoon screamed and at last fell from his horse, which reared and scrambled down the hill, trampling the body of his dying master.

Keane carried on. All around him his men were engaged with the enemy now, but their surprise had been total and the advantage was theirs. He hacked at a green-coated back, left the man for dead, then for an instant caught himself wondering how the Germans were faring on their left. Seconds later he found himself facing a tall dragoon sergeant who smiled at him knowingly through yellow teeth before lunging at his chest. Keane parried with a stroke to the right which deflected the blade, but in doing so felt the full force of the man's cut: strong and powerful against his blade.

Recovering, he made his own attack at the man's neck and was parried in turn with a skill that caught him off guard. This man was good, better than most French troopers he had met in combat, marrying a real finesse at swordplay with formidable strength. He was a veteran, Keane guessed, who must have fought through the revolutionary wars and earned his stripes in the blood of battle. The dragoon came at him again, with a stroke to the left, and Keane met it just in time. His riposte was clumsy but perhaps on that account it hit home and the man winced as Keane's sabre caught him in the ribs, cutting clean through the green serge tunic.

The man stopped for a moment and glanced down at his stomach, seeing the blood beginning to seep through the cloth. Then he looked up again at Keane and with a snarl attacked again, with fury born of pain. The blade swung towards Keane but he was ready for it now and, anticipating the force, parried it high and forced the man's hand down before sliding his own, deeply curved Arabian blade along the enemy sword, to connect with his chest. Keane's sabre slid in, helped by the force of the man's own stroke, and pierced the dragoon's body close to the heart. The man stared at Keane with wide eyes that quickly glazed over. Keane withdrew the bloodied blade and the dragoon slumped over his horse.

Looking to his left, Keane could see the hussars in the thick of a desperate melee with the dragoons. But now his prize was in sight. At last he was on the courier. At close quarters, the captain seemed to him no more than a boy of perhaps twenty at most. He glared at Keane and raised his slim infantry sword in a feeble defence. It would have been the work of an instant to kill him, but Keane did not cut at the officer. Instead, using the pommel of his sword hilt, he dealt the boy such a blow on the head that it knocked him senseless. Before he could fall from the saddle, though, Keane had grabbed him. He called out to one of his men, 'Martin, take this boy up the hill. We need him alive.'

Will Martin, Keane's fellow countryman, a farmer's boy from County Down, rode up fast and, grabbing hold of the courier, together with the reins of his horse, managed somehow to manoeuvre both of them with him slowly up into the cover of the pines.

Turning back to rejoin the rest of his men, Keane saw that, while two of them were busy dispatching two of the dragoons, the others had disengaged. From the direction of the hussars, the French were streaming past them now, apparently oblivious to their presence in their flight, eager only to escape from the deadly men in blue who had accounted for so many of their comrades.

Some two dozen of the cavalry fled along the road, pursued by a few of the hussars, their blood up. Others had gone already and the ground lay littered with the bodies of the rest. Perhaps a dozen of the Germans lay on the road while others sat in their saddles, clutching at their wounds. But it was clear who had had the best of the fight.

He scanned the dead for signs of the chocolate-brown, black fur-trimmed coat, which was the unique uniform of his own men, and thanked God that he could see none. Then, raising his hand in command, he shouted towards those closest to him, 'Guides, to me. Follow me.'

He led the way uphill, towards where they had begun, in the cover of the pines on the hillside. The French officer had regained consciousness and was sitting with his back to a tree, his head in his hands, watched over by Martin. Keane looked around him, eager to see that all his men had returned safely. He turned to Ross. 'Sarn't Ross, what's our state?'

'Good, sir. No losses. Heredia's taken a cut to his arm and Garland one to his back, but nothing worse.'

He looked at them as they dismounted and watched them loosen their tack and pat their horses. Heredia, the tall Portuguese cavalryman, inspected the cut on his forearm as he tied it up with a strip of torn muslin. Gilpin, the wily thief, short in stature but quick as lightning in a fight as he was in his previous profession, seemed unhurt and was laughing at his good fortune. Martin, still with an eye on the Frenchman, was wiping the blood from his sabre on a clump of grass, and Garland, the big ex-prizefighter, was removing his shirt so that another of their party could see how deep the Frenchman's sword had cut.

Keane watched as Gabriella, the common-law wife of another of the company, took a canteen of water to the young Frenchman.

Horatio Silver had been a sailor, or so he said, serving at Trafalgar under Lord Nelson. But then he had turned thief, his sentence commuted to service with the colours in the 69th foot. Once a thief, though, thought Keane, always a thief. And so Silver had been plucked by them from the jails of Lisbon the previous year, the first recruit to Keane's newly formed unit. Gabriella had come with him and, more than able to fight her corner, had been quickly accepted as one of the men.

The Frenchman took the canteen gratefully and Keane walked across to where he sat. He looked down at his captive. '*Parlez-vous anglais?*'

The man nodded. 'A little, yes.'

'You are carrying letters.' He pointed to the saddlebags, which lay on the ground some distance from them. 'Who sent them?'

The Frenchman looked at him and shook his head. 'I cannot tell you that.'

Keane nodded. He had come to have a respect for the French who carried these letters. They knew they had the most dangerous job in the Peninsula, that their life expectancy must be very low, and yet they continued to try. Most of them were young officers such as this, eager for promotion, keen to accept the danger if it meant reward. And most of them he knew would never see France again, but would die horribly and in agony, those that fell into the wrong hands, at least. This boy was one of the lucky ones and Keane would soon let him know it.

'Captain Keane.' The voice came from behind him.

Keane straightened up and turned and watched as the commander of the German hussars dismounted.

Captain Wilhelm von Krokenburgh was a tall man, of about the same height as Keane, with the aquiline looks of his country's aristocracy and a thin mouth, above which grew an abundant moustache. He walked across to Keane, smiling broadly. 'Good sport, Keane, eh?'

'Yes, von Krokenburgh, your men certainly had a field day.'

The German laughed. 'Did you see 'em run, Keane? The green lizards. Could have had a good deal more of them, given time.'

It was curious how the man spoke in almost an exaggeration of an English idiom, even though his accent was distinctly Teutonic. It was almost as if he needed to prove his rank and station. It betrayed, thought Keane, a certain insecurity. But then, he granted, who would not be insecure when your homeland had been overrun by the enemy and you were forced to live in exile in a foreign country?

The German hussars, or, to give them their correct title, 1st Hussars, the King's German Legion, had been attached to Keane's troop for a fortnight now, a necessity as the cavalry escorts to the French couriers had grown in number. They came from Hanover, formed by the exiled subjects of King George in his role as Elector of that state. The king had made them welcome in Britain, with their headquarters in Sussex, and over the seven years since their formation they had integrated with the local population, some even taking English wives. They were renowned as good fighters, ordered by a strict discipline and strengthened by a genuine hatred for the French who had taken their home. So, while von Krokenburgh might have irritated him from time to time with all his airs and graces, Keane was genuinely glad to have him and his men fighting at his side.

He knew too, even before he spoke, what the German's reaction would now be to seeing the captive who sat before them.

'This sprat's of no use to us, Keane. Better he'd have been killed, eh?'

'Not so, von Krokenburgh. You know as well as I do that he is of value to us. That is why we took him alive.'

'Surely all we need is in those bags. Why bother with the messenger?'

'Because the "messenger", as you call him, is often of more value than the papers he carries, and sometimes even the papers are themselves worthless.'

Von Krokenburgh shrugged. 'Have you looked at them yet?'

'All in good time, von Krokenburgh.'

The German cursed. 'As you will, Keane. But I would rather he was dead. With every dead Frenchman we grow another step closer to the liberation of my country. I wish you luck with him.

Now I must see to my men. Is your woman about? We have a few wounded.'

Keane nodded. 'I'm sure that Gabriella – our woman, as you call her – will be happy to help when she has finished with our own wounded.'

Von Krokenburgh grunted and shrugged, then walked away towards his men.

Keane turned to the Frenchman, who was staring into the mid distance. 'You're a very lucky man, you know.'

The captain nodded his head. 'Yes, I know that. Thank you. Thank God it was you and not those savages who took us. Did we lose many?'

'It's hard to say. Perhaps a dozen killed. More wounded. My sergeant will make a count. Most of your escort seemed happier to run away and leave you to us.'

'They're no fools. They think my journey is a waste of time. They don't want to be in these mountains. No one does. Only fools would stay here to be slaughtered.'

'Your emperor seems to want you to stay here.'

'He has his reasons.'

'And you. What is your reason for being here?'

'I volunteered. I need promotion.'

'You're a captain. Like me. Isn't that sufficient? You seem young enough.'

He shook his head. 'You don't understand, captain. In our army there are generals who are hardly older than me. In the army of the emperor there is the chance for any man to become a marshal of France. That is my dream.'

'Some dream. You chose to gamble your life against the guerrillas.'

The man shrugged. 'If you like.'

'You know what they do?'

The man's face grew pale. 'I've heard.'

'That dream must really matter to you then.'

'When you've come through all we've come through you would understand, captain. I was born into war. It's all that I know.'

Keane smiled at him. 'Then we have something in common, don't we? Captain . . . what did you say your name was?'

'I didn't, but it's Henri. Jules Henri.'

'So, Captain Henri, do you now suppose, as I have done you a favour in saving your life from both the guerrillas and our German friends over there, that you might find it in yourself to tell me who gave you the papers and to whom you were taking them?'

The man looked at him and Keane could see the despair and the resignation. 'My general gave them to me.'

'And who might he be?' Keane knew that he might find this out by simply looking at the letters, but he wanted the boy to crack, to become his. Then who knew what other information he might give up. It was all part of the game that he had perfected while interrogating couriers over the past year.

The boy said nothing for a few moments. Keane waited, knowing what was likely to happen. Then at last the Frenchman spoke. 'You said you had been born into war. Like me.'

'And so I was. It seems so at least. For I have been a soldier these twenty years.'

'And I was born twenty years ago. In the Revolution.'

Keane laughed. 'Ah, the Revolution. That was the start of France's trouble. And the start of all this. How many men has your country lost since then, do you suppose? In the name of liberty and then in the name of the emperor?'

The boy stared at him and said again, 'You said that you were born to war. Where did you fight?'

Keane smiled. 'In Alexandria, in the desert against your general Napoleon, as he was then. And in Flanders, before that. You beat us then.' The Frenchman smiled. Keane continued. 'But not since.'

'Corunna. You were beaten then. We drove you into the sea.'

Keane shook his head. 'No. We escaped across the sea. There is a difference, and now we're back. And you are here as my guest, for as long as I can keep you safe from the guerrillas. We deal with them constantly.'

The veiled threat was not lost on the boy. Keane looked at him and saw that his spirit was beginning to break. 'More water, Captain Henri? Or a little wine perhaps?'

The captain shook his head. 'No. No, thank you. I truly am most grateful, captain, that you took me prisoner.' He seemed about to say more and then looked down at his feet and said nothing for a long minute. Then he looked up and said, 'Perhaps I will accept your offer. A little wine might be nice.'

Walking over to his horse, Keane unslung a flask from his saddlebag and returned, offering it to the captain, who, having taken a long draught, continued. 'I am carrying papers from Marshal Massena to our army in the field. Of course you would have learned as much just by looking at them.'

'Nevertheless, thank you for telling me. You will travel with us back to our lines. And I promise you that neither the guerrillas nor the Germans over there will harm you. You have my word, captain.'

They camped for the night on a plateau high above the hills. It was a place they had first found some two months ago and

Keane had marked it on his master map for future use. Mapping out the country was just one of his many tasks. The place had the advantage of being sufficiently hidden in a dip to allow the flames of their campfires to go unnoticed. Keane made sure that the French captain messed with him and his men, away from the Hanoverians.

Silver and Gabriella had cooked up a stew of sorts from rice, tomatoes and salt beef in the big Flanders kettle that she carried slung across her mule. Even Keane admitted that it didn't taste half bad and their French prisoner seemed perfectly happy with his supper. The man had accepted some more wine with his dinner and had begun to speak volubly, as Keane had hoped he would.

There was not much of use as yet. Mostly he waffled on about his home in the Auvergne and the family he had not seen for two years, but occasionally he would drop in something that made Keane sit up: the fact that many of the animals in the artillery gun teams had become sick or the aside that Marshal Massena had a passion for peaches.

Keane encouraged it. It was just the sort of stuff that Wellington wanted. And it had been on just such a night that he had learned that Marshal Ney was moving across the Peninsula with half the French army. Another courier had spoken then, taken into confidence and in his cups. And so the boy went on and the fire crackled, and the wine flowed, although Keane was aware that while the flames would not be seen, the smoke would give them away. The last thing that he wanted was to attract the attention of an inquisitive band of guerrillas.

So he let the Frenchman prattle away and refilled his cup while the men spoke among themselves. He had ordered no singing this night, from the Germans too, lest they be heard from far off in the stillness that hung about the mountains of the high sierra. Instead the men told stories to each other or tried to grab some sleep.

Sitting close to Keane, Sergeant Ross was midway through a story about a witch who had terrorized south-west Scotland in the seventeenth century, holding the men spellbound, as he always did. Gabriella shook her head and muttered something in Portuguese.

Martin stared at Ross. 'Did they really have witches in the Scottish Highlands, sergeant?'

Gilpin laughed. 'Don't pay any heed to him, Martin. It's all talk.'

Ross shook his head and continued. 'Still do, boy. Just as they do where you come from, in Ireland. Brimful of witches, Ireland is. Didn't your mother never tell you that?'

'No, sergeant.'

'Well, that's what it is. Full of them. And if, like me, you had the second sight, you'd be able to tell just who might be a witch. Now take yon woman over there.' He pointed to Gabriella, who had walked off to stir her stewpot.

'She's not a witch, is she?'

Ross smiled. 'Well, laddie, what do you think? Do you think she might have a bit of the witch in her?'

Martin stared at Gabriella. 'Do you really think so?'

Ross laughed. 'No, laddie. She's no witch, though she's a magical way with a stew, wouldn't you say?'

The others laughed, as did Keane. He was well aware that Ross was from Glasgow and had no more of the Highlander in him than himself. And as for 'the second sight' . . .

Silver, who had seated himself beside Keane, spoke, quietly.

'Those Germans get on my wick, sir. Can't stomach them for all their preening and fancy ways.'

'But they're not bad in a fight, Silver.'

'True, but I'd rather be shot of them, sir. We can handle ourselves all right, sir, can't we?'

'Of course we can, Silver. But we must have someone to do the dirty work, mustn't we?'

Silver laughed. 'That's one way of putting it, sir. Yes, I like that. Doing the dirty work. I'll tell the wife that. She can't stand them neither.'

'She's had no trouble from them?'

'No, sir. Nothing like that. It's just they seem to treat her like their own skivvy.'

'And she's your skivvy, is that it, Silver?'

The man smiled. 'You might say so, sir. Well, she's my wife at least, ain't she?'

'You haven't married her yet, though, have you?'

'Not proper, sir, not church-married. With a priest. But we're army married, if you understand what I mean, sir.'

'Yes, I understand.'

Keane understood.

Like those of so many of the men who made up Wellington's army, Silver's marriage was by common law. When husbands were killed or died of disease their wives would take a new man, often within days. It was a matter of survival, particularly if children were involved. It was not an ideal situation and the unscrupulous could exploit it – on both sides. But it was the way that the army did things. Had always done things. And that, Keane knew, could not be changed. Even though other things might.

*

Plucked from his company in the Inniskilling Fusiliers, a distinguished infantry regiment from his homeland of Ireland, Keane had in the past year been propelled into a type of soldiering he had never known in twenty years with the colours in Flanders, Egypt and the Peninsula.

He had become what they politely termed an 'exploring' or 'observing' officer for the newly created general Wellington, his fellow Irishman, Arthur Wellesley. In effect Keane was a spy. One of a select group of officers who had been singled out to go either alone or with parties of chosen men behind enemy lines and liaise with the guerrillas to gather information on the movements of the French. Wellington wanted to know everything, it seemed, from the size of the French armies and their whereabouts, to what their commanders had for breakfast. Keane had not been enthusiastic. But he had warmed to his task and now took pride in his new-found ability.

It still amused and surprised him too that he should have gained his new position by default. The only reason that he had come to Wellington's notice in the first place had been on account of his having killed a brother officer in a duel. What was sure to be his apparent dismissal, or worse, had been commuted by the general to this new role. It did not help that since then he had killed another of his comrades in self-defence, nor that the sister of that dead man was the girl with whom he had fallen in love and who, as far as he was aware, still did not know the truth about her brother's death.

These things weighed heavily on Keane's mind as they had done every day for the last eight months, and he was glad to be out here in the field with his men and away from the questions that were sure in the end to come when at last he returned to Lisbon. He knew too that he commanded as fine a body of men as anyone might wish for. They might have been for the most part the scrapings of Lisbon's jails, but they had been turned by Keane and his sergeant, in a year's hard soldiering in the mountains of the high sierra, into a force on which he knew he could rely.

One of their number, though, was missing, had been missing for the better part of the year. Keane's closest friend in the army, Tom Morris of the artillery, as far removed from a felon as you could hope to meet, had been one of the first to join his troop and the only officer. But Morris had spent the past few months posted to headquarters, engaged on another matter of espionage.

Heredia, before he had joined their number, had discovered a French agent on the general staff – a distinguished British officer – and it had fallen to Morris to expose him. However, it was proving more difficult to do so than they had anticipated. Keane was concerned for his friend and intended, once they returned, to have it out with his superiors. Morris had been gone too long. Any longer and he might leave their number.

Their ranks, though, had been augmented. In the past few months they had been joined by two more men. One a gunner, Israel Leech, who had been recommended to them directly by Morris. Leech was no criminal, but handy with explosives and it was just possible that he might come in useful. He was a cool fellow, thought Keane, and inclined to swings of temper, but the men seemed to have taken to him well enough.

The other man was newly arrived just before they had set out on their current expedition.

Jack Archer had come to them expressly on Major Grant's orders and Keane was still unsure why. Certainly he seemed to satisfy enough of the criteria for their force; he could speak

passable Spanish and was a good shot and a fine horseman.
Keane supposed that was enough, but he wondered why Grant
had been so insistent.

Keane looked at them all as they laughed together at the
conclusion of Ross's ghost story and he knew they were his
men now. Even the newcomers. They would ride on tomorrow,
and the next day, he knew, would reach the lines. And then he
would hand over the Frenchman to his superiors and learn from
them what new task they had dreamt up for him.

Undoubtedly it would be some form of intelligence gathering.
But as to whether he might be sent to persuade a guerrilla captain to aid them or merely to intercept another courier, he did
not know. It was not of any great consequence.

The French were massing for an attack. Not under Napoleon.
The sort of fighting they engaged in here was not, Keane supposed, to the liking of a man who had made his name on the
plains of central Europe. Instead the Corsican had entrusted the
taking of the Peninsula to his great captains, Soult, Ney, Massena. Soon they would come, and it was Keane's role to discover
when and where they would make that attack. It was late June
now and the campaigning season had only a few months left to
run before the weather closed in and it became impossible for
an army to operate effectively, let alone fight and win a battle.

He had come to relish his role, although at times he longed
for the old life and action in line, meeting the enemy in battle.

The only actions left to him now were those such as today's
– harassing actions and skirmishes. That was all they had seen
since Talavera, and Keane presumed it would be all the action
he would be destined to see for the foreseeable future. It all
depended upon the commander-in-chief and whether or not he
should choose to meet the French in battle. The men were keen

for it certainly and Keane had heard talk that London was split in two as to what should be done. Some said that Wellington should sail home with his army. Beresford too, and abandon the Portuguese to their fate. Others, though, wanted action. He wondered which side Old Nosey would take in his wisdom.

All he knew was that he would take his orders and gather the intelligence that would give Wellington the all-important upper hand when the French push finally came. It was a waiting game they were playing now, and one thing Keane had learned since he had taken on his new role was that waiting gave them time, and while time might be the common soldier's everyday enemy, for the intelligencer it was the most precious commodity in the world.

2

The distinct clatter of spurred riding boots on a marble floor rang out shrilly through the salon of the large house in the town of Celorico that had been recently appropriated as the headquarters of the allied army. Sir Arthur Wellesley, lately created Viscount Wellington of Talavera, was agitated. Placing his hands together behind the small of his back, he turned to the similarly red-coated man who had been standing to one side for the last ten minutes as he had paced the room.

'Grant, I need to know more. Where is Massena and with how many men? I need numbers. Foot, horse ordnance, supplies. And I need to know where he intends to cross from Spain and when.'

Almost the duke's equal in height, Major Sir Colquhoun Grant nodded, an engaging smile lighting a fine-boned face whose most prominent feature, though not as distinctive as the duke's own, was its long aquiline nose. But, despite his amiable countenance, there was a seriousness about Grant's manner. 'Yes, sir. We will need to know all of that and more besides, if we are to outwit the fox. But you are aware, Your Grace, that we have the means to do it. Captain Keane is on his way.'

Wellington nodded. 'Keane? Is he, by God? Here?'

Grant nodded.

'Good. I need to hear his report. Don't let him tarry, though, Grant. I won't have men of that calibre hanging around head-quarters like a pack of lapdogs. We have officers enough, for that, to be sure. All purchase and too little talent. Best to get Captain Keane back into the field, where he's best used. He, with all the exploring officers in Scovell's Corps of Guides, are become my eyes and ears now. They are our best weapon.'

He stared at the map of the Peninsula spread on the table before him and then, apparently absently, traced a line with his finger from the border with France up towards the north and off into the air as if to some other country.

He sighed. 'The Corsican wins a battle in Austria and now we must suffer. Our friends the Austrians are, I suppose, wholly to blame. All that I won at Talavera, the archduke threw away at Wagram. So now Bonaparte has more men to throw at us here. Hundreds of thousands of them, Grant, marching down from the north even as we speak, to "push us into the sea".'

'Sir?'

'That's what he says, is it not, our man in Paris?' He waved a piece of paper towards Grant. 'You have seen this, have you not? Look at it. A missive from the French capital. The latest from that man we keep at Bonaparte's court. I forget his name. How much do we pay him?'

'I'll enquire, sir. Captain Radlett, as I recollect. He is invalu-able.'

'That's as maybe. But I don't need a spy to tell me what I know already. Bonaparte says that he will push us back into the sea "as he did before".'

He scanned the paper and read from it aloud. 'The emperor's order to Marshal Massena read as follows: "The leopard contaminates the land of Spain yet again."' Wellington raised an eyebrow. 'Since when were we a leopard, Grant?'

'I think Bonaparte refers to Britain as such, sir. The image, I think, being that of the lion couchant on His Majesty's coat of arms.'

Wellington nodded and grinned. 'Not a leopard, though, you see. No proper education, Grant. Peasant stock, Bonaparte.' He spoke the name slowly, as if the very word caused a sour taste in the mouth, then paused and seemed to dwell on the idea of Napoleon and all for which he stood. 'As I was saying, our agent in Paris writes that "Napoleon" intends to drive us into the sea. He is sending Marshal Massena.'

'I would reckon, sir, that the marshal will bring with him a good one hundred thousand men, now that the Austrians seem to have given up the fight for the present.'

'They have lost the stomach for it, do you suppose?'

'I could not comment on that, sir. But I would very much doubt it. It will surely be merely a temporary defeat. They are his principal enemy in the field, sir, have always been. Do not forget, Your Grace, the French cut off the head of an Austrian princess, their queen. And should Bonaparte prevail, he will seize their country as part of Greater France. They know they have much to lose.'

Wellington looked Grant hard in the eyes. 'We all have much to lose. You know the situation, Grant. If we are driven from the Peninsula, then Bonaparte has all of Europe at his feet. And through Spain and Portugal he will have land in the Americas. We may rule the waves at present, but should he sign a treaty with the Americans, what then?'

'Yes, sir. It is very grave.'

'It all devolves upon us, Grant. The fate of the civilized world.

If Marshal Massena can beat us here –' in emphasis he pointed to the map of Portugal – 'if he can invade Portugal with success and make a stand and keep to it, then we must leave. From the south of Spain this time. That is to be our route of escape. From here, by way of Cadiz. We shall embark in boats for the fleet. Just as we did at Corunna.'

He gazed at the map again. 'And the Portuguese will away to the Brazils. Those are the orders. The Cabinet believes that we cannot hold. What say you, Grant?'

'I am with you, Your Grace. I believe we can do it.'

'Yes, I too. I'm damned if they will make of me another Sir John Moore, God rest his soul. We merely need to make sure of certain things and then we can beat them. We must train up the Portuguese. I will not fight alongside the Spanish. Not any more, not after Talavera. The men are of good quality, sure enough, but their generals are impossible. General Cuesta in particular. Second, we must hold on to the key forts of Elvas, here –' again he pointed to the map – 'and Almeida, here. And finally we must make for ourselves a fortified camp. The whole of this benighted country, the entire Portuguese frontier, must become a fortress from which we can then take the initiative – to sally forth and beat the French. When the time comes. The autumn, Grant. That will do.'

Grant nodded. 'Colonel Fletcher and the engineers have the project of the defences advancing by the day, Your Grace. The lines are rising, from the Tagus to the sea.'

'And all that is secret, is it not? Nothing is known to the French?'

'Nor even to our own government in London, Your Grace. Just as you instructed.'

'Pray God then that the press in London do not get hold of it.

They are Bonaparte's chief source and my hidden enemy. Those gentlemen do me more harm than ten thousand of Bonaparte's sons.'

He muttered something that Grant could not make out and stared at the map for a few moments, before going on. 'You said that Keane was on his way?'

'He's only lately returned from the field, sir. Brought with him a prisoner and dispatches.'

'A prisoner?'

'Courier, sir. From Marshal Massena.'

An orderly officer entered the room. 'Captain Keane is waiting outside, Your Grace.'

'A timely arrival. Well, show him in then, Ayles, show him in.'

Grant signalled to the young ADC, who opened the door to admit Keane.

Wellington's face brightened. 'Captain Keane, I hear that you have news for us.'

Keane entered and, advancing towards the commander-in-chief, nodded his head in salute. 'Yes, Your Grace. Marshal Massena has crossed the border, at Ciudad Rodrigo.

Wellington smiled. 'You know that for certain?'

'I have it from a courier whose word I do not doubt and from the dispatches he carried . . . His word was better.'

Wellington smiled. 'At Ciudad, damn me, as I had thought he must. With how strong a force?'

Keane hesitated for a moment, knowing the gravity of the information he was about to give the duke and how vital it was that it should be accurate. 'Over three hundred thousand men of all arms. He received one hundred thousand fresh troops, sir, before the advance.'

Wellington looked at Grant. 'There, Grant, I told you. Come down from Austria.'

He turned to another red-coated officer, who up till now had stood, almost unnoticed, a little way off from the duke and Grant, in conversation with a fourth, similarly invisible officer.

'Murray, remind me again who holds Ciudad for us?'

Colonel George Murray, the duke's quartermaster general, and de facto chief of staff, did not need to consult the notebook he carried inside his coat, which contained information on the locations of every brigade, battalion and regiment in the Anglo-Allied army. The answer was ingrained on his brain.

'General Herrasti, Your Grace, with five thousand Spaniards.'

Wellington nodded. 'Herrasti. He's a good man, one of their better officers. Brave as you'd like. But he's old, Grant. He won't surrender, though. He'll go down fighting.' He shook his head. 'It'll be a bloody business. I cannot do anything immediately to raise the siege. I have neither the men nor the equipment to help. To try would be to weaken our position. But you can be sure Massena will take the town too soon, unless we act.' He looked at the map and, as if his mind had completed an equation, barked the answer. 'Murray, have General Craufurd's Light Division move to Ciudad directly, with a brigade of cavalry in support. I can spare no more. Instruct the general not to engage the enemy but to observe him and to harass him if possible. The Rifles and a few squadrons of Light Dragoons will do the job nicely.'

Murray nodded. 'Yes, Your Grace. We could send a division of Portuguese also. Or more cavalry.'

Wellington shook his head. 'No. No more. I told you, I cannot afford to raise the siege. I can merely divert the French. To move on Ciudad would imperil our own lines. There is nothing for it. Herrasti will have to succumb eventually. There is no need to go on wasting men on him. But Craufurd will hold them up for long enough, long enough for us to act. And he knows not to commit his men. No point in sending the cavalry. Once they're off, they're off, and we lose them. Good in the saddle, but damned uncontrollable fellows. Every one of them.'

He turned back to Keane. 'In the meantime, Keane, I shall need to know more if I'm to outwit Marshal Massena. I have not the men nor the resources to meet him on equal terms in the field, so we shall have to achieve by guile what we cannot by force of arms.'

'Yes, sir.'

'You have the Germans with you?'

'Yes, sir.'

'Good. You will take them with your own men and make a reconnaissance in force. Attach yourself to General Craufurd's force, but keep out in front of it. I don't want you drawn into any large actions. By all means you may give the French a bloody nose, Keane, if you find the opportunity. But just that. No more. Remember, your job is not to fight; it is to observe and report. That is how you are of the best use to me.'

He looked back to the map. 'Once Ciudad falls, Marshal Massena can do one of only two things.'

He pointed again. 'He can advance down here, to the south, towards Elvas and Badajoz, or he can move here, quickly to the west. Against the fortress at Almeida. It is my guess and indeed my hope that he will do the latter. The road through Elvas is too heavily defended and soon he must know that. If he comes by way of Almeida, we can hold him off there for two months. Which will give us the time we need to complete the lines of defence. Then we can meet him, or part of his army, on ground of our choosing and beat him before we take to the lines. That way we can force him to withdraw.'

Keane looked at the map and saw the simple, brilliant genius of Wellington's plan by which he would win against a force three times his in number.

'That is what I require from you, Captain Keane. Assurance that Massena will advance upon Almeida. I know that you cannot change the marshal's orders or his decision. But let me know what he intends and I will be able to steal a march on him. That is all I need: time. I must have three months to complete the fortifications. Three months. We are now in June. The engineers tell me that it will take until September.'

He looked away and gazed out of the window across the town. 'London is opposed to me, Keane. Outside here, in the anteroom, as you came in, you will have noticed another officer waiting to enter.' He turned quickly. 'Did you know him?'

'No, sir. I can't say that I did.'

'That, Keane was a Major Cavanagh. Lately arrived from the Horse Guards. Major Cavanagh enjoys the patronage of the prince regent and he comes bearing a message for me.'

'Sir?'

'A message, and with it an order. He bids me to engage the French immediately. The prince regent wants a victory. He wants me to dazzle our friends in Austria and his own friends at court. But he cannot have it.'

'No, sir?'

'He will not have it, Keane, because should we engage the French as he would wish, my army would be beat and pushed from this country into the sea.'

He paused and then engaged Keane with his piercing blue eyes before continuing. 'The prince regent will have his victory,

Keane, God willing. But in my time and on my terms. Three months. You must do what you can. We must delay the French as much as possible. Anything, Keane. We must do anything that buys time.'

He looked at Murray. 'Very good, gentlemen. You may go.'

They nodded and made to leave, and Keane made to go with them. But Wellington held up his hand in a gesture that indicated he should stay.

'Captain Keane, a moment further, if you will.'

Keane stopped and turned back. Grant, who had remained in the room, closed the door behind the others.

Wellington spoke. 'There is another matter which we now have to conclude, is there not? A matter somewhat closer to home.'

Keane had known that this would come. The matter of the spy.

Wellington looked at Keane directly. 'We must rid ourselves of this traitor. It has been harmless enough to play him these few months, and we had hoped he might betray himself, but the time has come.' He picked up a sheaf of printed papers which lay on a desk at his side. 'Have you seen these?'

Wellington thrust them towards Keane, who scanning the topmost of them saw that it was a copy of the *Morning Chronicle*.

Wellington continued. 'How is it that I can read in the British press, in our own newspapers, the exact size and dispositions of my own force? How the devil can such a thing happen?'

Keane responded. 'There are tongues that wag everywhere around us, Your Grace. That and the fact that we know the French have spies of their own, here and in Lisbon and London.'

'And not least this viper in our own midst. We must act now. Keane, what news on this?'

'My man has not yet managed to find the damning evidence that we had sought, sir.'

Wellington shrugged. 'Yes, I thought as much. He's clearly a canny one. Like his masters. Well, we shall simply have to confront him. That is, you will have to do it, with your man. Remind me of his name.'

'Morris, sir, Tom Morris, lately of the artillery.'

'Ah yes, Captain Morris. A popular figure in the mess, is he not? The two of you must do it. Take the man, before it is too late. And don't delay, Keane. I know how quickly you tire of life with the upper echelons.'

Wellington was right. Keane was not a natural staff officer. His life had been in the field, and every time he was confined to business of the headquarters he grew restless within a few days. Others took to it as ducks to water, and indeed there were some who while in later years told great tales of their exploits in the Peninsula, in truth had spent most of that time behind a desk at Lisbon, Coimbra or here at Celorico.

But he knew that there were times when his presence was needed and that now was one of those times.

There was, as Wellington had said, a snake in their midst, a serpent who for a year and more had been stealing information and passing it to the French. Keane knew who it must be, but they had agreed that to out the man, it must be done subtly and with guile. But it was clear that it should be done soon. Last year's campaigning season had been a triumph, culminating in the rout of the French at Talavera, and the winter had yielded little of note for the French spies, but now, with Massena's men about to descend upon Portugal and Wellington making plans designed to engineer his destruction, it grew too dangerous to tolerate the presence of the traitor any

longer. His time had come. But Keane had not thought that it
would be he who would be selected to confront the man. Of all
that he had done, from common soldiering to meeting with
guerrilla captains and any number of fights, this task he now
faced was surely one of the most onerous. To have to accuse a
brother officer of treason, to his face, even though he felt sure
that his information was right. Heredia had sworn as much
and had been acquitted on the proof. Nevertheless it rankled
with him.

'You want me to do this, sir?'

'I can think of no one who would do it better.'

'Can you tell me where I might find Colonel Pritchard?'

Grant spoke. 'He is attending to some paperwork, I believe.
His quarters are close by, in the Rueda della Casa. When will
you take him?'

Keane nodded at Grant. 'I'll do it now, sir.'

Wellington spoke. 'He was a fine officer, you know. Connec-
tions with Ireland, I seem to recall. Joined shortly after the
Egyptian affair. I would never have had cause to suspect. But
Grant is convinced of his guilt.'

Grant nodded. 'There is no doubt in my mind, Your Grace. I
would have taken him months ago.'

'Yes, I am aware that it is my insistence on proof that has
caused us to delay in this matter. Still, that's in the past now.
It is too late for him. The fact is that the French seem to know
our moves to the extent of cheeking us by passing the news to
hacks in the Strand. It must be Pritchard's doing, and I will not
have it. And I should like to see our turncoat, Keane, before he
stands trial, if you will.'

'Yes, Your Grace. I'll bring him here directly.'

They left the room and, once outside, Grant stood with him

at the closed door. He was about to speak when one of the aides rushed up to him.

'Major Grant, sir. May I have a word? It is a matter of some urgency.'

He noticed Keane. 'My apologies, Captain Keane. I must have Major Grant for a moment.' The young man moved away with Grant, and Keane heard only the words 'very drunken lieutenant . . . Portuguese lady . . . inexcusable . . . relations.'

Keane smiled, concluding that some young fool of an officer had taken advantage of the amicable relationship between the two nations and imperilled the honour of one of their allies. He pitied the major his responsibility for such things. Knowing that Grant wished to speak to him, Keane waited, staring at the map of the Peninsula that stood propped up on a table by the hearth. It was then that he noticed Major Cavanagh. He stood close to the window, a slender man in his forties with greying brown hair tied back in a queue. As Keane looked, the major caught his eye, then smiled at him and approached.

'Captain Keane, is it not?'

Keane nodded. 'Sir.'

'Major Cavanagh. Late of St James's.' He looked Keane up and down and nodded. 'We've heard of you, Keane. You've come to our attention. The prince keeps a watchful eye on the Gazette, you know. He's taken notice of you. Oporto, weren't it?'

'Indeed, sir. I'm honoured.'

'And Talavera. You're a spy, ain't you?'

'Exploring officer, sir. Yes, sir.'

The major nodded again. 'You know, you're just the sort of fellow that might profit from the prince's patronage. He's most generous.'

Keane knew instantly that he was being suborned. He nodded

and smiled. 'Do you really think so, sir? How might that be.'

'The prince will reward officers well who are inclined to do his express bidding. We have a task on our hands here, Captain Keane, do we not?'

'Sir?'

'The French, Keane. The prince is most anxious that we should engage the French with the utmost speed and defeat them. We cannot delay. Agree?'

'Of course not, sir. Quite agree. I will not pass up any opportunity to engage the enemy. My men are the eyes and ears of the army. We see them first. I will ensure, sir, that as soon as we find the French I will report their position and their state.'

Cavanagh nodded and smiled. 'And you will, naturally, Keane. You will advise in any report you make that an immediate attack would be advantageous. For whichever general as should receive that report? Whether or not it might be the commander-in-chief.'

'Naturally, sir. I only have the victory of the army in my mind.'

Cavanagh smiled and nodded. 'I see that we have an understanding, Captain Keane. I will make sure that I acquaint the prince of your particular loyalty.'

Grant had broken free now of the aide, who hurried from the room. He walked towards the two men.

'Apologies, gentlemen. A domestic matter. Most embarrassing. But nothing more. Major Cavanagh, His Grace will see you shortly. May I trouble you for a moment? I must speak to Captain Keane.'

Grant took him to one side and moving across to another end of the large room, spoke in hushed tones. 'You met our Major Cavanagh then?'

'He spoke to me, sir, yes.'

'And?'

'He attempted to persuade me to go against the commander-in-chief's orders, sir, and contrive some means by which we should engage the French at once.'

Grant laughed. 'Did he, by God. The man's a sly one, right enough. And you said . . . ?'

'I replied merely that it was clearly vital that we should have a battle and that personally I would lose no opportunity to engage the enemy.'

Grant laughed again. 'By God, Keane, we'll make a diplomat of you. Well done, my boy, and thank you for warning us. We'll need to keep an eye on the major. But you'd best be off now. You will find Captain Morris in his quarters. I know he is anxious to see you.'

Keane nodded. 'Yes, sir. Morris will know the colonel's ways better than I, should anything go amiss.

'You'll need a few men, Keane. Take the provosts. Morris will find them. They know him well enough.' He patted Keane on the shoulder and turned to Major Cavanagh.

'Ah, Major Cavanagh. What news from the court? The general cannot wait to see you.'

Walking away from the headquarters building, past the lines of redcoats being drilled on the square, Keane smiled to himself to think that he had duped Cavanagh. The man was an ass to suppose that he could persuade him to turn on Wellington for the sake of patronage. Mind you, he thought, there was something to be said for such a patron, and he worried for an instant whether if he were found out that things might go badly for him were he ever to present himself at court. But he dismissed the thought. He was a soldier and his business was here, helping to defeat the French in whatever way his commander-in-chief saw fit. He was Wellington's man, come hell or high water, or the prince regent and his toadies. Besides, he had more pressing matters on his mind.

Pritchard must be taken. It had long been known to the commander-in-chief and others that the man was a spy. In truth they might have outed him long ago, but Grant had thought that it might be useful to play him until there was more damning evidence. Who knew how many men's deaths he might have taken the blame for? One thing was certain: Pritchard would die. After he had given account of himself to Wellington.

He found Morris at his lodging, a tawdry little house, deserted by its owners, down a close near to the church of Santa Maria, which was acting as a hospital. Even from the street, Keane could smell the faint stench of putrefaction that haunted the place, which was home to cases of disease and sunstroke for the most part. He pushed open the door to Morris's billet and found his friend seated at a table.

'Tom. How good to see you, friend.'

Morris stood and clasped Keane by the shoulder. 'And it's good to see you, James. Thank heavens. I wondered when you might return. You have news?'

'I come from Wellington. We've to fetch Pritchard. This instant. Have you any men?'

'My orderly. But the provosts have a post close by.' He smiled. 'Thank God. I cannot tell you the agony it has been to have this role these few months. Now at last to be relieved.'

'He gave you no cause before now.'

'It was almost as if he knew.'

'Perhaps he did. For all we know, there are others like him.'

'Surely not, James. One man such as Pritchard I can stomach, but not to think that our staff might be a nest of vipers.'

'I hardly think so. I wonder merely if he has an accomplice. One thing is certain in this war, Tom, that we can be certain of nothing.'

He moved quickly towards the door. 'Come on. We must arrest him before he hears of his fate.'

With Morris leading the way, they left the house and were once again enveloped in the stink of the place. They hurried past the church, across the main road and along the narrow back streets of the town, back in the direction of the headquarters building. Morris stopped. 'This is the provosts' post, James.'

The door was half open and from within they heard the sound of English voices. They entered the small single-storey house and disturbed a half-dozen men of the Blues and Royals who were seated around a small table, playing cards. Seeing the two officers enter, one of the men, a sergeant, snapped to his feet. 'Officers present.'

Instantly the men rose and returned the salutes offered by Keane and Morris.

'Sarn't Baynes,' Morris said, 'we have need of your men. It is a rather delicate matter. Don't ask any questions, if you will. Merely come with us.'

The sergeant nodded. He was a lean man who had twenty years' service with the regiment, the last two with the provosts, for which duty his unit had been selected for its reliability and courtesy as well as its prowess at arms. He knew better than to ask questions of an officer and had in his time seen some things that were best forgotten. Nor would he have expected to have asked questions when that officer was Lieutenant Morris. He knew that the artilleryman had been taken on to the duke's staff some months back and no one was quite sure what he did, but the sergeant held his own ideas about that. Now, though, was not the time to delay.

He turned to his men. 'Right, you heard the staff officer. We're needed. Boots and spurs, all of you.' He turned to Morris and Keane. 'Shall we bring our mounts, sir?'

Keane spoke this time. 'No, sarn't. No horses. It's only you that we need, just in case. Best bring your carbines.'

Keane and Morris left the room, followed by the six troopers, each of whom as they emerged put on his crested helmet, which served to emphasize their already remarkable height and build, and collected his carbine from the pile in the corner. With this formidable force behind them, led by Morris they made their way towards Pritchard's billet.

They rounded the corner of the street. Two children playing in the gutter stopped and stared at the sight of so many tall, finely dressed soldiers, so unlike the red-coated men they were used to seeing here, or even the officers who came and went from the only house that was anything other than a hovel. Further down the street a man in a long coat and broad-brimmed hat walked out and stared at them for a moment before turning sharply and returning the way he had come. They did not see him.

As they approached the house Keane stopped for a moment and turned to the sergeant. 'I should tell you, sarn't, we've come to arrest Colonel Pritchard.'

Baynes said nothing and his unchanging, poker-faced countenance gave no hint as to what his thoughts might be. He simply grunted. 'Sir.'

'I'm not at liberty to disclose the reason. You might want to post two of your men at the rear of the house. Lieutenant Morris will show them where to go.'

Baynes pointed at two of the troopers. 'Fletcher, Johnson, go with the officer.'

Morris led them off down an alley to the rear and Keane walked with the others towards the front of Pritchard's billet.

They were scarcely a hundred yards away when, without warning, there was a huge explosion. It came from within the house, smashing the walls and throwing the windows out into the street. Masonry flew in all directions.

Instantly, instinctively, Keane turned and ducked, protecting his head. The blast picked him up and threw him against the door of a house on the opposite side of the street. A man of lesser stature might have been bowled over, but Keane manage to stand and, recovering, he shook his head and looked about. The sergeant and most of his men had done the same. One man, though, had been unlucky and as he had begun to turn had been hit on the head by a flying block of stone, which had killed him just as if it had been a roundshot, taking away half of his cheek and a portion of his skull and spattering another of their number with his brains.

His dead body lay close to Keane among the shards of tile and pieces of masonry that now littered the street. Keane stared down at him and thought it ironic that such a man not have met his end on the field of battle, even though it had been done in the same way. Then, feeling that his own mouth was cut, he brushed away fragments that had been blown on to his face, spitting the dust from his caked lips. The air was filled with powdered stone and Keane spat again to clear his mouth. He wiped his eyes and turned towards the sergeant. Baynes, like Keane, was covered in white dust and rubbed at his eyes before brushing off his blue coat.

'God, sir. What in the name of all that's holy was that?'

Keane looked across the street and stared. 'That, sarn't, was Colonel Pritchard's lodging being blown to smithereens.'

The sergeant followed Keane's gaze and saw that where the house had stood there now lay only an empty space with, sticking up like some painful jagged tooth, the ruins of its ground floor. Of the upper floors, where Pritchard had had his rooms, nothing remained. He looked around and, seeing the near-decapitated body of the trooper, managed only, 'That's Briggs. Poor bugger.'

Keane looked down the street and saw that one of the urchin children too had been hit, her leg gashed and broken, it seemed, by a piece of flying masonry. She was screaming and her shrieks filled the street, giving human expression to the catastrophe. But Keane could not hear them. His ears were ringing with the noise of a hundred bells; the blast had rendered him half deaf.

Keane thought of Morris and the two others. He shouted at the sergeant and in his deafness, just made out his own words. 'Christ, come on.' Together the two of them, followed by the remaining two troopers, walked towards the ruined building. The smell of burning wracked their throats and grew more acrid the closer they came to the site of the explosion.

Keane reached the house first and punched at the door, which remarkably was still standing. It fell in at his touch. Smoke and dust were rising in a cloud and as Keane looked inside he could see tongues of flame licking up at what had been the staircase.

He pushed past the shattered door and entered, picking his way across the steaming stones. 'Tom, Tom?'

There was no answer, or if there was, Keane did not hear it.

Surely, he thought, his friend had not perished like the unfortunate trooper, or even been blown to atoms so that nothing of him remained. He called his name again and, walking towards the rear of the house, noticed a pair of legs protruding from beneath a huge block of stone, which must have crushed the owner to a pulp. For a moment he paused, frozen. But then he saw that the legs wore bloodied top-boots, cavalryman's boots, and realized that they were not his friend's. There was a faint cry ahead of him and he found Morris sitting on the ground, cradling his bleeding head in his hands. Keane could see that a single buttress wall had shielded him from the force of the blast, although he had clearly been hit on the head and arms.

Morris looked up. 'James. You're alive.' Looking past Keane he saw the boots of the crushed man. 'Where's the other fellow?'

Keane shook his head, but as he did so there was an answering shout from behind Morris. 'Here, sir, I was out in the street.'

The man came tottering towards him, blood streaming from a gash on his shoulder.

Keane looked at the smoking ruins. 'Our friend Pritchard's been blown to pieces, I imagine. Unless he did it himself and escaped.'

'You think that likely?'

'Anything is likely.'

'A bomb?'

'Without a doubt.'

With some effort, Morris pushed himself to his feet, blood coursing down his leg. 'If there was a bomb, then there must be evidence. A fuse or some such. A fragment.'

Keane nodded. 'We should at least find Pritchard's body.'

The two upper levels of the little house had collapsed in on the ground floor and sticks of wooden furniture lay mingled with orange roof tiles and blasted rubble. Morris began to kick at the smoking remains.

Keane picked up a long piece of wood and poked it into the masonry. 'Damn your fuse, Tom. I need a body.'

Morris was moving through the house now, rubbing at his injured thigh, looking for some trace of the device. 'This is bad work, James. It's a bomb, I would say. Smells like it, and the way the explosion worked – could only be. Where's Pritchard, dammit?'

They had reached the very back of the house now and as they walked on, amid the dusty pallor, a patch of vivid bright red caught Keane's eye and looking more closely he recognized that it was an arm. He was not sure at first whether it was still attached to a body but, looking more closely, he saw that it did not protrude from a block of stone, but lay quite separate.

Keane had a desire to turn away and retch but suppressed it and went on. For all they knew, this might well be all that was now left of Colonel Ambrose Pritchard. He moved to it and looked more closely. Apart from the patch of red uniform, the rest of the arm had been scorched black by the explosion. At what had been the shoulder, close to where it had been torn off by the blast, he saw something else. Traces of the strands of gold bullion that would have hung from an epaulette. The gold epaulette of a senior officer. He called to Morris. 'Tom, look here.'

Morris, though, was otherwise occupied. Bending down, he had retrieved something and, bearing it before him, walked across to Keane. His smile revealed a sense of triumph. 'There, James. What did I say? A bomb, as sure as I'd know one.'

He held out a still-hot fragment of blackened iron. A piece of spherical shell casing and, in it, in the semicircle where the aperture had been, Keane could make out a blackened stump of fuse.

Keane spoke again. 'Look over there.'

Morris looked and instantly the smile fell from his face, as he caught sight of the severed arm.

'Good God. Pritchard, d'you think?'

'So it would seem. It's the arm of an officer, certainly.'

'Where's the rest of him, d'you suppose?'

'You, of all men, know better than to ask that, Tom. You know the effect of a shell and gunpowder upon the human body. How frail is our flesh.'

'My guess is that anything more that's left of the colonel, if it is him, is scattered in fragments in there.' He gestured to the smoking ruins.' 'Who did it? The French, d'you think? Were they wise to us? Got to him before we were able?'

Keane thought for a moment. 'It's possible. Yes. Perhaps.'

Or might it be something else? he thought. The questions came fast. Was it possible that there was another spy? Could he have done this? Or was Pritchard dead at all? What proof did they have that this was him?

Morris was searching among the debris, looking for further clues. At length he called, 'James, I think you should see this.'

Keane walked over to him and saw that he held in his hands a sword. It was curved, not unlike Keane's own blade, which he had acquired in Egypt as a young subaltern. But instead of the white mother-of-pearl hilt of his own sword, it was fitted with a grip of black onyx.

Morris held it out towards him. 'It belonged to Pritchard.'

Keane took the sword, whose blade had been twisted by the force of the explosion, and stared at it. Morris must be right. But it was still not conclusive proof that the man who had owned it lay among the rubble of the building.

He shook his head. 'How can we be sure?'

'James, surely.'

'No. It's not enough.'

It was a desolate scene and Keane was desperate to leave as

quickly as possible. Surely, he thought, this place would yield no more secrets.

Morris gave a shout. 'Christ almighty! James, come here.'

Keane picked his way through the stones and found his friend standing over all that was left of a man. The head had gone and the right arm – presumably the one they had already – but the torso remained intact, though blackened by flames. Morris was pointing down at it and Keane followed his gaze to the dead man's hand. Keane could see that the little finger bore a gold ring engraved with a crest.

Morris spoke again. 'There's your proof, James. That's Pritchard. No doubt.'

Keane, though nauseous at the sight, stooped and lifted the hand. He shuddered. It was still warm from the explosion, in a mockery of life. Then, carefully, he grasped the ring and eased it off the finger. 'This will do as proof for Grant. Well done, Tom.' It was enough for Grant, he thought, but it still did not tell them who had set the explosion. The business was far from concluded.

Placing the signet ring in his pocket, Keane turned and with Morris walked carefully through the ruin and into the street, which was alive with people. They stood, dazed and deafened by the explosion, some of them nursing wounds from blast fragments. One woman was wailing and running from house to house and person to person, screaming someone's name, a husband or a child unaccounted for. The blast had travelled upward and sideways, ripping a hole through the two houses to the left of Pritchard's dwelling, with the bizarre random ill fortune that typified such explosions. And thus a device intended to kill one man had brought death and suffering to a neighbourhood.

Keane thought for a moment and, as they walked, turned

to Morris. 'Have you realized, Tom, that had we been but two minutes earlier, we too might have ended up like Pritchard?'

Morris blanched. 'No, I had not. You don't suppose it was intended for us?'

'Not for a moment. But what luck.' Though, for an instant, Keane half wondered whether Morris might have been right. They stood together in the street and, as the dust cleared, Keane saw bodies lying closer to the house. A woman lay in the gutter, much of her head taken away, and beside her one of the urchin children, half eviscerated.

Morris shook his head. 'No matter how long I serve in the army, James, I cannot countenance the death of the innocent. Yet the longer this war continues the more civilians seem to die. Is that to be the future of all war, d'you suppose? That all should die? Not merely soldiers such as you and I, but entire peoples.'

'That has always been the way, Tom, you know that. The innocent have always suffered in war. War has no favourites. Singles out none for its special attention.'

'Yes, but this war, James, is somehow different. These people. It has become a way of life for them. Why should they die?'

It was a thought, he knew, that had often troubled his friend, as it did Keane himself and many others, but he had not heard Morris speak with such passion about it before. This war might be different, but there was something about his friend which was different also. It worried him and he wondered if he was witnessing a change in Morris's temperament that had not been there previously.

'They all fight now, Tom. You know what the guerrillas say: this is a war to free their country. These people – women, children – are simply justified casualties in the struggle. Just as any soldiers might be.'

Morris nodded at the mangled corpses. 'Yes, but they didn't deserve to die like that.'

'No, no one deserves such a fate. And of course they didn't. But you must agree that their death and that of the provost in there are but a small price to pay for our being rid of the spy. Who knows how many lives Pritchard's death today has saved?'

'Yes, put like that, I can see there must be a greater purpose to it, although my mind still has so many questions left unanswered.'

Keane nodded. 'Mine too, dear friend. And chief among them now is, who it was killed Colonel Pritchard?'

3

Keane drew the spyglass from his saddlebag and clicked it open before putting it to his eye to survey the plains of León. The landscape stretched away from him – parched midsummer fields under a blazing sky – and there, rising in the middle distance, the city of Ciudad Rodrigo: isolated, helpless and besieged.

Keane stared at it through the glass and considered the situation. The city of ten thousand souls, with a garrison half that number, had been invested since the end of April, almost two months, and for half that time had been under constant bombardment from some two hundred French guns.

Keane knew how that must feel – the constant whine of the incoming rounds of shell and ball shot which smashed into the masonry or exploded high above your head, raining down death and lethal shards of red-hot metal upon anyone below: soldier and civilian alike. He thought for a moment of the two bodies at the wreckage of Pritchard's house. His mind was filled with the image of the woman and child, innocent victims, caught in the bomb blast, lying in the gutter in Celorico, and he amplified it a thousand times. This then would be the extent of the human catastrophe that was about to unfold here, at Ciudad. And he was powerless to prevent it.

It was relentless, although Keane knew too that General Herrasti must still hold out hope that Wellington would march to lift the siege. But if what Wellington had told them was to be believed, those hopes would soon be dashed. Keane slid the glass together and replaced it in his bags, then looked at the surrounding countryside. León was as flat as any place he had ever seen, even the deserts of Egypt. It would have been suicide for Wellington, with his inferior numbers, attempt to relieve the place. It was precisely what Massena would have wanted. The ground was perfect for his large, mobile army and for the French tactics. The British and their Portuguese allies would have been swallowed up and run down by Massena's cavalry, arguably the finest in the world.

No. It was impossible to think that Wellington would come. He would sacrifice the city and its inhabitants to safeguard his army. There were times, thought Keane, when the end justified the means. And times when he thanked God that he was not in the general's place.

He thought of the people of Ciudad, the women and children, and recalled not only Celorico now but what he had witnessed the previous year at Oporto, when the army had liberated the city after it had been ravaged by the French. Eight thousand people, they said, had been butchered, the women raped, the houses ransacked. He had no doubt that the same must happen in Ciudad. And then the name of the British would be cried out by the dying and a curse called down upon the name of Wellington.

He and his men, together with the German hussars, were based at the town of Gallegos, some three miles distant from his current position overlooking Ciudad. This morning he had taken a small patrol out to the hill. Just six of them, all his own men. His boys.

There was, though, one man missing. He had left Morris at Celorico. The excuse had been that, even with the death of Pritchard, he had things to resolve about the spy. Paperwork which must be completed and allegations to be addressed in order at last to secure Heredia's lasting innocence.

But Keane knew that there was more to his absence. He had seen it at the blast site. Something in Morris's eyes that he had not seen before and which troubled him. Something hidden and new.

In fact, he felt, with no little guilt, glad that his friend was not here. There would have been nothing worse than having to deal with Morris's lack of faith in their mission and their command in the open, before the men.

They were under orders to observe and, if he saw an opportunity, seize information. But in the ten days he had been here no such opportunity had arisen. Keane had watched the French from the rear as they went about their business. Today was no different, he thought. Some time soon, surely, the place would fall. But not today.

Sam Gilpin was beside him. The gutter thief he had liberated from jail and whose talent at mimicry had already been used to good effect as a spy.

'Queer, ain't it, sir, how we can't do nothing to help them. Makes you feel useless as a whore's rosary.'

'Yes, Gilpin, I know exactly what you mean. If only there was some means of aiding them. But all we can do is sit here and watch. And we know what must happen in the end.'

It's a bloody shame, sir. And those poor women and wee children in there too.'

'We have our orders. There is nothing we can do.'

'The general's not going to come is he, sir?'

'No, Gilpin, I don't think we need have any fear of that.'

He was about to turn and head back once again to join the others at Gallegos, when there was a shout from behind him, where Will Martin, keen-eyed as a hawk, had been looking out across the barren landscape.

'Sir, over there, on the right. In the distance, there. Something's moving.'

Keane took out the glass again and put it to his eye. A dust cloud was billowing across the plain, suggesting men on the move. The boy was right. From the French lines it appeared that someone or something was moving in their direction. And it was moving fast. He handed the glass to Ross.

'There, sarn't. What d'you make of that?'

The Scotsman put the telescope to his eye. 'Someone's coming, sir, I'd say so. Horsemen. Quite a few of them too, by the look of it. Can't see who they are.'

Keane stared at the dust cloud. 'But I think we might guess. Best not take any chances, eh?'

He took the glass back from Ross and, having stowed it, pulled on the reins and turned his horse. 'We'll pull back. We may have been seen.' He cast a glance behind him and saw that, as he had feared, the dust cloud was drawing ever nearer. He could see horses in it now, and above them something catching the light of the sun which sat high in the sky. Something glistening. A touch of gold.

'Dragoons. They're dragoons, lads. Come on.'

The word was enough. They needed no other command. Together the six horsemen dug their spurs into the flanks of their mounts and headed away down the far slope of the slight hill on which they had been standing to observe the city.

They were certainly dragoons, thought Keane, but why the devil would Massena send them out from the French lines?

He was well aware that their mounts were not the equal of those ridden by the dragoons. In fact, they were hugely inferior animals and could not hope to outrun the French for long. He prayed that they would make it back to Gallegos and the rest of the force.

They reached the bottom of the slope and rode on, spurring into the flanks of their horses. Though sorely tempted, Keane did not look behind. The slightest delay might cost everything. He wondered why the dragoons were bothering to give chase. Surely Massena would simply want the observing British and Portuguese to be driven off their post overlooking the city?

Then another thought struck him. What if it was not merely the forward positions Massena wanted but the outposts as well. The marshal must know about his and others like it which formed a half-circle around the French lines. If that were the case, then it was possible that not even his full force would be a match for whatever men Massena had despatched to take their post.

He dug his spurs in deeper and urged on his horse. And at last the roofs of Gallegos came into view. Keane overtook the others and as soon as he entered the village pulled up and swung himself out of the saddle. He looked around and at last saw the man he sought.

Von Krokenburgh was leaning against the door of a deserted village house, puffing on a cigar.

'Keane, what news?'

Keane was breathless. 'The French . . . French dragoons . . . on our tail. They'll be here in minutes. Stand your men to, quick, man.'

The German needed no retelling. He turned and barked an order to his sergeant major, then, finding a lieutenant, directed him towards his men.

Keane's men were dismounting now; pulling their carbines from their long leather holsters, they left their horses to one of the German farriers, who led them to the rear with those of his own regiment. This was no work for mounted men.

Ross shouted, 'Carbines. Draw carbines and form a line across the street, two deep.'

Keane turned to von Krokenburgh and pointed to the first four houses in the street. 'We need men up in those houses, captain. At the upper windows.' Unquestioning, the German yelled a command and two of his sergeants ran for the houses, followed by a dozen hussars, carbines in their hands.

This was the sort of fighting Keane knew best. For although he was handy with a sabre, he was no cavalry officer but an infantryman through and through. Twenty years with the colours in the Inniskillens had seen to that. He was never more at his ease than when standing behind a line two deep with muskets levelled at the French. His men, while drawn from various arms, were likewise at their best when used as infantry. Their role was that of skirmishers, though. They were, almost to a man, keen shots, and he often thought that, had they been equipped with the Baker rifles issued to the riflemen of the 95th, they might have accounted for a great deal more of the enemy.

It said much for the Germans that they too formed line with ease, and not for the first time Keane admired their ordered efficiency. But it was not before time. For hardly had they been given the command to load and make ready than the lead dragoons appeared at the entrance to the village. Seeing the line of brown- and blue-coated soldiers across the street between two buildings, the first of the horsemen pulled up and turned to shout to the others. But it was too late. Those behind had already careered into the leaders, and just as they did so Keane gave a command and the carbines blazed.

The leading horses reared up and several of the dragoons recoiled sharply, jerking like puppets as the rounds tore into them. In the crush the following ranks could not advance and there was no need for Keane's men to be told to reload. It was natural. Four rounds a minute they could manage, as good as any infantry battalion. They raised the carbines to their shoulders again, just beating the Germans by a whisker, and again the bullets whipped into the green-coated enemy.

The French were whirling in a confused mass as Keane and Ross yelled at the men to keep firing. Hands fumbled with cartridges as teeth bit paper and spat the ball down the hot barrels. From the windows of the houses the carbines of the German hussars cracked as they caught the horsemen in a deadly crossfire.

It did not take long for the dragoons to realize the hopelessness of their position. A moustachioed captain held up his hand to give the command and the men wheeled around and rode hell for leather away from the village, leaving their comrades dead and dying before the line of exhausted defenders.

Keane yelled, 'Cease firing.' And at last the men relaxed.

A dragoon clawed the dust and sank to the ground as an injured horse raised its head and whinnied in agony. One of the hussars walked across and despatched it with a single shot to the head, and for a moment Keane wondered if he might not do the same to the man who lay beside it, gasping for water. But the hussar knelt down and gave the Frenchman a drink from his own canteen. It was hard, thought Keane, to gauge the Germans. At times they were like men possessed, fighting for their homeland at any cost. At others they displayed all the courtesies of a soldier of a hundred years before. In this case, though, perhaps there was another motive. He walked across to the hussar. 'Will he live?'

The man replied in a heavy German accent. 'I think so, sir.'

'Then bring him in. I need to speak to him.'

Walking over to the house, Keane passed Martin. 'We did well, Will, to stop them.'

'Yes, sir. Do you think they'll try again?'

'I don't know, Will. Don't know why they chased us back here. I'll let you know when I do.' He motioned the hussar and another trooper, who was helping him carry the wounded dragoon, to take him into the house. Inside, in the cool dark of the single room which was kitchen and living space, Keane swept the table clear of the few possessions left on it by its owners in their flight and had the men place the Frenchman upon it. The man groaned and Keane looked at his face. He was young, probably still in his teens. A carbine ball, smaller than a musket round, but no less deadly, had hit him in the shoulder, and Keane wondered how mortal a wound it might be. He knew from experience that such a shot could travel towards the heart.

Ross entered. 'Sir. What was that about, do you think?'

'That's what I want to find out, sarn't. If this lad will tell me. Do you know if any of Captain von Krokenburgh's men has any medical skills?'

'No, sir, I don't, but I could ask.'

'Yes, do that. And you had better get Gabriella, if you can find her.'

Ross went and as Keane was staring at the pallid face, contorted with pain, another figure appeared at the door. It was Archer, the new arrival. 'Begging your pardon, sir, but I heard from Sergeant Ross that you were seeking medical assistance.'

'Yes, this poor bugger needs help. And I need his help to find out what those French bastards were about.'

'If I might take a look at him, sir.'

'You, Archer? What do you know of medicine?'

'A little, sir. Before I joined the ranks I was training to be a physician. In Edinburgh.'

'Were you, by God?' Of course Major Grant had not mentioned the fact. His idea of a joke, thought Keane, allowing him to discover when the time came and not before. It was typical of the man's dry sense of humour. Nevertheless Archer's experience would be invaluable now.

'Can you help him?'

Archer walked to the table and, peering down at the boy, touched the entry wound. The dragoon winced and cried out. Archer whispered an apology in French. '*Pardon.*'

'Is it a bad wound?' asked Keane. 'I know with a shoulder a ball may travel to the heart, isn't that so?'

Archer nodded. 'The danger, sir, is that the ball will reach the great vessels and cause a fatal haemorrhage. It's hard to tell how close this ball is without cutting.'

'Then cut, man, if it will save him. We need to know what the French are about and if they intend to return. For heavens' sake, cut him if needs be.'

Archer shot him a glance. 'Sir, with respect, if I cut him he may die. If I do not, he may well die also. I have to take a considered course of action.'

Keane nodded. 'Yes, of course. You will know best. But make it quick, man.'

Archer reached into his pocket and produced a roll of material. Carefully unrolling it on the table, he revealed an array of steel instruments of the sort that Keane had often seen in the surgeons' tent. Taking a pointed steel, Archer gently poked at the area around the entry hole. The dragoon screamed.

Ross was in the room now, along with Gabriella and Silver, who spoke. 'A gag. We need a gag. A bit of wood. Anything.' Looking around the room he saw a small wooden spoon which he placed across the open mouth of the dragoon. The man's teeth closed upon it and as Archer probed he began to writhe.

Gabriella found a pitcher standing in a corner and pouring from it into a beaker, tried the water. She poured more and brought it to the dragoon, whose open eyes were rolling in agony.

Silver spoke. 'Christ, the poor devil. Have we no brandy?'

Archer, still working carefully at the wound, spoke quietly. 'No, no brandy. It will have little effect on the pain and it will thin the blood. He may have some later, if he lives.'

Keane watched closely and found himself praying for the Frenchman's life.

Archer changed tools, selecting a pair of tiny silver pincers. Pushing hard on the dragoon's shoulder he inserted the head of the instrument into the wound. The man's screams could be heard even through the wooden gag, and for a moment Keane thought he must die. At the crescendo, Archer held the pincers up and Keane could see that in their teeth lay a small lead ball.

Archer grinned. 'Got it, the little bugger.'

The Frenchman lay motionless and again Keane presumed that he was dead. Archer dropped the ball on to the cloth and, laying down the pincers, leant close to the man's face. He looked at him and reached for a small mirror, one of the tools that had been rolled in the fabric, which he held to his mouth. A few seconds later he withdrew it and looked at it before showing it to Keane. It had misted over. 'He's alive.'

Keane slapped the table. 'Thank God. Can we bring him round?'

'Not for at least an hour, I'm afraid.'

'That's impossible. Quite out of the question. The French might return at any moment.'

'What is even more out of the question, sir, is bringing him round. The man is still in a state of shock and needs rest. To bring him round might result in trauma, even death.'

Keane scowled. 'Very well. An hour. No more, though.'

He walked to the door and was about to leave when he turned and looked back. 'Oh, and well done, Archer. Quite a surprise. I would never have guessed. Come and see me when you've tidied up.'

Keane walked along the street and watched as the hussars dealt with their few dead and wounded. He thanked God there were not many. He met Archer as he left the house. 'Where did you say you had studied?'

'Edinburgh, sir, under Doctor Ramsay.'

'And you never entered the profession? Why on earth not? What went wrong? And why did you end up here, for God's sake? What did you do, man?'

'Didn't they tell you, sir?'

'No, evidently not. It was Colonel Grant who appointed you to my unit, was it not?'

'Yes, sir. He's one of my mother's relations.'

'Well, that would explain something at least. But why? Where did he find you?'

'In the jail, sir. I stole a loaf of bread.'

'Well, that's not a hanging offence, is it?'

'Not yet, sir, anyways. No, sir. Twenty lashes.'

'Not so bad. And he managed to get you out, but how did you come to the army in the first place?'

Archer said nothing.

'You'll have to tell me, man. I'll find out somehow if you do not.'

'I lost my way, sir.'

'Lost your way?'

'Fell in with the wrong crowd. I gambled, sir. Debts. Couldn't see a way out.'

'But you found one, nevertheless.'

'Yes, sir, I was a resurrectionist.'

'You mean you . . . ?'

'Yes, sir. I dug up corpses newly dead and sold them to the college of surgeons.'

'Good heavens, and that made you enough money?'

'Enough to pay my gambling debts, yes, sir. There's no law against it. They're no one's property, the dead. Long as you strip them of everything. Rings, clothes, anything, they're fair game.'

'So how did you come to be here?'

He buried his head in his hands. 'It all went wrong. It came to it that I was getting them before they were cold and not even buried but straight from their beds. That was when they got me. One night I pronounced a woman dead. She'd stopped breathing and no heartbeat. We stripped her and everything. Got her in the wagon. We were taking her body from the carriage into the college to sell to Doctor Barclay.'

'What happened?'

'What happened, sir? She only came round, didn't she? Sat

up and screamed the place down. Said I was trying to kill her. Of course they took me. Had me for attempted murder.'

'You were tried?'

He nodded his head. 'Yes, sir. Convicted for attempted murder and other counts too. People they said I'd killed. They pinned them on me, sir. I never killed anyone.'

'Nevertheless you were convicted.'

'Yes. Sentenced to death. The judge offered me the chance to join. Take my chance with the colours. So I did.'

Keane thought for a moment. 'You stole a loaf of bread, you say?'

'Yes, sir. From one of the men in my company.'

'Just a loaf of bread. Nothing more. Is that true?'

Archer looked away. 'Stole some money too, sir.'

'Gambling?'

Archer nodded.

'You're a bloody fool, Archer. Carry on like that and you will end up on the end of a rope. Major Grant has given you another chance with us. He must have seen something in you.'

'He's family, sir. That's why.'

Keane nodded. 'Yes, that'll be it.'

But Keane knew Grant, and he knew that the man would not have plucked the boy and placed him with them, whatever relation he might be, without some further motive. He guessed that it might be his medical skills. Or his expertise as a thief and a grave robber. It was evident from his gambling debts that it was not his skill at cards.

'You seemed very adept with your instruments.'

Archer smiled. 'They said I was the best student in my year, sir. That I would go far. Look at me.'

'You're young. You have another chance now. Don't waste it. The dragoon, will he be sufficiently recovered now?'

'He might be, sir. I couldn't say for certain. Could go either way.'

'I'll take that chance. Come with me.'

Together they walked back to the house, where Gabriella had been sitting with the Frenchman. Like all her compatriots, she had no love for them. But she knew how vital it was for Keane to get information from the man and so she made sure he remained alive. Who knew what might happen later?

They found the man in the same place, but now his eyes were open. Sweat streaked his forehead, and on seeing Keane and the other man a look of panic spread across his face.

Keane spoke, in French. 'It's all right, there is no need to fear. All I want is some information.'

The man stared at him, still terror-stricken.

Keane continued. 'I need to know how many of you there are. Are there more of you?'

The man opened his mouth, but seemed unable to speak. Archer motioned to Gabriella. 'Get him some water. He's parched.'

She poured a beaker of water and held it to his lips. The dragoon gulped and swallowed and as he did so the look of fear seemed to slip from his face.

Keane asked again, 'How many are you? How many more?'

The dragoon said nothing. Merely looked hard at Keane, who asked again, 'Tell me your strength. I need to know. I've saved your life. I need something in return.'

The dragoon continued to stare at him.

Keane tried another tack. He gestured towards Gabriella. 'She is Portuguese. Do you know what your countrymen did to her family? Can you imagine? And to her? What do you suppose she would like to do to you?' He paused as the dragoon looked at

Gabriella, who, not understanding a word, smiled back at him. Keane carried on. 'Perhaps you're right. You have nothing to tell me. Come on, Archer, we'll leave this poor bugger to Gabriella. I don't want to watch her at work. She's better than one of your surgeons with a knife. Poor bastard.'

Keane led the way to the door and Archer followed.

Suddenly the dragoon called out, 'Don't go. Please. I'll tell you what you need to know.'

Keane turned and retraced his steps. 'Tell me.'

'We are brigade strength. Under the command of Général de Brigade Sainte-Croix.'

'A mixed force?'

'Yes, sir. Five battalions of infantry, six squadrons of dragoons and artillery. Six-pounders.'

'How many of you in the advance party?'

'Two hundred. All dragoons.'

'Thank you. And one thing more: does Marshal Massena believe that Wellington will raise the siege and come to the rescue of the Spaniards?'

'I am only a sous-lieutenant, sir.'

'Monsieur, the French army, it is well known, is very different from our own. Any officer or even a man in Napoleon's army knows or can guess what his commander intends. I could ask you again.'

'He does not know. He saw some of your patrols. Here to the west. That is why he ordered General Junot to send us after you. To find out.'

'So your friends and maybe more besides will return to see how strong we are and if we mean to raise the siege.'

The man shrugged. 'If you say so, captain.'

'Thank you. You have been most helpful. Archer, stay with

him and see that Gabriella does nothing untoward. We need to get him back to General Craufurd in one piece. Call Silver if you need to, if she tries anything.'

Archer looked across at her and she shot him a smile. 'Will she?'

'Who knows. She hates the French.'

He walked to the door, where Ross had been standing during the interrogation.

'Do you think he was lying, sir?'

'No, I think he was terrified. He was telling the truth, sarn't.

'Well, Sainte-Croix can come. We'll fall back on the Light Division. Perhaps he will think we really are the vanguard of the main army. It will waste time and that is precisely what Wellington wants – anything that wastes time and pins down Massena while we finish the defences.'

As they walked from the building Ross asked him, 'Would you have left him to her, sir? Really?'

'What do you think?'

'I don't think you would, sir. You're not made that way. You don't like cruelty or pain.'

'I'll not be known as soft, sarn't. I'm as happy as the next man to dish out any amount of pain if it has a purpose. But I got more with the threat of pain then than any amount of torture could have uncovered. Besides, he would have died and then we would have less than nothing.'

'You're no fool, captain, sir. I'll say that.'

'I'll take that as the compliment it was intended, sarn't.'

'Others would have tried to beat it out of him.'

'And others would have failed. I happen to believe that there is more to soldiering than brute force. Right. We'd better get saddled up before his friends come back. We need to beat them to General Craufurd.'

4

The road took them west, from Gallegos, towards the river Côa, away from the plains of León, through a parched landscape of brush and barren rock. Keane's horse trod carefully, picking her way through the scrub and the boulders that lay across the roads, which, little used before, had lately seen the passage of thousands of travellers.

Such was the discipline of both Keane's men and the Germans that they had managed to leave the village before the dragoons had returned, though not, Keane guessed, with much margin of error. He and his men rode at the head of the column, with the German hussars following. Keane himself took the lead, with Ross beside him and the others tucked in close behind. Trotting quickly, as they climbed the long hill road out of the village he spoke to Ross.

'Did you know that Archer was a physician?'

'No, sir. No idea. He kept that quiet, right enough.'

'We're damned lucky to have him, sarn't. It's not just the enemy who'll benefit. We might all have to put that skill to good use before long.'

'Yes, sir. Things are getting hotter, ain't they? Them dragoons are close behind and half the French army with them.'

'Not quite half, sarn't, but certainly a good portion, according to our green friend there.'

'Sooner we reach General Craufurd, sir, the better.'

'Yes, he needs to know the extent of the force on its way to him. And even he will be hard pressed to hold them up.'

Brigadier General Robert Craufurd, or 'Black Bob' as he was affectionately known to the rank and file, on account of his volatile temper and liking for strict discipline, had positioned his command, the recently formed 'Light Division', just before the village of Alameda. Although a division by name, it was actually no more than an oversized brigade, comprising two English battalions – the 43rd and 52nd – two of Portuguese 'cacadores' riflemen and the 95th Rifles.

Keane knew that Craufurd was their only hope. If he could make it to the Light Division's lines then at least they had a chance of halting the pursuing French. If not, it would all be up for them. Even the Hanoverian hussars, attacked on the march in column by enemy cavalry, would stand little chance. A handful of guides and a couple of squadrons of hussars, however bravely they fought, could not hope to take on an entire brigade.

He yelled back to the men, 'Spur on, come on,' and dug his own spurs into the flanks of the mare. Within a few minutes they had picked up speed and were galloping fast. Looking into the distance Keane could see the village, which he knew from his map must be Alameda, beyond which lay the Portuguese border.

Before it an old stone bridge lay across a narrow river – the Duas Casas. He could make out a body of troops now, formed up in line behind the bridge. Craufurd's men, surely.

He yelled again: 'Across the bridge. Get across.' Turning, he glanced behind and what he saw filled him with dread. For there, still distant but nevertheless closing fast with the rear of the column, he could see another body of horsemen. 'Dragoons to your rear. Come on.'

Lashing both sides of his horse's neck now with his reins, Keane again dug in the spurs and muttered oaths. The animal pushed herself hard and Keane could feel her limbs throbbing and sense her distress. All of them were riding hard now, Silver holding the wounded dragoon in the saddle as they neared the bridge. From behind, the crackle of gunfire told him that the French dragoons had opened up from the saddle with their weapons and he wondered whether von Krokenburgh's hussars would have replied. He was on the bridge now, and beyond, in front of the village, he could see the line of battle deployed in green and red with the brown of the Portuguese cacadores. Craufurd's vanguard was formed up two deep across a wide front and Keane counted the four battalions, with the Rifles in front in skirmish order. He noticed that there were cavalry too, posted on the wings. He laughed and shouted to Martin, 'See, Will, there we are. Salvation.'

Martin gave a whoop and pushed past Keane, arriving at the lines first. He jumped from his horse and turned to pull off his carbine before sending the animal to the rear. Keane followed suit and with him the others. Gabriella alone remained with the horses, and the wounded dragoon.

Keane called, 'Silver, make yourself known to General Craufurd. Tell him that we're here and that there's a French division on our heels.'

Silver nodded. 'Sir,' and went to find the general.

Keane turned to Ross. 'Sarn't, we'll join the line. Stop those bastards a second time.'

There was a shot as a rifleman on picket, seeing Keane and his men, discharged his weapon above their heads.

'Who goes there? Friend or foe?'

Keane yelled back, 'Friend, rifleman. Captain Keane, Corps of Guides.'

The rifleman waived them on into the lines.

The hussars were coming in now along with a few riderless horses that told a tale of their own. Von Krokenburgh led them off to the left flank and Keane reported to the first redcoat officer he could find, a callow lad of the 43rd who greeted him with a stammer and a grin.

'Good day, sir. We thought you might be French. You're fortunate that you were not killed.'

Keane stared at him. 'Really, Lieutenant . . . ?'

'Steerforth, sir.'

'Lieutenant Steerforth, it is you that are fortunate that you still live. We might as well have taken you for red-coated Swiss in the French service, might we not? And you should know, lieutenant, that my men are not particular. They prefer to fire first and then ascertain their target.' He paused. 'May we join you? We do have an enemy, as you can see, and not a minute to waste.'

He pointed across the bridge to the dragoons, and the boy, dumbfounded, nodded before turning to his men. 'Company, ready. Prepare to receive cavalry.'

As he had been talking, Keane's men had formed up two deep at the end of a file and there he joined them, preferring to stand in the ranks. They readied their weapons and waited for the dragoons, who were now less than two hundred yards distant.

Keane watched as Leech, the gunner, bit the end of his cartridge, spat the ball down the barrel and rammed it home with the expertise of an infantryman.

'Ready, Leech?'

'Ready as ever I'll be to die, sir.'

'I didn't mean that.'

'I know, sir, but you might as well be ready for it, mightn't you?'

The French were on them now, near as dammit. He could hear their yells and their officers' commands. The sun glinted on their drawn sabres.

In their own lines he heard the young lieutenant bark the command to 'present' and a company of muskets were pointed at the enemy as his own men raised their carbines. But then, to his surprise, the dragoons veered away across the lines and towards the north and it was there they struck at the line, the 43rd's volley hitting them at an angle as they went. Looking more closely he realized they had gone deliberately for a regiment of brown-coated Portuguese.

He waited for the clash as sabre met bayonet, but instead there was another crashing volley, and as Keane watched, still waiting for the attack, through the white smoke he saw dozens of green-coated cavalry in retreat. streaming back across the bridge.

Steerforth had seen them too and waved his hat in the air. 'Hoorah. Well done, my brave lads.'

Led by their sergeant, his men, whose trust and affection he had not yet gained, gave a ragged, reluctant chorus.

Heredia spat on the ground and then turned to Keane. 'Did you hear him? He thinks that was his doing, does he? Doesn't he know it was my countrymen? The cacadores?'

Keane chose to ignore the insubordination. 'No, Heredia, I don't think he does, and if you told him he wouldn't believe you. That sort will never hold that any Portuguese soldier is the equal of the worst-led Englishman.'

Keane knew Heredia was right. It had been the Portuguese riflemen, albeit British trained and equipped, who had driven off the French, and the enemy would know next time not to expect an easy victory from them. They watched as the French turned tail, a few shots chasing them across the bridge.

Heredia had turned to Keane and was about to speak again when a red-coated British officer rode up and cut him short. The colonel wore a hat cocked fore and aft and what looked as if it might be a permanent sneer. His coat was trimmed with gold bullion and he was heavy-set, with a shock of grey hair that almost matched the coat of the handsome hunter on which he rode and which Keane rightly guessed had come from his own stable in the shires. He looked down at Keane. 'Who the devil are you?'

'James Keane, sir, captain, Corps of Guides.'

'Oh, guides, are you? A spy, eh, captain? We shall have to watch ourselves.' Keane ignored him and the man continued. 'Well, being a spy, you probably know it already, but the news is, we're on the move, Captain Keane. Whatever your business may be here. General Craufurd's orders. We're all to fall back. Including your lot. There's a brigade of the French coming up here.'

Keane smiled. 'I know, sir, I passed the general that message. We came from the front. From the outposts above Ciudad.'

The man's face, already florid, grew even redder. 'You did, did you? And then I suppose you joined our lines?'

'Yes, sir.'

'And you engaged the enemy and drove them off?'

'Yes, sir, although we did not see them off. That was done by the cacadores.'

Heredia smiled.

The man, seeming at a loss for words, stared at Keane's brown uniform. 'What the devil d'you call that guise? That's no uniform for an English officer. You're Portuguese yourself, aren't you?'

'No, sir. Corps of Guides, as I said before.'

He stared at Heredia. 'But this man here's a Porto isn't he? How's that?'

'He is one of my men, sir. Late of the Portuguese cavalry. We have all sorts in our company.'

The colonel frowned. 'Yes, so I can see. Well, you're to join us now, for our sins.'

Silver arrived. 'Sir, General Craufurd asks if you will attend him at once. He would know more of the French force.'

The colonel stepped back in astonishment, stuck for speech. Keane smiled. 'Thank you, Silver. Right, lads, you'd better follow me.' He turned and looked up at the colonel. 'Colonel, I think you might be as well to follow your own advice and General Craufurd's orders and retire before the French arrive. They have a division on its way, you know.' He turned before the officer could reply and led the way at the head of his men, knowing the air behind him would be blue with oaths.

Once they were out of earshot, Ross laughed. 'You're a danger to yourself, sir. One of these days you'll go too far.'

'But not today, Ross, eh?'

'Even so, sir, you'd be better not to do the same to Black Bob.'

They found Craufurd standing on a large rock which gave a view out over the plain below them. He was raking the landscape with the telescope and it seemed at first as if he had not noticed them. But after a few moments, still with the glass to his eye, he looked down at them and spoke.

'You're Keane?'

'Yes, sir.'

The face was instantly familiar and yet at the same time not that of anyone he could call friend. General Sir Robert Craufurd was a legend in the army, as feared as he was loved. Black Bob, along with the late Sir John Moore, had created the Light Division as it now existed.

The Light Division. A division of light infantry. A relatively new concept of units which fought using the tactics that had been developed in America during the revolution with such devastating results. There was something more. The individual intelligence of each and every one of the men was far above that of the rank and file. It took them, it was said, a mere seven minutes to get themselves under arms at night-time and just a quarter of an hour to form line of battle, day or night. The Light Division was Crawford's child and he used it with care and good judgement. Wellington trusted him completely.

Craufurd stared at Keane. Seemed to be judging him, as if he could read into his soul. 'Good. Perhaps you can be of more use to me than this damned glass. How many of them are there? Exactly.'

'As I understand it, sir, there is the best part of a division, but with support. Five thousand men, of all arms.'

'Who commands?'

'Général de Brigade Sainte-Croix, sir.'

Craufurd nodded. 'Sainte-Croix. Yes. I see.' He climbed down from the rock and stood facing Keane. He was a little shorter, with straight dark hair parted in the centre, heavy eyebrows and a deeply furrowed forehead that seemed to warn of his quick temper. 'Go on, Keane. How many cannon?'

'Only some light guns as far as we could see, sir. Perhaps a half horse battery.'

Craufurd nodded and thought for a moment. 'That's good work, Keane. Major Grant spoke well of you and he was as good as his word.'

'Do you have any further orders for me, sir? Anything from Major Grant?'

Craufurd shook his head. 'No, nothing. Were you expecting something?'

'I had hoped that I might return to headquarters at Celorico. I have some unfinished business there.'

'No, Keane. I have received no such order. What will you do now? Your post is driven in. You cannot return. Sainte-Croix will be there already. I presume that, failing any new instruction, your orders were to remain with us?'

Keane nodded. 'Yes, sir. Just that.'

'Then that is what you must do, captain. We will stand here against General Sainte-Croix and you alongside us. I need every good officer I can muster and in battle as in the work of a scout your name precedes you, Captain Keane. You did well at Oporto.'

'You are kind, sir.'

'Kind, man? Kindness has nothing to do with it, dammit. Praise where it's due, Keane. Only where it's due. You did well.'

Keane nodded. Had he done well at Oporto? He had defended a half-built monastery for the best part of a day against a French division with no more than his own men and two companies of redcoats. And in doing so, they had bought just enough time for Wellington to cross the Douro and take the city. Yes, he supposed that he had done well.

Craufurd spoke again. 'It's a damned shame we can do nothing for the city. But there it is. We can hardly take on the entire French army. But the Spaniards see my force here and presume I will attack. It's what a Spanish general would do,

isn't it, Keane? Go and save his people. But my orders expressly
forbid it. Look at this.'

He held out a note, written in a scrawl on a piece of parch-
ment. 'Sent from General Herrasti in Ciudad, two days ago. You
read Spanish?'

'Yes, sir.' Keane took it and looked at the paper. It bore few
words: '*O venir, luego! luego! a secorrer esta plaza.*'

It was beyond doubt the last desperate plea of a doomed man
and it seemed to Keane that it must have been written in the
full knowledge that all it asked was in vain. He handed it back
to Craufurd.

'Is there really nothing we can do, sir? Surely to allow the
palace to fall will be unbearably grievous a dishonour for the
army.'

'It is, I would guess, one of the hardest decisions that our commander has ever been forced to take. The world looks on and
wonders if his promise to protect Portugal is a hollow sham. It
wants an indication of our earnestness. But this we cannot give.
The duke cannot go to help Ciudad. You realize that, captain,
as well as I do.'

Keane nodded. 'Yes, sir, in truth I do. But I have seldom felt
so sick at heart.'

Craufurd nodded solemnly. 'And I share your sentiment. But
five thousand ill-disciplined and useless Spanish brought off
from Ciudad will not recompense the duke for the same number
or more of our own good troops who would certainly be lost in
the taking of it.'

It was sound sense and Keane knew it. The soldier in him
asserted its truth and, as was always the way, it was the soldier
who won against the man of humanity. And it was clear, he

thought, that Craufurd was not in Cavanagh's camp, in favour
of an all-or-nothing battle. He was Wellington's man.

Craufurd spoke. 'God knows when Sainte-Croix will reach us.
His dragoons will have told him of our presence. I only hope
that he will believe we are the vanguard of the army, come to
raise the siege. That is the impression we must aim to give. I'd
be glad to have you and your men here.'

Keane wondered if the general would have had the same
enthusiasm had he found Heredia as he discovered him a few
minutes later. He was apart from the others. The man was sitting on a rock and staring into the distance while puffing on a
cheroot. He seemed preoccupied.

Keane stood beside him. 'Heredia, you are very thoughtful.'

The Portuguese trooper was not exactly insubordinate but he
was not now accustomed to rising in the presence of an officer.
He looked up at Keane before replying. Again Keane chose to
ignore the fact. 'I have cause to be, captain. As you well know.'

'Meaning?'

'Colonel Pritchard.'

'Colonel Pritchard is dead, man. Blown to atoms, well, almost.
Dead for certain in the ruins of his house.'

'Yes, I know. That is what troubles me.'

'What? Why?'

'Now I can never be completely clear of the crime of which I
was accused. He takes his secret to his grave.'

'But Major Grant attests for you. And Captain Morris assured
me that he would undertake paperwork that would prove your
acquittal.'

'Is that enough? When Major Grant is gone, as he may be,
then who will plead my case. It might be forgotten that I was
innocent.'

'For your information, Heredia, the Duke of Wellington believes Major Grant.'

'Are you sure? I think he would rather have believed Colonel Pritchard.'

'You're a free man. Isn't that all that matters?'

'Am I truly free? It's a question of honour, captain.'

'There is nothing that can be done to that end. Pritchard is dead.'

'Unless Pritchard was not working alone.'

Keane paused. 'Do you think that might be the case?'

'I don't know. Just something I noticed. Captain Morris mentioned it to me. Pritchard always took two copies of everything.'

'That's standard practice on the duke's staff, isn't it?'

'Perhaps, but he paid more attention to detail than most. Did Captain Morris not tell you about this?'

'No, actually, he did not.'

'In that case perhaps it is not important. Perhaps I should not think so hard.'

But Keane knew that Heredia had an agile mind. It was one of the qualities that he valued most in him. There must be something to Morris's having noticed Pritchard's modus operandi.

But if so, then why, if it were something so fundamental, should Morris not have mentioned it to him? He did not doubt his friend for a moment and half wondered whether this might be a ploy by Heredia to drive some barrier between them. It occurred to him that the Portuguese was adept at playing off one man against another. He had seen it with Silver and Gabriella. Heredia would get into an argument with the girl and it would end in a screaming match between Silver and his common-law wife. Quite how Heredia achieved it was beyond him. As was the reason for it. Perhaps the man was jealous.

Perhaps he just disliked one, or the other. But he knew that he should be on his guard.

Heredia shot him a glance, almost as if he could read his thoughts, and again Keane felt uneasy.

'What are we doing, sir?'

Keane was slightly caught off guard by the word from a man who was not as inclined to use it as perhaps he should.

'We're staying here. For the moment at least.'

'Staying to fight? That's a waste. That's not our job, is it? We are scouts, captain, not cannon fodder.'

'I have given my word to General Craufurd that we will lend our support to his defence. Would you have me go back on it?'

Heredia smiled and took a puff of the cheroot. 'Just an opinion, sir. Nothing more.'

Keane almost found himself coming out with the time-worn riposte that other ranks were not intended to have opinions, least of all express them, when he realized that in this unit, in his company, such a response was absurd. What bound them together was their ability to act independently, to use their intellect or their particular skills to their best ability. They were unique in the army. That was why he tolerated their ways: Heredia's rudeness and Silver's lack of punctuality. Garland's ham-fisted bouts of temper and Gilpin's wry, sarcastic wit.

His encounter with Heredia had filled his mind with misgivings. He thought back to the ruins at Celorico. To the shattered, dismembered body of the officer. It had to be Pritchard. Of that there was no doubt. But the question still remained as to who had planted the bomb. Why would anyone want him dead? The obvious answer was that he had an enemy.

Of course, it might have been a personal grievance. God knew there were enough in the army. Hadn't Keane himself aroused one such passion by killing a brother officer in a duel? But a bomb seemed an unlikely means of taking revenge and, besides, Pritchard was a spy. A traitor. And, hadn't the duke told him, a fellow Irishman to boot. It occurred to him now that that might have been his motive. There were many in the south of his homeland who would drive the British out. United Irishmen, they called themselves. Catholic and Protestant alike. Hadn't they risen up in '98? He recalled the militia officers' heads impaled on pikes at Wexford and wondered if Pritchard had seen them too. Or indeed if he had given the order.

Morris had suggested that the bomb must have been the work of another French spy. It had seemed likely to him at the time that the French might have learnt that Pritchard had been discovered and sent in someone under orders to eliminate the risk. But why a bomb? he wondered. Something so very destructive.

What, he asked himself, in passing, if the bomber had been Morris himself? But not to trust a man who had been his friend for years and with whom he had seen service? How could he even begin to think in such a way? He dismissed the thought as quickly as it had come to him.

Perhaps, he thought, the assassin had been Heredia, intent on killing the man who had done him such harm. Keane had guessed that he had sworn to manage such a thing.

And, there again, how did they know for certain that the bomb had been intended for Pritchard? Perhaps it had been meant for himself and Morris. Perhaps it had been Pritchard who had made it, and had been killed by mistake. The ideas buzzed inside his head, addling his mind.

Then another thought came to him. Perhaps the bomb had

been intended to accomplish something other than merely killing Pritchard. Perhaps its purpose was to destroy some fabric of evidence or material which might be damaging to the French should it fall into the hands of the allies. The more that he considered it, the more this last cause seemed the most likely. He knew the answer must lie in the ruins of the house. How, though, was he to return there when his orders confined him to keeping a watch on Ciudad?

He wondered if, in the absence of Morris, he should confide in any of the men. But Heredia could be ruled out, and Silver, given the animosity between the two men. Ross perhaps might offer an opinion. But there again, he thought, another opinion was the last thing he wanted. So Keane kept his silence and dwelt on the options and waited for the moment when he might have the chance to get back to Morris at Celorico, make sure of his friend and not least have a chance to investigate the ruins. He hoped it would not be too late and that he would live through the French attack.

But the French did not come. For four days they waited at Alameda as June drifted into July and still Sainte-Croix did not appear.

The men were nervous and hard-pressed to find something to do. Ross had them cleaning their weapons every day, but the usual tasks of the camp were not theirs. There were no white belts to chalk, no buttons to polish. They sat around and played dice and talked and thought about the French and the fire they were raining down upon the people of Ciudad.

At length, Craufurd summoned Keane. 'You're restless, captain. Your men too.'

'Restless, sir?' Was it so obvious?

'It isn't hard to see. But at least you're mobile. You might do

me a service. Take your men. Not the hussars – just your own
men – and carry out a reconnaissance as far as you can, until
you see the French. I need to know what has happened. I've
heard nothing from Herrasti since that last note. We need to
know if Ciudad has fallen. The minute that you know anything,
you must return. Are you clear on that? Do not on any account
engage the enemy.'

'Yes, sir. Quite clear.'

Leaving Gabriella behind, with Craufurd, they rode back down
the road along which they had come in such haste, retracing
their steps in silence, keeping a careful watch for any sign of
the French.

But there was none. At length they came within sight of Gallegos, but the little village appeared to be unoccupied. Silver,
who was riding close to Keane, spoke in a whisper. 'They've
vanished, sir. Thought they'd be here at least, getting ready to
attack us again. Finish the job.'

'So did I, Silver. It seems very strange.'

Perhaps, he thought, the dragoons had reported that Craufurd's command was greater than it actually was. Panic could
affect a man's perception. In that case it seemed likely that
Sainte-Croix might have decided it would be prudent not to
follow up. There was little evidence of the fight. The French
had taken their dead, and only a few bullet holes in the white
plaster and some patches of brown dried blood told the story.

Riding on through the village, they carried on into the
country and reached a piece of rising ground.

As soon as they did, Keane pulled up and patted his horse on
the mane. He did not require an eyeglass to tell him what he
needed to know. The pall of black smoke said it all. Ciudad was
in flames. So that was why Sainte-Croix had not come again. He

and his men had been called back to the siege, or gone voluntarily, to take part in the rape of the city.

Flames leapt up from the walls and from deep within. It seemed that even at this distance he could detect the smell of burning. A sweet, sickly scent that he knew from experience meant that people had died, were dying, in the flames.

It had been his worst fear.

He knew, though, that as soon as the French were done with that, their orders would be to engage Craufurd as quickly as possible to gauge the strength of his force.

Ross stared at the smoke. 'Poor buggers. And we did nothing to help them, sir. Not a bloody thing.'

'We could do nothing, sarn't. What could we have done?'

He turned and looked back at the others, all of whose faces wore the same blank stare of unforgiving despair and bitterness and he knew that somehow they must blame him.

Heredia cursed. 'Look, look there. The flames. You know what is happening, don't you? This is your general's idea of saving a nation. Can you see?'

Ross tried to calm him, but even his words were not in earnest.

Martin spoke quietly as he looked. 'How many people did you say were in there?'

Keane spoke, still staring at the city. 'I didn't.'

Silver provided the answer. 'Ten thousand souls, God help them.'

They stood there for what seemed like hours but was in fact but a few minutes, until at last Keane spoke and there was a coldness in his voice. 'Well, there's fewer than that now. There's nothing to be done. We need to get back and warn General Craufurd. The French won't waste any time. As soon as they've had their fill in there, they'll come for us.'

He turned his horse, thankful not to have to look any longer at the burning city, and rode down the hill fast and back to the road, followed by the others. No one spoke for the entire journey back to the bridge, and on entering the camp, past the green-jacketed sentries of the 95th, who presented arms, Keane made straight for the general's tent.

He found Craufurd writing a report.

The general looked up. 'Keane. Well? What news?'

Keane shook his head. The gesture and his expression would have been enough, but he replied nevertheless. 'Ciudad is lost, sir. In flames. Taken this morning, I'd guess. And all within it.'

Once again the image came to his mind of the dead woman and child in Celorico.

Craufurd shook his head. 'This is a sad day for British arms, Keane. But there was nothing to be done. To have risked relieving Ciudad would have lost us Portugal.'

'And Europe with it, sir.'

'Yes, Europe with it. Though I'm sure that our own army will soon be wondering what it is we are doing here. This benighted country is in a parlous state. Its men fight well – regular army, that is. But the militia are deserting in droves. They have either lost faith or they just want to gather the harvest. They have no conception of what may befall them. In any case they won't have any harvest to gather very soon. And what they have may be destroyed.

'The Portuguese regency are utterly opposed to the duke's policy of a "scorched earth". They see British soldiers destroying their people's livelihood. And who can blame them for protesting?'

'I can see why we do it. But at what cost? We lay waste the crops to prevent the French from taking them.'

'Now your British soldier must pay for everything. Every last scrap and morsel. And if he did not you would flog him. And you'd be right, Keane.'

'Yes, sir.'

'Those are Wellington's orders. But the French, as everyone knows, live off the land. Loot, pillage . . . it is their way. They take everything they can find. That's the way the emperor likes to manage his campaigns.' He laughed. 'You must admit, it has a certain simple brilliance about it. In one stroke he can ensure his army is fed and at the same time instil a sense of terror into the people they invade. You and I know the soldiery, Keane. Any soldier, whatever his country. Leave a soldier to fend for himself and he'll make damned sure he gets what he wants. And no questions are asked. It's a stroke of brilliance.'

'Yes, sir. It is clever,' Keane agreed. It was sheer genius and utterly immoral.

'But we cannot sanction such a thing. And so we burn the crops. Mark me, Keane, if we carry on as we are, very soon we shall have the Portuguese turning on us, as well as the French.'

'Sarn't Ross, stand the men to, throughout the night.'

'Are you sure, sir? When there's divisional pickets of the Rifles posted anyway? The lads might save their energy.'

Keane glared at him. 'I'm not requesting you to do so, sarn't. It's an order. Yes, the Rifles are good enough, but I want to know what's happening before anyone else. It is our business to be ahead of all others and I do not intend to lose face. They can take turn about at guard duty.'

Ross snapped to, suddenly back in the regular army, seeing in Keane the manner of an old-style officer which lately he seemed to have abandoned. 'Yes, sir.'

'And I won't have any slacking. Any man asleep at his post will be on a charge.'

Ross went to break the news to the others and Keane wondered if he might have gone too far. In recent weeks the men had come to see him in a new light. He had created, he felt, a new form of officering, more suited to his role and that of his men, in which he allowed each of them more head and in return expected more of a sense of responsibility. But in that moment, while they had been staring at the burning city, he had sensed the faint whisper of dissent and that, he knew, could not be tolerated. Certainly he might not treat them as if they were the ordinary rank and file. But they must all agree to respect his authority. About that there could be no question.

The following morning Keane was woken by Ross from a deep sleep and a dream in which he and Kitty Blackwood were sitting by the banks of a stream, somewhere in England. He glared at the sergeant and snarled, 'What? What the devil d'you mean?'

'Sir, you said to wake you. It's past dawn.'

Keane came to, all thoughts of home and Kitty lost to the moment. Instinctively he reached for his sword, which lay close to the camp bed. 'The French?'

'No, sir, nothing of them all night. And the lads were on picket, just as you ordered, sir. They must still be in the city.'

'Yes, Ross. I've no doubt that will occupy them for a few days.' He wondered how many had died and how many women had suffered.

Ross spoke. 'And we wait here, with the men straining at the leash to get their hands on a bloody Frenchie.'

'They'll come, sarn't. They'll come.'

And come they would, he knew. To test their strength, as Massena took the bulk of his force on to the great border fortress of Almeida, the key to Portugal. But how many would he send now? Based on the reports of the dragoons? More, he guessed, than Sainte-Croix's division.

He pulled himself from the camp bed and, sitting on the edge, scratched through his shirt under his armpits and across his chest. The damned lice got everywhere, and no amount of fumigating would ever clean them entirely from their home in the stitching of his clothes. He scratched again and, picking up his overall trousers from the floor, pulled them on over his stockings. He wrapped the black cotton stock around his neck and tucked it into place before pulling on his tunic. The boots came next, half-length and hessian style for comfort. He had had them made in Lisbon, paying for them with some of the proceeds of some French silver they had liberated the previous year, and they had been worth every penny. Good dependable footwear was the one thing a soldier needed and valued. Without good footwear you were sunk.

Emerging from his tent, Keane blinked in the sunlight. The camp was alive with activity. To the right the Germans were watering their horses and scrubbing them down as if on parade. Closer to his tent two of his own men, Martin and Leech, were washing their faces in a bucket. Silver sat with Gabriella a little way off, eating some form of breakfast from wooden bowls.

Craufurd was walking towards Keane. He held a piece of paper before him. 'Keane. I have orders for you. Newly arrived by courier from the commander-in-chief hisself.'

He presented Keane with the letter. Keane took it and unfolding it saw that it had not been dictated but was in Wellington's own hand and written on a piece of mule skin, which

Keane knew the general kept in his saddlebag when in the field for just such a purpose.

He began to read and looked up. 'You have read it, sir?'

'I have. You are to proceed at once to meet with a Spaniard. A certain Don Julian Sanchez. You might have heard of him?' Keane shook his head. Craufurd went on. 'This Don Sanchez, it seems, is little short of a marvel. While the French were still besieging the city, he managed something others had tried and failed. He broke out of Ciudad and galloped to Gallegos.'

'Good God! He deserted?'

'Not quite. He managed to save himself and a fair number of his own men. They're good fighters, although it's a miracle they got through the French lines. He has taken command of a band of guerrillas in the hills and has offered us his services as a colonel.'

'Sir?'

'You are to join him and, under cover of bringing him and his men in to fight with us, investigate him and ascertain for Wellington exactly what sort of a man he might be. Lord knows what you'll find. He's quite a character apparently. Colonel be damned. Began as a private soldier, a farmer's boy. Promoted to officer in Ciudad only last year. God knows where he acquired the 'don', but they all seem to call him by that name. Hates the French.'

'Don't they all, sir?'

'Indeed, though Sanchez has more cause than some. They killed almost all his family in cold blood.'

Keane read the rest of the note. It was as Craufurd had described. The duke wanted him to find Sanchez and give an account of his character. He was assembling, by all accounts, a personal army. Reports varied as to its size, but according to

George Scovell it was estimated that he might be as many as a hundred strong in horse and twice that in foot, with more men flocking to his banner by the day. The tone of the note seemed to imply that the duke wanted to know if Keane felt that Sanchez might need to be brought under the thumb. 'I am sure that you will know how to deal with him', it concluded.

Craufurd, seeing that Keane had finished reading, spoke again. 'The word is that you are quite adept at dealing with the guerrillas. Is that the case?'

'Sir?'

'I did hear that you worked with them last year to liberate a sizeable sum from the coffers of the French and that most of this was passed on to the duke to pay the men. Is that correct?'

'Yes, sir, we did manage to take a deal of silver from Marshal Soult's baggage train in the rout from Oporto.'

'Well done.' He paused. 'I also heard that some of that money was never recovered.'

Keane said nothing.

'Sorry, captain. Were you not aware of that?'

'I'm sure, sir that we did not recover the entire amount. And I know that the guerrillas made off with some.'

'The guerrillas? No one else?'

Keane blanched. 'No one else, sir. Are you suggesting that I . . . ?'

'Merely a rumour I had heard, Keane. No more than that. Among the staff. Fair game, I'd say. Wouldn't you, Keane? Spoils of war?'

'I couldn't comment on that, sir. The duke might not agree with you.'

Craufurd looked down and played with his sword knot. 'Nor he might, Keane. There was something else, wasn't there? Someone died. An officer.'

Keane felt suddenly alarmed. Surely Craufurd could not know about his killing of Blackwood. Only Morris, Grant and the duke knew the truth of that day. He managed to steady his nerve.

'Sir? I don't follow you.'

'A duel. You killed someone in a duel, did you not? A fellow officer?'

A faint smile touched Keane's face and he breathed again. 'You seem well acquainted with me, sir. Is that how I'm known among the staff, sir?'

Craufurd laughed. 'Touché. No, captain, it is not how you are known. Although your predilection for cards and pretty women precedes you. Principally you are known as the hero of Oporto and quite the rising star. You have the duke's ear. He likes to have himself surrounded by bright young men. If you keep your nose clean and don't do anything stupid, you'll advance far.'

Keane wondered how Craufurd could know that he and his men had appropriated a quantity of the French silver. A quantity which had bought him not only the boots but the soft cotton shirt he now wore beneath his uniform jacket. And he also wondered whether that was all he knew. Whether he might be aware of the identity of Blackwood's killer and, if so, whether the fact meant anything to him.

Fastening on his sword, which in his haste he had not done, he saluted the general. 'If you will excuse me, sir, I'll take my leave. I must find my men and make ready to leave for Don Sanchez.'

'Yes, of course, you must go by all means, but remember what I have said. Oh, and one thing more, Keane. The French will be aiming for Almeida now. The duke craves further knowledge about how they will advance. Do not disappoint him, Keane. On any count. Nor me.'

5

According to Wellington's note, Don Sanchez had left his base near Richioso and crossed the border into Portugal, and was now based at San Pedro, an old citadel town built around a central tower and the remains of a palace. Even in this time of crisis, for the Spanish officer to lead his company quite independently into Portugal and occupy such a place, redolent with history of the border wars between the two peoples, was, thought Keane, a presumptuous action. Not only did it count on the hospitality of the Portuguese; it also took for granted that the British would necessarily want or need to work with him. Presumptuous perhaps, he thought, but it was also undeniably good strategy. The man was shrewd, of that there was no doubt.

Once Sanchez was in Portugal it would be hard to get rid of him, and so he had come to the British for better or worse. And it was Keane's job to find out which.

From such a position Sanchez would be able to keep an eye on the fortress of Almeida in the valley below and the surrounding area and to eventually establish contact with Wellington at Celorico, which lay directly to the west. The plan was to attach Sanchez and his men to the hussars, with Keane acting as liaison, and to move the whole force down to the line of the Duas Casas river in order to guard Craufurd's right flank.

Craufurd himself had elected to fall back to a better position by the ramparts of the old Fort Concepcion to the north of Almeida and to await Massena's onslaught there.

Keane consulted his master map and traced a line between Sanchez's reported location and the bridge. It was not far. Perhaps a day's march at most.

From experience, Keane knew that the guerrillas would have spotted his column long before he was aware that they were near their camp at San Pedro. He would not attempt to outwit Sanchez, but allow them to be taken. The only way to ingratiate yourself with these people, he had come to learn, was to let them believe that they had the upper hand. Be taken by their sentries without protest.

He turned to Ross. 'Don't concern yourselves about the guerrillas. We'll let them take us, sarn't.'

'Yes, sir, just as we always do.' Ross recalled their first encounters with the guerrilla leaders Morillo and Cuevillas the previous year. That had been an eye opener and no mistake. He turned to Keane. 'Sir, what d'you reckon to this Sanchez? Will he be the same as Cuevillas, do you think?'

'I've heard, sarn't, that he's somewhat more civilized. But we can take nothing for granted, as you well know.'

'More civilized. That would be easy. Those heathen bastards.'

Keane had come to understand that this was his sergeant's way of describing any Catholics. A natural trait for a man who had been brought up a strict Presbyterian among Glasgow's Ulster Scots.

They climbed steadily. This was not the huge rocky outcrops of the Serra da Estrela that they had negotiated the previous

year. They were further north and these hills were more for-
giving and seemed less inclined to put Gabriella into the cold
sweat that had been engendered by the eerie atmosphere and
massive, lowering presence of the 'mountains of the stars'. At
the same time, though, Keane felt a sense of apprehension. It
was all very well for the duke to offer the opinion that he knew
how to deal with guerrillas, but in truth he still felt something
of a novice. He wished he had Grant's consummate coolness, or
even the bluff confidence of George Scovell.

What troubled him most, however, was the knowledge that
they would not be able to return to Celorico until they had carried out the duke's instructions with regard to Sanchez. He had
decided on one course of action at least. He would send a rider
off to Morris and tell him to explore the ruins of Pritchard's
house. Apart from that, there was nothing he could do, save
disobey a direct order from the commander-in-chief. And while
Keane was capable of going against orders and using his own
initiative at all times, even he knew at what point he would be
overstepping the mark.

They travelled to the north-west in a long, snaking column,
Keane and his men as usual at the front, the hussars following
on.

After four hours Keane began to have the feeling that he was
being observed. He pulled back until he was level with Ross and
spoke in a whisper. 'We're being watched, sarn't.'

'Yes, sir. I felt the same myself, since a mile back.'

Von Krokenburgh came riding up from the rear. 'Keane, do
you feel it? The eyes in the hills?'

'Yes, we both do. Sanchez's men, no doubt. Just do as we
agreed. Let them take us.'

Von Krokenburgh dropped back and they carried on until they

came to where the road crossed a little stone bridge and then split, the left forking up towards San Pedro. Without warning, four horsemen appeared from either flank. All were dressed in a form of uniform, a combination of elements of Spanish, French and British items and all had drawn sabres. Keane pulled up and barked, 'Halt.' As the column came to a stop more men appeared to their left and right armed with a variety of weapons. One of the leading horsemen, a gaudily dressed young man in a purple-and-blue lancer's dolman, a scarlet French hussar pelisse, grey British overall trousers and the bicorne hat of a Spanish officer, presented himself to Keane.

'Sir, you are to come with us, please. Follow me.'

Keane nodded and signalled to the others to follow. They rode behind the four horsemen, followed by the hussars, and climbed up the narrow road towards San Pedro. Above them the old citadel towered, silhouetted against a clear blue sky.

The town had been deserted many centuries before, after the Portuguese forces, keen to stamp out the Spanish influence and sympathies of the local lord, had attacked and razed the fine palace to the ground. But Keane could see what it once must have been. The stronghold of a warlord, dominating the surrounding countryside and exercising his rule by force and reputation. It seemed to him that Don Sanchez might be attempting to do the same. As he had discovered in his previous dealings with other guerrilla leaders, while their common purpose might be the saving of their nation, ultimately these men operated as individuals whose priority was their own interest. He wondered whether Sanchez might be any different.

The man who now called himself Don Julian Sanchez sat close to the ruins of the main tower of San Pedro in a tented area which one of his men had constructed by throwing a scarlet blanket between two trees. He was a little under medium height with a distinctive shock of curly black hair and a moustache and side whiskers to match. He was dressed in what bore a close resemblance to the uniform of a French hussar or a British Light Dragoon, with dark blue overall trousers and a matching pelisse trimmed with brown fur. Around his waist he wore a broad scarlet sash and on his head a shako which had undoubtedly once belonged to a French officer, although this had been subtly and wittily altered by turning the brass eagle plate, the symbol of the triumph of the emperor's armies, upside down. On either side of him stood a young man, similarly dressed and of a smart appearance. Aides de camp, thought Keane, who liked to think he could recognize the breed, to whatever army they belonged.

Sanchez grinned widely at Keane and rose from his bower to greet him. 'Captain. It is Captain Keane, is it not? Welcome, captain. My scouts have been tracking you.'

Going against his own advice, Keane found himself answering, 'Yes, I know; we were watching you also.' Why, he wondered by all that was holy, had he said that?

Sanchez smiled. 'Really, captain? You surprise me. My men are masters of disguise and fieldcraft. Where did you first see them?'

Keane was thinking on his feet. 'I have been aware of their presence, colonel. My general sends his best wishes, sir, and offers his sincere congratulations on your escape from the city.'

'Your general Wellington is kind. It was in truth the hardest thing I have ever done. But we managed it. Me and twelve others. The men you see here.' He indicated the louche young men who seemed to Keane an unlikely group to have escaped in such a daring exercise. But perhaps their looks belied their worth.

Keane chose his words with care. 'How on earth did you

manage it? It must have been almost impossible to evade their sentries.'

'We have our ways, captain. The garrotte and the knife are our friends.' He made a gesture with his hands as if pulling on an invisible rope held taut between them. 'We stole some horses and here we are. Not like those poor devils we left behind.'

'Have you had any word from the city?'

Sanchez shook his head. 'Nothing. It is not good. We know what has happened to them. And so do you, captain. You know the French as well as we do.' Keane knew what was coming. 'Perhaps your general Wellington should have helped them. It would have been better for the way the people of this country feel about him, and all of you.'

'He did it for the greater good.'

'Tell that to the innocent women and children in Ciudad. He swore that he was coming back to save Portugal, and to send the French from my homeland also. And what has he done? First he destroys all the crops and ruins people's lives, and now he refuses to come to the aid of five thousand innocent people and leaves them to their fate.'

'As I said, colonel, it was for the greater good.'

'Yes, I heard you. You and I understand that. But not the peasants.' Sanchez paused and, extracting a cigar from his pocket, bit off the end and spat it on the ground before lighting it by striking a long match upon a nearby stone. Then he spoke again. 'I think I will make a unit of men like yours. But maybe without those hats. I will have my own explorers as Wellington has his. Then I will know all the movements of the *ingléses*. Just as you know all of the French, and then we will know where we are. No?'

'Yes, sir. A splendid idea. You must have a great many men here if you are able to make a corps of guides such as ours.'

'I have many men. Horse and foot. Many men.'

'How many would you say. Two hundred? More?'

'You are clever, Captain Keane. Perhaps I will tell you, soon. Just how many men I have. Perhaps I myself do not know.'

A rider, dressed like a French lancer in what was mostly captured uniform, came galloping up to Sanchez and spoke fast, gasping for breath. 'Don Sanchez, sir, French infantry and artillery have been seen at the Quinta Buralda. Their cavalry are at Barquillos.'

Keane took out his map and opened it. Don Sanchez looked down with the others and Keane spoke, pointing to the villages.

'Craufurd was right to move back across the river. The French have made some ground.' He traced a line to Quinta and the road from it that led south across the river Turonnes. 'This is dangerous. He might well be heading for Almeida, but Marshal Massena believes that there is a sizeable force of British and our allies here and he is not inclined to let it go.'

Sanchez spoke. 'Stay with us. You must stay with us if you want to discover how well we know the French. I would have you return to Wellington with a good impression. I am anxious that we should become friends and allies. I am sure that there is much that we will be able to do for one another.' He paused. 'I did hear tell that you had succeeded in liberating a great deal of silver coin from Marshal Soult's train last year. You were in the company of one of my brethren?'

'We worked with a guerrilla leader, yes.'

'Name of Morillo, wasn't it?'

'Yes. You are well informed, Don Sanchez.'

'I make it my business to be nothing less. How shall I put it?

Should a similar possibility arise again, we would be only too pleased to work alongside you. For a consideration, of course. I'm sure that you would do no less.'

Keane let the insinuation drop. He had not come here to pick a fight. But he recognized it for what it was. So, he thought, Sanchez is against the French but on his terms. He wants money from us. A straight deal.

He smiled. 'Of course, Don Sanchez, if I ever have the opportunity again, I will think of you first.'

'Till then we wait. Always we wait. What do you do to pass the time, captain? I hear you play cards.'

'Yes, but not today, I'm afraid.'

'But we still have time for some fun, yes? Something to take our minds off the horrors of this war.' He thought for a moment or two and then smiled at Keane.

'We will have a contest. A contest of marksmanship, no? You will put in the man who is your best shot and I will do the same. The prize will be . . . what? The pretty girl in your party?' Keane could sense Silver bristle. Sanchez went on, laughing. 'No, of course, I was joking. The prize will be ten silver pieces. Yes?'

Keane smiled and nodded. 'It seems fair.'

It did indeed seem a harmless enough wager and one that he was guaranteed to win. On past performance, Keane suspected that Will Martin could outshoot anyone in the army and carrying Keane's own gun, as he did, he would have more than a good chance of trouncing Sanchez's man.

Sanchez's man shot first. The targets were to be two French infantrymen's shakos, thrown into the air by one of Sanchez's men, a giant, with huge hands and muscles to match. The marksman by contrast was a wiry fellow. Thin and gaunt, with taut skin the colour of a walnut, he walked towards the two men and shot them a grin that slit his face with a flash of yellowed teeth. Sanchez introduced him. 'This is Ramon Garcia. Surely he is one of the finest shots in all of Spain. He will go first. Show your man what he has to beat. Where is your man, captain?'

Keane beckoned Martin towards them. As he approached, Sanchez raised an eyebrow.

'But he's hardly more than a boy. Are you sure of this, captain?'

'Never been more certain.'

Garcia squared up and held his gun before him at the ready. Keane could see now that it was a Baker rifle, clearly appropriated from some poor rifleman who no longer had need of it. Its owner fondled it with the care one would accord a woman, rubbing his hand over the polished stock. It was already loaded and as he cradled it against his thigh, Garcia pulled back the lock to cock the weapon. He looked across at the big man and nodded. With a huge throw, the Spaniard sent the shako soaring up beyond the trees into the blue sky. Garcia brought up the rifle to his shoulder and fired just as the target reached the apex of its climb. The shako came tumbling to earth like a wounded game bird and landed close to his feet. Sanchez walked over and picked it up. Keane could see that the shot had gone through the front of the hat, just where the eagle had been attached, and exited at the rear. Had a Frenchman been wearing it his brains would have been blown away.

Sanchez smiled in triumph. 'There. What do you think of that? A kill, wouldn't you say, captain?'

Keane nodded. 'Yes, without a doubt a kill. Very nice shooting.'

Garcia smiled and nodded and patted his gun with affection.

The big man had found the second hat by now and stood ready and waiting for the command.

Martin let the gun hang loose in his hands, although it had been loaded and was already primed and cocked. At a signal from Sanchez, the second shako flew high in the air and in what seemed almost like slow motion, but was the work of an instant, the boy raised the fowling piece to his cheek and pulled the trigger. The cap seemed to stop in mid-air, like a felled cock pheasant. Then it fell to ground, hard-hit and as the smoke cleared, Martin walked across to see the damage. 'A hit, sir. I hit it.'

Keane nodded. 'Well done, Martin.'

Sanchez walked across to where they stood and stooped to pick up the cap. The shot had taken out the crown completely. Somehow, against all odds, Martin had contrived to get his shot to travel up through the hat. It was as central as anyone could have hoped.

Sanchez stood staring at it. He smiled at Martin. 'Good shooting, boy. Very nice. I will have to admit defeat.' Then he looked at the gun. 'Now that is a remarkable weapon. A truly magnificent gun, captain.'

'Yes, I know,' said Keane. 'It was my father's, so I'm told.' It was in fact one of the few things he owned which had come to him from his father.

Keane still remained unaware of his identity. It was his father who had purchased him his ensign's commission those twenty years ago, and his mother had told him that he had been a high-ranking military man, but more than that she would not say. The mystery of his father's identity troubled him. It was Keane's burning ambition to learn who his father might be. But for the moment, all that he had to link him was the gun, mysteriously sent to his mother before his fifteenth birthday, along with a lock of hair in a locket, a silver snuffbox and an ivory-backed hairbrush.

Sanchez held out his hand to Martin. 'May I hold it?' The boy handed it over and the Spaniard ran his fingers along the walnut stock. 'It is something any man would be proud to own.'

Keane smiled, with a little apprehension, wondering where this was going. 'Yes, indeed it is.'

'I don't suppose I could make you an offer . . . ?'

'No, I'm afraid the gun is most definitely not for sale.'

Sanchez looked at it again in his hands, raised it to his shoulder and placed his cheek against the stock. 'Truly wonderful. Such a weapon.' He thought for a moment and then turned to Keane. 'Another wager, captain?'

'By all means, Don Sanchez. New targets?'

'Yes, of course.'

He clapped his hands and a man brought two small leather cartridge boxes and gave them to the giant.

'And another stake, captain.'

'Shall we say twenty livres, colonel?'

Sanchez shook his head. 'No, I have something else in mind. Your gun, captain. We shall play for your gun. Double or quits. If I win, then it is mine. If you win, then I will give you one tenth of all the gold I hold in this camp. And let me tell you that is not a little.'

Keane went suddenly cold. He would do all that he could not to lose that gun. But how to keep the friendship of Sanchez without agreeing to the wager?

Sanchez clapped his hands and two men appeared dragging a handcart. Looking at it, Keane could see that it was piled high with gold ornaments of every kind. Looted, he presumed, from

French and Portuguese alike. It was clear that Sanchez had been planning this since their first wager. The gun had ever been his objective.

He answered. 'Very well. I accept your wager. One tenth of all the gold.'

Then walking across to Martin, he spoke quietly. 'You must lose.'

Martin looked at him incredulously. 'Sir?'

'I said, you must lose. You have to lose if we are to keep Sanchez on our side. He has to win the gun. Don't worry, I'll get it back somehow. And it shan't be your fault. But for now, you have to lose.'

'Don't know if I can, sir. I just shoot and it works.'

'Martin, listen to me, you have to lose.'

Sanchez called across to them. 'Captain Keane, are you ready?'

'Quite ready, colonel. I was just offering Martin some advice.'

They walked over to where the thrower was standing. Sanchez spoke. 'You may shoot first this time, captain.'

Keane shook his head. 'No, why don't you? We prefer to follow on.'

'Very well.'

Sanchez looked at Garcia, who had loaded his gun. Once again the man took up his position and the thrower made ready. On the given signal the big man hurled one of the cases high into the air. Garcia brought up the weapon and squeezed the trigger. The gun spat flame and shot and the box stopped short in mid-flight and fell to ground. Keane watched it fall and saw the hole neatly drilled through the centre.

'Good shot, colonel.'

'Now you.'

Martin took up his post and gave a nod to Keane. Once again

Sanchez nodded his head and the giant threw the second box up into the air. Martin brought the gun up and followed through the trajectory of the fall, then pulled the trigger. The bullet caught the box on the top lid and spun it around. Keane gasped as the box fell. And Martin let out a low curse.

It hit the ground and Sanchez ran across to pick it up. There was a small nick taken out of the flap, but apart from that it was intact.

'Captain Keane, I claim the victory. Fair?'

Keane walked over and took the box from Sanchez, staring at it intently in disbelief. 'Good God. I wouldn't have thought it possible. Martin, what's this? You missed.'

He looked across at the boy who was standing a little way off, his head down. 'Sir. Yes, sir. Sorry, sir.'

Keane looked back to Sanchez. 'Yes, colonel, quite fair. The gun, it seems, is yours. Martin, give it to the colonel.'

Martin surrendered Keane's gun and the Spaniard took it, his face suffused by a look of pure, almost childish joy. 'Thank you. What a prize. I am a lucky man, captain, am I not?'

'Indeed you are, colonel, and fortune is evidently not with me today.'

Sanchez clapped him on the back. 'That is the way of life, as we soldiers know. It is perhaps fortunate that today did not find you on the battlefield. A lack of luck there can mean something far worse than losing a gun. Now come and eat with us and console yourself in fine wine and good company.'

They ate together in the shadow of the old fortress and, while Keane dined with the colonel and his officers, the men, as they had been instructed, contrived to socialize with Sanchez's guerrillas.

Silver took Martin to task over his poor marksmanship. 'How

the deuce did you do that? You're a dead shot any day. You couldn't have missed that if you'd tried.'

Martin said nothing.

Silver narrowed his eyes and stared at him. 'That's it, isn't it? You did try. You missed on purpose.'

Martin remained silent. Silver shook his head. 'Was that the captain's doing? I'll be bound it was. He lost his own gun to keep Sanchez on our side.' He looked across to where Keane was sitting drinking wine with Sanchez. 'He's a clever man, our captain, and no mistake. Sell his own mother to trick the Spanish into our hands or bugger the French.'

Martin smiled. 'I really thought he was angry with me, Silver.'

'No, lad. It was his doing. He told you to pull the shot. He'd not be angry with you for that. He's just a good play-actor. Decent man he is. Might be a sharp one otherwise, but not with us, his own men. He won't do us wrong, lad. Loves you too, he does. Specially, like his own son, if he had one.'

Martin shook his head and smiled. 'You're talking twaddle, Silver, and you know it.'

Now Silver shook his head. 'Ask Gabby. She sees it. Sees it all. Mister Keane looks after you, lad. You mind that. And he'll get that gun back. You'll see. After he's used Sanchez, or got him by other means.'

Keane listened to Don Sanchez's tales of his career as a soldier. How he had come from humble origins and risen to fame and fortune and how he had sworn to drive the last Frenchman from his country or die doing it with the last drop of his life's blood. As more wine flowed, they drank toasts. To Spain. To the death of the French. To Lord Wellington. To Sanchez. To Keane. And by the time they finally crawled away to sleep, where there had been suspicion there was friendship, and where there had been fear there was trust. And Keane, who had been making sure that he drank half of what the Spaniard put away, knew that in Sanchez's command there were a hundred and fifty horsemen in two squadrons and a troop of lancers, along with three hundred foot soldiers split into five companies of sixty apiece. This private army was well organized. Far better so than those he had encountered in the hills last year. Officers and NCOs were aplenty and Sanchez had told him that he was careful to promote on merit where it was due. Of course some of his officers owed their position to purchase. But that did not mean he thought them any worse. They had come with him from Ciudad. He had seen them murder the French. Lying awake in his blanket, by daybreak Keane had gained a good impression of Sanchez's strengths and weaknesses. He also reckoned that, in the gift of the gun, he had won him over. That and the promise of silver that he had felt obliged to make in the course of their evening. Now perhaps, he thought, he might be able to return to Celorico.

Of course, it was not that simple.

They were compelled, by courtesy as much as anything else, and by a semblance of duty, to pass another two days in Sanchez's camp. It was, though, time well spent. Keane observed his daily routine and instructed his men to do likewise. In the early morning after the night-watch had stood down, Sanchez would send out scouts into the hills and others down into the plains. At around midday these men would report back, sometimes with news of the French, and would be replaced by others who would remain on patrol until evening. On the second day two of the parties did not return. Keane quizzed Sanchez. 'Are they in trouble?'

'No, they are merely making camp further out.'

'Advance positions.'

'Is that what you would call them? They will lie low and then in the night will creep into the French camp and take one or two Frenchmen and bring them here.'

'And then?'

'Then we find out what we need to know.'

The following morning, as predicted, the two parties returned and with them three French prisoners. Two of them were of little value and Sanchez berated his men for their poor choice. The third man, though, was as good a prisoner as they might have taken. A French major of artillery.

'You plan to torture him?'

'I will interrogate him.'

'I know what that means. I've seen your countrymen too many times.'

Keane found himself floundering. He knew that Don Sanchez was a vital ally to Wellington and had already sacrificed much to keep him. But his conscience refused to coerce in barbarity. Nevertheless, where before swift action and brute force had sufficed to save the skins of French prisoners, this time he knew that such tactics would not work. He could not lift his hand against this man.

Sanchez looked at him. 'You are weak, captain. You don't approve of our methods. But they work.'

Keane said nothing, then, 'Give him a choice.'

One of Sanchez's officers spoke. A neatly scrubbed moustachioed young man in red breeches and on his head a French lancer's czapka. 'What? He's a prisoner. He deserves no choice. I say we strip him and use the knife.'

Sanchez waved him down. 'No, wait. Captain, what do you mean?'

'By all means strip him, but do no more. It's my bet that he will be so terrified that if you give him the option of talking to me or submitting to you, he will choose the former. Try it. What do you have to lose? If he refuses then he's yours and God have mercy on him.'

At least I have tried, thought Keane. It was all he could do.

Sanchez nodded to one of his men and while two of them held down the French major, another man ripped his clothes from him until he stood before them naked. He spat on the ground and cursed them, but Keane could see the terror in his eyes. The men bound the major's hands tightly behind him and led him across to Don Sanchez.

The Frenchman stared at Keane, trying to work out what his uniform might mean, with its Portuguese brown tunic and British light cavalry helmet. He spoke. 'English?' Keane nodded. 'Help me.'

Don Sanchez spoke. 'There is no help for you. But I, Don Sanchez da Estrella, I will give you a choice. I am a man of peace and mercy. To prove that, I am willing to let you choose your fate. We need to know what plans your marshal has. You can tell the captain here and we will not harm you. If you choose not to do so, then my men will make you talk. Either way you will tell us in the end. But I have decided to give you the chance to avoid the agony of torture. You see, I am a most thoughtful and intelligent man.'

Keane smiled at the way in which Don Sanchez had used his offer. The Frenchman said nothing. Don Sanchez spoke again.

'Well, what's it to be? Will you talk or would you have me hand you over to them?' He pointed to his men, who were waiting close by. One of them, the giant who had presided over the shooting competition, was holding a length of rope, another a long knife.

'Oh, very well, you may have him.'

Suddenly the Frenchman began to speak. At such a rate that neither Keane nor any of the others could make out what he was trying to say.

Keane said, 'Begin again,' and the major began to talk more slowly now.

Twenty minutes later, Keane covered him with a blanket and left him to sob. He went across to Don Sanchez.

'He says that they have a plan to outflank your General Craufurd.'

'You have a map?'

Keane took the map from his valise and laid it out across a flat rock, Ross helping him weigh it down with stones.

Sanchez pondered it for a moment and then pointed and spoke.

'He says they will move here. To this bridge.'

'We can do something about this. Have you any explosive?'

Sanchez looked at him. 'Of course.'

Keane addressed Ross. 'Find Leech and send him to me.'

Don Sanchez looked intent, 'What do you intend to do, captain?'

'I intend to blow the bridge. To stop the French getting across.'

'It's a good idea. Can you do it?'

'I have an expert in such things.'

'Your men have many talents, captain.'

'That's why I chose them, colonel.'

Ross brought Leech, and Keane briefed him quickly.

'We will patrol by the river. Leech, you're to take two men of the hussars and destroy the bridge at Nava d'Aver. There. Across the Duas Casas river. That at least will prevent the French from crossing and taking General Craufurd in the flank.'

'The explosive, sir?'

'A present here, from Colonel Sanchez. Just make sure that you blow it. And then return.'

It was simple, flawless.

Leech looked at the map and turned to Sanchez. 'You know this bridge, sir?'

'Yes, it's not big, but the French could use it well enough.'

'How big, sir?'

'Three spans, maybe twenty feet high at most and three files wide.'

Leech thought for a moment. 'How much black powder do you have?'

'Enough. We took it from the French.'

'I'll need fifty pounds of it. You're sure you have enough, colonel?'

Sanchez nodded. 'Yes, that's not a problem.'

'And could I prevail upon you for a cart, sir?'

Sanchez nodded and called to one of his men.

Leech turned to Keane. 'That's all I need, sir. That and a linen tube to act as a fuse. But I'll make that from sacking. Shall I find the Germans?'

'No, I'll ask Captain von Krokenburgh to select them. I'll get you a driver too. You load up the powder. Good luck.'

Within half an hour Leech had gone, with his small escort, the explosive loaded on to a wagon driven by another of the hussars.

Keane paced around Sanchez's camp, talking to Ross. 'I can't help thinking that we might all have gone with him.'

'Sir, it's a simple enough exercise. Leech said so himself. He'll blow the bridge and then return. The French are miles away. He has plenty of time. Better to go fast and not be burdened with too many men.'

'Yes, sarn't, I know you're right. But it's me who will take the blame if anything happens to him.'

'Always is, sir. You're the officer.'

'Yes, Ross, you're right. I'm a captain now. Though when the bloody paperwork will come through from Horse Guards to confirm it, God only knows.'

'That's the army for you. Happy to march us all ragged but won't do nothing it doesn't want to do any faster than dead slow.'

The evening was coming in now and even up here above the river plain the mosquitoes were gathering in the lights of the campfires.

Sanchez wandered over to them. 'Come and eat with us, captain, and your men too. And don't worry about your man. He will be back soon. Maybe tomorrow. Come and I will tell you a story of the old Spain. Before any of this happened. And maybe then you will understand more of my people.' And Keane allowed himself to submit, and under the stars at the campfire, with Sanchez's stories and the sound of guitars in his ears, he thought that he was perhaps starting to understand.

6

Keane wondered how long it could take to demolish a bridge. It had been three days since Leech had left with the demolition party. He was never content when he had to split his small force and he cursed himself for not having sent a larger escort to accompany the artilleryman. For his part, the days had been spent watching for the French, expecting a party of dragoons to come upon them at any moment. But at heart Keane knew that his men had the upper hand. They were the army's eyes and ears and a damned sight better than any Frenchman. Besides, the guerrillas travelled with them.

He shot a sideways glance at Sanchez, who was riding alongside him at the head of the column of their combined forces. The guerrilla had left most of his men in the camp at San Pedro, but the small number he had brought with them bolstered Keane's command. Keane had deliberately left von Krokenburgh back at the Spanish camp with most of the Hanoverians and taken only a single troop of the hussars as escort.

He had thought it politic, for there was a hierarchy to any column of march, just as there was to a line of battle. Don Sanchez, with his grandiose ideas, demanded a position for his men close to the front, where Keane, as de facto commander, had naturally placed himself. To have posted the Hanoverians further back along the column to bring up the rear would not have not gone down well with von Krokenburgh. As it was, to place the single troop of hussars behind Sanchez was less of an affront to German honour.

He turned in the saddle and watched the little column as it snaked through the defile which led from the citadel town towards the river. Behind his men came the first of Sanchez's cavalry: twenty lancers, dressed in the uniforms of captured or killed French and Polish cavalry, but with the eagles either removed from their czapkas or reversed, like that of their commander. Their fluttering pennons of red and yellow, the national colours of Spain, had replaced those of white and red which had previously adorned the original owners' lances. Behind them came Sanchez's hussars, as motley a crew as Keane had ever seen, again in captured uniforms but in a rainbow of colours which reflected the regiments of that arm who served Bonaparte in the Peninsula. Then came the Germans, under the command of a young, recently commissioned cornet by the name of von Cramm.

Keane turned to Sanchez. 'Is it much further? It's hard to tell from my map.'

Sanchez laughed. 'Your map. You British. You place so much faith in your maps but they tell you nothing. You should just take some of my men with you wherever you go. It will take us another hour before we come in sight of the bridge, if it is still there. Then another half-hour before we come to the village. I'm sure that your men will be in one of those places, captain. My scouts say that the French have not yet begun to advance against the bridge. They will be fine.'

But there was something about his voice which did not convince Keane that he was as certain as he appeared.

They had emerged from the hills now and on to the plain which led down to the river. Away to either side it stretched, dotted by occasional farms, and for the first time, as they rode on, Keane noticed the change in the landscape. Fields which at this time of year should have been billowing with waving crops of barley and maize now lay barren, their crops burnt down to blackened stumps. This was Wellington's doing. His policy of a 'scorched earth', denying everything to the enemy. It was as if some great fire god had passed over the countryside, razing everything that would yield food and succour to the French. At the same time he knew that it would make the peasantry resentful. He knew farmers. Had grown up on a farm himself and knew too the nature of tenants and those who depended for their lives on reaping a meagre income or subsisting from the land.

He spoke to Silver. 'Have you noticed the fields, Silver? What's happened to them.'

'Yes, sir. Sad, ain't it.'

'Worse to know it was our own men that did it. You can't help feeling sorry for the poor buggers who make their living from the land. What will they do now, do you suppose?'

'Can't say, sir. But it'll be hard for them. Damned hard. Bound to be. It's all they've got. But if it stops the Frenchies and leaves them blue bastards with their bellies hanging out, then it's got to be worth it, ain't it, sir?'

Keane supposed that it was. Like anything in war it had to be weighed on the scales of what was right and what was wrong. What made any war 'just'? Was the decision to sacrifice the livelihood of thousands of people justified if it confounded the enemy's strategy and forced him to retire through lack of supply? Military thought dictated that it was. Even if humanity was outraged and babies starved. He wondered whether he could have done it, had the decision been up to him, and doubted it. He had seen too much as a boy: babies dead in their mother's arms and men driven mad by loss and famine, railing against their plantation-owning masters. No, he thought, it would not have been his way.

Descending a slight incline among the ravaged fields, they came in sight of the crossing place. Even from a distance it was not hard to see that the bridge had gone. Heartened, Keane spurred on and hurried down towards the river.

The bridge was no more, but of Leech and the two hussars there was also no sign. Nor could they see the cart or the horses. Keane rode up to the river and dismounted, followed by Ross and Silver, who was the first to speak.

'What d'you make of it, sir? Where's Leech?'

'I don't know, Silver. It's very strange. By the look of it, he's most definitely finished the job. No one could attempt to cross that.'

He looked towards the space where the bridge had stood for the past two hundred years. All that now remained of it were the end piers on both sides, sticking up like great, jagged teeth; of the two central supporting arches there was nothing but four stone stumps barely visible beneath the water. Rubble had been thrown either side of where the span had been, as far as thirty feet in all directions, and Keane imagined that it had gone up with a huge explosion.

It was as good a job as he could have wished for. But where the devil was Leech?

Ross spoke. 'Must have been a hell of a bang, sir. Perhaps they were caught in the blast. Hurt bad, I mean. Killed even.'

Silver was down by the water's edge now, kneeling down. He called back to Keane. 'Look, sir. There's cart tracks here, leading back up to the road.'

Keane joined him. Silver was right. You could see quite clearly where the cart, heavily laden with the powder, had been taken down to the water's edge and other tracks leading away, less deeply scored after the explosive had been unloaded. The two of them traced the tracks back up on to the road in the direction of the village.

Silver spoke. 'Maybe the villagers took care of them.'

'Perhaps you're right. We will only discover in the village. I think that we might go there directly, don't you?'

He walked back to his horse and said nothing more, although he felt certain that Leech was sufficiently competent an engineer to ensure that neither he nor the other two men would be caught up in the blast. Something was quite clearly not right. And Keane was impatient to find out what.

Sanchez was standing beside him. 'He did a good job, your man. No Frenchman will try to get over that.'

'Yes, thank you, colonel. He knows his business. But where do you suppose he is?'

'We will try the village. His job is done, you know. Knowing you British, we will most likely find him sitting in a posada, with a drink in one hand and the other around the waist of a pretty girl.'

Although he had not known Leech for more than a few weeks, Keane did not think it a likely explanation. But he nodded at the Spaniard and smiled. And kept his worries to himself. They remounted and turned to join the others, riding down to the road, which ran parallel, along the line of the river for the few miles towards the village.

Nava d'Aver, when they came to it at last, was nothing remarkable. It consisted of a single street ending in a little church, with the usual cluster of houses, the better, bigger ones closest to the house of God. It amused him, this country of Catholics in which the rich, thought Keane, always showed their willingness to buy their way into heaven by making sure they were close to its representative on earth.

The streets seemed unusually quiet. A wild dog barked at them as they trotted past and a young boy ran across their path, laughing and pointing, causing Silver's horse to shy. At one of the houses a woman looked out of the door and then shut it abruptly. At another the shutters were being barred as they rode past.

Keane turned to Silver. 'That's curious. They can see we're friends, so where are they? I don't like it. There's something not right here. Not at all.'

They rode on and Sanchez, who had been riding slightly in front of Keane, dropped back. Instead, though, of the smiling face of earlier, his expression had now grown serious.

'This is very strange. Where are the other people? The French have not been here. The houses are still standing. I don't understand.'

They passed a posada, its inn-sign blowing in the breeze. Sanchez reined in and dismounted. 'Come on, captain. I think we might look for your men in here.'

Keane slid his leg across the saddle and jumped down, followed by Silver and Ross, who had motioned to the others to remain with the troop. With his hand on his sword hilt, Don

Sanchez pushed open the door and went in, followed by the three others.

The inn stank of old wine and sweat and the stench of two hundred years of village life. To their astonishment, it was empty. But the half-empty glasses and tankards on the tables made it clear that it not been so for long.

A fire was still burning in the grate and Sanchez walked over and poked at it, seeming to hope that it might yield evidence of the whereabouts of the population. 'It is very strange,' he said quietly. 'Where are they all?'

Keane counted the glasses and bottles and estimated that until a short time ago there must have been at least fifty people, no doubt men, sitting there. 'What do you suppose made them leave in such a hurry? There's no sign of a struggle.'

Silver stood staring at the tables, a frown furrowing his face. 'Have you noticed something else, sir?' he asked. 'They even left their hats and coats.'

He was right. Various items of clothing littered the tables and chairs. It was as if they had rushed out in a moment of madness, forgetting everything else.

Keane spoke. 'Yes, but no weapons were left behind.'

They left the inn and, as they were remounting their animals, Keane heard a shout. It sounded like a cry of jubilation or triumph. He turned to Sanchez. 'Did you hear that?'

'Yes. It sounds at least as if they are enjoying themselves. It must be a fiesta.'

There was another cry, almost a hurrah.

'Where would that be?'

'Most of these villages have a space set aside for such things, a plaza, away from the centre. We have only to follow the noise.

Your men must have got themselves involved in the celebrations. It will be a saint's day or something like that, I expect.'

They went in the direction of the shouting, which was louder now, riding in column, and still, despite Sanchez's relaxed manner, Keane felt uneasy.

They reached a clearing at the end of the village, where the houses stopped and the road opened out into a flat area of dusty open ground, framed by olive trees. But they could go no further. The way ahead was blocked by a crowd of people. They were mostly men, dressed in simple pleasant clothes. The spectators were oblivious at first to their presence, so intent were they on the spectacle. They remained standing, with their backs to the advancing party. Keane strained over his horse's neck, eager to see beyond the dense crowd, to catch a glimpse of the focus of their attention. But, tall as he was, he could not manage it. The crowd continued to shout and laugh – whatever the entertainment was, it had them gripped. It was clear that many of them were drunk.

At length, one of the peasants, a short, swarthy man with a red handkerchief tied around his head, heard the jangle of harness and the whinny of the horses, impatient to move ahead. He turned, and as he did so, saw the uniforms and the horsemen and, after a moment, began to shout.

But it was not the welcome that Keane had expected. It was clearly intended as a warning. Other men turned, and soon the whole place was in uproar. Keane signalled to the column to halt and draw arms and Sanchez looked at him, his easy manner transformed into an expression of alarm. He called to the troopers to keep their ranks and Keane shouted back to von Cramm to have his men do the same.

Sanchez looked anxious. 'There's something wrong here, captain. Something very wrong. These men are afraid of us, but we are meant to be their friends?'

The crowd was fleeing now, as fast as it could go, running away from the column of horsemen in all directions. Men too drunk to run fell to the ground in the rush. Not just men were here, but women and children too. They streamed past the troopers and down the street back into the village, darting into houses, closing the doors behind them. Within what seemed like seconds the *plaza de fiesta* was cleared, save for two dogs fighting over a chicken bone and three men, one unconscious and two too drunk to get up. But there was something else left behind as well.

On the far side of the clearing, in the direction towards which the spectators had been facing, stood six trees, laid out in a neat row. And tied by ropes to four of them were the bodies of four men.

Silver saw them first. 'Christ almighty! What's that?'

Keane and Sanchez spurred across the plaza towards the trees, followed by the others. Keane leapt from the saddle and ran up to the men. Their uniforms, although covered in blood, let him know that his fears had been well founded. Three of the men were the German hussars and the fourth was Israel Leech.

He went to Leech first and lifted his head. The man's eyes were open though glazed over and he was breathing, just.

Keane spoke to him, gently. 'Leech, you're all right, man. You're still alive. You'll be fine. We'll get you out of here.'

He turned and yelled. 'Archer. Over here. Quickly.' Then, moving to one of the hussars, he felt his chest and then lifted his chin, but the man was dead. Like Leech his face was a mass of cuts and gashes, and his body too, though still clothed, bore signs of violence, with deep cuts made through the serge of the tunic and overall trousers. Keane turned to the third man, who had been similarly savaged. He too was dead, a huge, bloody hole in the side of his head where a blow had taken away part of his skull to expose his brains. He walked on to the last hussar and, raising up his head, he recoiled in horror for a moment, for one of the man's eyes had been smashed from its socket. The hussar, though, was not yet dead.

Keane looked to Leech and saw that Archer was with him and, as Martin untied him from the tree, was trying to make him swallow some water and looking at the worst of the wounds. 'Archer, I think this poor bugger needs you now.'

Archer left Leech for a moment in the hands of Martin and came to the hussar. He lifted his head. 'Good God.' The man was trying to speak, but no words came, merely a bubbling froth. Tearing a bandage from the piece of muslin he carried in his knapsack for just such a purpose, Archer tied it around the man's head across the sightless eye and surveyed the damage.

As he did so, Ross approached Keane. 'Who could have done this, sir? Those peasants?'

'It would seem so, sarn't.'

Von Cramm was with them now. He stared down at the three hussars. He said nothing at first, then just, 'Was it really them, sir? The peasants?'

Keane nodded. 'I can't think of any other cause. You saw them too.'

The young officer muttered something in German, then spoke in English. 'It's obscene. What can we do, sir?'

Sanchez, who all the time had remained mounted with his men on the edge of the clearing, had said nothing and still he continued to hold his silence.

It was Silver who spoke next. 'Have you seen the ground, sir? Look at it. All around them.'

Keane looked down to the dust, where the blood of the four men stained the dry earth, and saw that around each of them lay a pile of white rocks, some of them also heavily bloodstained.

'My God,' he said. 'They've been stoned. Stoned to death. By the very people we're trying to save.'

Sanchez, who had now dismounted, had been looking on. 'It is just what I spoke of, captain. The peasants do not understand. To them you are just soldiers, like any others. You come and burn their crops. Ruin their living. Take away what little they have before the French come to finish the job because there is nothing here for them. So when they find soldiers, any soldiers, they do this. Who can blame them?'

Keane felt a fury and hatred whose like he could scarcely recall. He tried to speak and his voice seemed to come from deep within. 'No, colonel. You are wrong. Quite wrong. What right do these people have? No one has the right to do this to a British soldier. We come here and try to save their land, to save them. And how do they repay us? Like this.'

He shouted to von Cramm, who had remained with his men, mounted by the opening to the clearing. 'Cornet, have your men dismount and take their carbines. I want prisoners. Martin, Sarn't Ross, Silver, all of you. Do the same. House to house. I want the men who did this. Failing that, I want a dozen of the villagers. And be on your guard. Shoot anyone who resists or runs away. You have my authority.'

He looked at Sanchez, whose horsemen had remained in their saddles as the hussars dismounted and drew their guns. 'Colonel, what about your men?'

Sanchez shrugged. 'I cannot order them. I don't know if they will do the same. They may not agree with you. They are farmers too, some of them. They understand these people.'

Keane shook his head. 'Understand? What's to understand? They're murderers. No less. You're mad. Quite mad to think anything else.'

Keane's own sympathies for the peasantry had suddenly vanished. It was one thing to support their cause against Wellington's scorched-earth policy, quite another to condone the terrible behaviour to which the ghastly scene bore witness. He called over to Ross. 'Sarn't, get the others back into the village and kick down the doors. Do whatever you must to bring them all out. Any you can find. Use force. I want them all in the plaza. Now. Line them up.'

Archer was attending to Leech now. They had cut down all four men from the trees and laid them on the ground.

Keane walked over to Archer. 'The other German?'

'Dead, sir. Loss of blood and a massive injury to the head. He couldn't have lived. The rock dashed his brains out.'

Leech's eyes were rolling and he was trying to speak. Archer calmed him. 'Quiet now. No need to talk.' He had unbuttoned the man's tunic and Keane could see where the jagged rocks had struck home again and again. It was clear that the men had been tied to the trees for some time. Probably overnight, left out to become sport again the next day. This presumably explained the swift departure of the people in the inn. They had been impatient to get back to their victims.

He felt a passion rising in him, like a wall of red mist. A fury, pure and implacable.

The village was in uproar as the hussars, together with Keane's men, forced their way into the houses and dragged out their occupants. Many of the villagers had fled away into the fields, but more than two score remained. He heard firing and knew that von Cramm would have taken him at his word and shot anyone who did not come willingly. He was aware that the Germans would want revenge for what had been done to their comrades and that he had to turn a blind eye to it.

Whatever the shots had signified, within a few minutes the remaining villagers had been assembled in the plaza. They huddled together, surrounded by the hussars. There were, he noticed, mostly women, the old and the young. Most of the men had made it into the fields. Some, though, remained.

Keane shouted to Ross and von Cramm, 'Get the men. Bring the men forward.'

Roughly, the Germans pushed their way into the crowd and dragged the men out so that they formed a line in front of the huddle. Keane counted eleven of them. They stared at him with hard, emotionless eyes. Only three of them looked away, down at the dusty ground.

Keane rested his left hand on his sword hilt and spoke to them in Portuguese, in a slow, measured tone that they might understand.

'Tell me why you did this? Why? Why kill these men?'

There was no reply. One of the children began to whimper and a woman sobbed. He went on. 'This is inhuman. You're savages. All of you. Animals. No better than animals.'

He took a pace back and addressed the crowd. 'I'm taking these men back to my general. They will stand trial for what they have done. And they will pay.'

One man walked forward. He was almost as tall as Keane and heavily built, with a muscular frame.

The man spoke. 'You are the inhuman ones. Your English soldiers were pigs and they died like pigs. You take from us all that we have. This is the punishment we keep for those who betray us. It is the same for a woman who betrays her husband. The stones are the people's punishment. No one of us is the killer. We all have our say in the death. It is the only way for them to die. You're no better than pigs. All of you.'

It was too much. Keane had stood and taken it, but suddenly the red mist rose again and what remained of his self-control disappeared. He walked towards the man and, before he or anyone else knew what he was doing, took a swing at him. The punch connected, his fist crunching home against his jaw, knocking him off his feet. The villager sat up, shook his head and rubbed his face, as the blood oozed from his bleeding lip. He spat on the ground, blood and teeth, and then pushed himself to his feet. Keane stood glowering at him, his fist still clenched. Just as Ross was walking forward to assist, without warning the man flew at Keane, headbutting him in the stomach and knocking the wind from him. Keane fell to one knee, clutching at his diaphragm as the peasant prepared to attack again. But as he did so, Keane pushed upward and deliberately raised his head, so that the top of his skull caught the man hard on the chin, smashing into the bone and knocking his head up and back. The villager reeled away holding his jaw, and Keane straightened up, still recovering from the blow to his stomach. As he regained his balance, he saw a thin sliver of silver catch the light, as the man drew a knife from his boot. Ross began to run, but it was too late. The man was on Keane now and the knife flashed upward towards his neck. But Keane had seen it coming. He moved fast and, parrying the man's hand with his left arm, landed a huge haymaker on his right temple. It looked like a random punch, but Keane had been careful to deliver it so that the point of his knuckle struck hard into the side of the man's head.

The man reeled from the punch, his head jerking sideways. Then he seemed to straighten up. The knife fell from his hand, clattering to the ground, and for a moment he seemed to hang in the air, his eyes, round and staring, looking into nothingness. Then his knees buckled and his body crumpled to the ground. He did not get up. Keane stood over him, blood streaming from his knuckles where it had connected and he knew that the man would not get up again.

Keane held his head. It felt as if a thousand hammers were pounding at it, but at the same time he experienced that sense of elation that only came to you when you knew you had triumphed. It was hard and basic and it was something that you didn't speak about. It came at the kill. He looked down at the man. It was not hard to see that he was not breathing.

Silver came up and held his shoulder. 'Bloody hell, sir. You've killed him. Not that he didn't deserve it.'

Keane turned to him and spoke quietly, breathless. 'No one deserves to die, Horatio. But sometimes your time just runs out.'

He was aware of Sanchez standing beside them.

'Well, so, you've done it, captain. You have made an enemy of a nation. Your general will not thank you for it.'

Keane tried to regain his breath and faced the colonel. 'No, Colonel Sanchez. I have simply shown these people that you do not throw our sacrifice back in our faces. And now I intend to teach them another lesson.'

Sanchez looked alarmed. 'What? What are you going to do now? Kill the rest of them?'

Keane wiped a gobbet of blood and spittle from his face. He turned to Ross. 'Sarn't Ross, arrest ten men.'

'Sir. Yes, sir, and then?'

'You tie them up, good and hard, so they can't move. And

then you find a wagon. And you put them in the wagon. We're taking them back to Celorico to be tried for murder. Fair and square.' He looked down at the dead villager. 'I've done my bit. And more. I've avenged the poor bloody Germans and Leech. That's enough killing for one day, isn't it?'

Yes, he thought, I've avenged one of them, and I've behaved as badly as the peasants themselves. He wished that he had been able to keep his head, to exercise some self-control. But when the red mist came upon him, there was nothing to be done.

Sanchez stared at him and at length, as Keane was adjusting his uniform, he spoke. 'I'm surprised at you, captain.'

'Really, why?'

'You seemed to me to be the model of an English officer. A real gentleman. And now you turn on a man and kill him with your bare hands. I'm impressed, of course. But also I am appalled. Where is your decorum? Where are your famous rules and regulations? Where is your honour?'

Keane stared at him. 'You mistake me, colonel. I have never claimed to be an English gentleman. I am an Irish gentleman and I learned my trade the hard way. I was taught to fight back home as a boy and I honed my skills on the battlefields of Europe and Egypt and in the cathouses of Dublin and Londonderry. That's how much of a gentleman I am. I have honour. I'm steeped in the stuff. Honour and loyalty and rules. And I'll tell you something, colonel, no one does that to one of my men. And no one talks about my men like that. No one.'

Sanchez nodded and said nothing.

Keane retied his stock, which had come loose around his neck during the fight, and walked across to where the others were standing. Garland, the giant prizefighter, grinned at him.

Keane smiled back. 'Good as you almost, eh, Garland?'

'If you say so, sir. It was well done, though.'

Keane looked at his bloodied hand. 'Hard bloody head he had, though. You might give me a lesson.'

Archer, the newcomer, had been watching the while and now he walked over to Keane and looked at his hand. 'I've never seen that done, sir. Not ever. Killed with a single punch.'

Keane waited while Archer bound up his hand. He spoke quietly. 'To be honest, Archer, I've never done that before. But don't tell anyone, will you? I surprised myself. Only supposed I'd knock him out. Always wanted to try it, though. A trick taught me by an old Indian hand. Fellow in the 33rd who said he'd learnt it from a kaffir. One of Tippoo's thugs. How to kill a man by punching him hard on the temple. Always wondered if it worked.'

Ross had done as he'd been ordered and rounded up ten men from the crowd. They had come without a struggle, cowed and shocked by what they had just witnessed. He reported to Keane. 'Ten men, sir, like you ordered.'

'Very good, sarn't. Find a cart and make them load the bodies on to it. And you had better put Leech into it too, and Archer with him. We're heading back to Celorico. All of us.'

It was then that he realized that he had not seen Heredia for some time. Not, in fact, since they had entered the plaza and discovered the dead hussars. 'Sarn't Ross, where's Heredia?'

'Couldn't say, sir. He was with me when we cleared out the village. Haven't seen him since, though. Shall I get the men to look for him? He can't be far.'

But hardly a moment later Heredia appeared. He walked into the clearing from the direction of the village and Keane could see from his manner that something had happened.

'Heredia? We wondered where you'd got to were. Where the devil were you?'

'I chased two of the villagers into the fields. Two men. They were running away.'

'Do you have them? Where are they?'

Heredia said nothing. He shook his head.

Keane frowned. 'They got away then?'

Heredia looked across at the villagers, who were loading the dead hussars on to a wagon. He turned to Keane. 'Please believe me, captain. This is not the way my people behave. These people are savages. You were right, sir. Well, now I have become one of them. I am a savage too.'

'What do you mean?'

'Nothing. I did what I had to do. Just that.'

'You killed one of them? You know that I did the same.'

'You do not want to know what I did, captain. Please do not ask me again. I have restored my people's honour.'

Keane noticed that Heredia's overalls were heavily blood-stained on the right leg and saw too that blood had dried on his scabbard and at the top of his right arm. 'Are you wounded? Have Archer look at it.'

Heredia looked at him and shook his head. 'It's not mine. I told you. I have restored my people's honour. Isn't that enough?'

7

Something had changed in Celorico. There was a new spirit abroad in the town. Keane had sensed it the minute they had entered the main square. He could not place it exactly, but it was there in the eyes of the people as they looked up at the strange party.

Keane and his men rode at the head of the column, followed by two wagons containing the prisoners and another, smaller cart carrying Leech and Gabriella.

They had buried the three hussars at San Pedro and, still distrustful of the mood of the villagers, Keane had thought it wise to leave Sanchez and his men there. He had, however, brought von Krokenburgh and every one of the German hussars, anticipating a potential antagonism between them and Sanchez's men following the commander's refusal to involve his troopers in the arrest of the villagers.

He wondered what it was that might be troubling him. A sense of suspicion, resentment or just fear? The expressions on the faces of the townspeople seemed to speak of all of these things. Keane supposed that it might be simply his imagination playing tricks. A consequence of the shock of seeing the

Portuguese villagers turn on his men. But there was no denying that there was definitely something amiss.

He had returned to the town too in some trepidation, aware that his presence there might not be what Wellington had intended. But he had justified it to himself, secure in the conviction that it was of paramount importance that the murderous villagers should be brought to justice and receive their punishment, which he presumed would be death.

Had he but been truthful with himself, however, he would have admitted that this was not the prime reason for his return. There were in fact two more powerful reasons, neither of which he could admit to either Grant or Wellington.

He pondered Pritchard's fate and knew that he would not rest until he had searched the ruins of his house once again. Something was not right. He could not pinpoint it. He knew that any such investigation must be done as soon as possible. Before the place fell to pieces or was too much looted. But apart from that, he had a burning need to gain any news he could of Kitty Blackwood.

They took the prisoners directly to the town jail, which was now a military prison, and handed them over to the care of the provosts. Keane had detailed Ross, Garland and Martin to do the job, but the sergeant soon reappeared outside.

'Sir, I think you had better come in. Something you should see.'

Keane tethered his mount to one of the irons outside the building and walked in. He was met by the same provost sergeant who had accompanied them when he and Morris went to arrest Pritchard. The man saluted and Keane acknowledged him.

'Sarn't Baynes, good day. Good to see you again. What's all this about?'

'I was just saying to your sergeant, here, sir, that these ain't the first of their kind we've had here in recent days. Not by any means. Whole place is full of Portos. Makes a change from the usual drunks and brawlers from our army, I suppose. But it's a queer thing, sir, ain't it?'

'It is, sarn't. Very curious. How do you come to have so many locals? What are their crimes? Have they all been thieving from us?'

'Oh no, sir. Far worse than that. Same as your lot there. They've been murdering us, or trying to, the bastards. Don't know what's got into all of them. Thought they was on our side, sir. But I reckon we'll have a few hangings before the week's out. And good riddance to them.'

'Can I see them?'

'If you're quite sure you want to, sir.'

The sergeant took Keane from the guardroom and into the prison, to where Garland, Martin and two of the provosts were shutting the ten villagers away in a common cell.

'They're in there, most of them. There's a couple of right wild ones cooped up on their own in another cell, but I don't think you'd want to see them, sir. Have your eyes out soon as look at you, they would. I'd shoot them now and be done with it if I had my way.'

Keane peered into the dark cell, his sense assailed by its rank stench of slop buckets, damp stone and sweat. At a guess, including his own prisoners it contained some forty men, all dressed in civilian clothes, all of the same peasant stock.

'And you say they're all here on account of having attacked British soldiers?'

'That's the long and short of it, sir. There's three there that's actually done murder on us as far as we know. Leastways that's what the officers who brought them in swore to be the case.'

'And where are they from?'

'Seem to be farming villages mostly. Far as we can make out. All along the river. Where our cavalry have been doing the burning.'

So, thought Keane, it was not an isolated incident. Half the populace was in arms at Wellington's policy. He thanked Baynes and with the others walked from the prison and out into the sunshine and fresh air.

At some point he knew he would have to make his report to Grant and Wellington and there was no way in which he would be able to cover up his actions at San Pedro and that he had killed a villager. Nor would he be able to disguise the fact that he had returned to Celorico. He wondered whether it might not be better to do so, however, after he had visited Pritchard's house, lest they should insist that that he return to Don Sanchez without further delay.

'Sarn't Ross, take the men and find a billet. You might try our old hovel. Failing that, you had better go with the Germans and see what they can offer you. We shan't be staying more than a single night, I imagine.'

Leech was lying in the small cart, tended by Gabriella and Archer. His eyes were open and, though it was clear he was in some pain, he managed a smile on seeing Keane.

'Feeling better, Leech?' He turned to Archer. 'We had better get him to the hospital.'

'Not if you want him to live, sir.'

'Is it that bad a place?'

'There's too many that goes in there with no more than an

ailment that comes out in a box. Best that I look after him, sir, at least until we return to the front.'

'Very well, Archer. We're lucky to have you. But I can't spare you here. You'll have to leave him when we go.'

He walked to where von Krokenburgh and his men stood dismounted by their horses. 'Captain, I suggest that you return to your unit. I daresay you'll want to explain about your three men. We'll leave here tomorrow. I'll give a good account of you to the commander.'

Von Krokenburgh nodded and thanked him and led the hussars away to the lines of their parent unit, which had remained with much of the light cavalry close to the headquarters, from where they and others had made their daily sorties to ravage the land in accordance with the standing orders of the commander-in-chief.

Keane, having given his horse to Martin, set off into the town. He had decided that he would find Morris first, at least visit his house, and then, after a tour of Pritchard's ruined billet, stiffen his nerve and make his report. He walked from the prison in the direction of Morris's billet on the Rueda della Casa.

On his way there he noticed again the changed nature of the place and began to think that it might indicate a change in the attitude of the Portuguese as a whole. What had previously been gratitude to their liberators had he thought been replaced by resentment at their presence.

At length he came to the little narrow close beside the church of Santa Maria. The church was still in operation as a hospital. Now, though, a good deal more of the disease had been replaced by wounds from battle, but, as before, Keane smelt the familiar odour of infection and suffering. He stooped at Morris's door and was surprised to find it shut and locked. He banged at it a few times and called Morris's name. But there was no response. At length a window opened in the house opposite and an old woman looked out at Keane. Seeing her, he smiled and asked as to the whereabouts of the officer *inglêse*.

The woman shrugged and said simply, '*Partado.*' Morris had gone.

Keane was baffled. In theory, with Pritchard dead, he was once again part of Keane's unit and had only remained in Celorico on account of various things to which he had to attend. Once again Keane found his mind inventing solutions. No doubt all would become clear when he made his report to headquarters. A moment he was still keen to delay.

He walked from Morris's house along the way the two of them had taken on the day of the explosion, past the church with its twin bell towers, then across the main road and through cramped back streets, towards the granite buildings of the old town and past ornate gothic windows, in the direction of the headquarters building.

Pritchard's house looked much as they had left it. Some of the sticks of furniture which had been left intact after the blast had gone, he thought, but apart from that, the site was the same pile of rubble it had been. The bodies, or parts of bodies, had long been taken for disposal and were he presumed now either interred or burnt. He was not even sure quite what it was he was hoping to find here. He only knew that somewhere in this place there must lie a clue as to who had planted the bomb and the identity of the body parts. Curiously, although it had been a good ten days, the house still smelt of burning.

He walked through the rubble, kicking at the stones as he went. Here was the spot where he had found the severed arm and over there the place where the torso had been. Fragments of the bomb still lay where they had fallen, but nothing yielded any further clues. Keane wondered at himself for having returned.

He left the site and walked up the road to the headquarters building, wondering all the way what he was going to say to the commander-in-chief.

Lieutenant Ayles showed him in to Wellington's office. Grant was standing with Wellington.

The duke appeared to be genuinely surprised by his appearance.

'Captain Keane? I had not expected to see you. I had thought you were with Don Sanchez. Explain yourself, if you will.'

'Sir. I am sorry to say that I have to report a problem.'

'A problem? With Don Sanchez? This is not the news that I wish to hear from you, captain. This is not the purpose for which you were engaged. I expect you to bring me intelligence and news of cooperation between your two forces along the enemy lines. What is this problem?'

'You will not have heard, sir, that we have just now brought in ten Portuguese peasants under arrest.'

'Arrested, eh? Really? You do not surprise me, Keane. The place is full of them. For what were they taken?'

'Murder, sir. Murder of your own soldiers. Sir, do you realize that the whole countryside virtually is rising against us?'

'I think you exaggerate, captain. We have had a few incidents. Nothing more.'

'Sir, they killed three of the German hussars in cold blood. Stoned them to death. And almost did the same to one of my men who had just demolished a bridge, thus denying the French passage across the river.' He paused, then spoke again. 'In fact, I killed one of them, in self-defence.'

Wellington raised an eyebrow and shook his head. 'Did you, indeed? Captain Keane, I am only too aware of the unpopularity of my policy of a razed earth. That was always to be expected. But it is a necessary evil.'

'Yes, sir, of course. I do understand. But coming so close as it does to your being seen to have abandoned the poor people in Ciudad. Ten thousand of them. It cannot surprise you that it has come to such an extent as this. This is more than isolated incidents, Your Grace. Surely we must alter our plan?'

Wellington turned on him. 'Our plan? What do you mean, Captain Keane, coming in here and challenging my strategy? It is not your place, sir, to tell me how to run the war. This is how we shall do it.'

Keane knew that he had overstepped the mark. 'I am sorry, sir. Please accept my apologies. It was not my intention to challenge you.'

Grant interjected. 'Captain Keane is distressed, Your Grace. I don't think he intended to be insubordinate. And in truth, he does have a point.'

'I am aware of that, Grant. Some of what you say is true, Keane. I did not anticipate that destroying the crop would have such a widespread effect. I had thought that the people were behind us, that they would sacrifice anything to defeat the French. I have to admit that it has taken me by surprise.'

He began to pace the room. 'There have been moments in the last few days when I even felt that the Portuguese alliance might be doomed. I begin to question our very presence here.'

Keane glanced at Grant. He had never seen Wellington in such low spirits. The major gave nothing away and the duke continued. 'I am out of favour at St James's. In my own headquarters Major Cavanagh hovers like a buzzard over prey, awaiting the slightest slip. In Lisbon, the Portuguese royal family opposes me. Across the country the very peasants I am tasked to defend are killing my own men, and all the while Marshal Massena is advancing. Now he besieges Almeida. Should the fortress fall before our defences are complete, we are lost and everything with us.'

He turned to Grant. 'He does know about the lines of defence?'

'Yes, sir. Naturally. Captain Keane, in common with all your intelligencing officers, knows of their existence and their progress.'

'Good. So it should be. But Keane, word is to go nowhere beyond this room. Not even to your men.'

Keane saw an opportunity. 'Speaking of whom, sir, might I enquire as to the whereabouts of Lieutenant Morris?'

Wellington raised an eyebrow and looked at Grant. 'Morris?'

'The artilleryman, sir. Transferred to Keane's company. Of late he was here at headquarters. The unpleasantness, sir.'

'Of course, your man outing our spy. Dreadful business. Lucky thing that the traitor died in the end. Blew himself up apparently, here in Celorico. In his own house. Making a bomb. Isn't that right, Grant?'

'Yes, sir, that would seem to be the case.'

'Where's Morris now?'

'Requested leave, sir. A few days in, Lisbon I believe. Had to see someone on an affair of his estate.'

'Quite. That's where you'll find him, Keane. Lisbon. Not that you will be going there. I need you to remain with Don Sanchez. He's more valuable to me than a thousand German hussars, poor devils. I need Sanchez, Keane, more than ever now, and it is your task to ensure that he remains both loyal and anxious to assist.'

'I have done my best, sir.'

'Have you, by God? Well, you had best continue doing so. He is of a mind to assist us?'

'Yes, sir. I believe so, even with the recent business of the hussars. He did, though, seem to express interest in recompense.'

'He wants to be paid for his trouble?'

'He is aware that certain other guerrilla leaders have benefited from a bounty.'

'Doesn't he understand, Keane, as you must surely do, that I have no money. It was your action with Marshal Soult's baggage train enabled me to pay the army last year. The government at home votes me the £300,000 that I request for the maintenance of a Portuguese army trained and commanded by my officers under General Beresford. Apart from that my purse sits empty. From where exactly does Sanchez think I can pay him?'

'I do not know, sir. But he is open to other forms of bribery. I myself gave up my father's own gun to him to keep him onside.'

Wellington stared at him. 'Did you, by God? That was a damned fine thing to do, Keane. Grant, make note. Have Captain Keane recompensed for his loss. Uh . . . whenever we are able. It was a good piece?'

'The very finest, sir. I was loath to part with it. It was one of the only links with my father.'

Wellington stopped short at the mention of Keane's father and looked at him for a moment. 'Your father. Yes, of course. A good man, Keane. That was truly a hard choice to make.'

Keane stopped. Here was the duke admitting in so many words that he knew his father. Certainly that he knew who he was. It was as he had thought then. Wellington was the key to his identity. It was vital that he should remain in favour with the general. For an instant Keane was tempted to ask there and then what he had meant. He had long supposed that Wellington might have known his father. Even entertained the possibility that they were related. But here at last was the hint of proof that the duke might hold the clue to his father's identity. But of course, this was not the time to mention such a thing. Keane held his tongue.

Wellington, realizing the reaction his comment had brought, looked at him with a curious expression and Keane knew that one day he would have the answer to that question. But for now it would have to wait. 'You are a most extraordinary man, Captain Keane. Most extraordinary. And most fortunate.'

Keane bit his lip. 'May I ask, sir, what you intend to do with my prisoners? I should like to tell Leech – that is, my man who was gravely wounded by them – what their fate is to be.'

Wellington looked away out of the window at the town and said nothing. 'Tell him, Grant.'

'I'm sorry, Keane. We cannot try them. You must see that. Were we to do so, they would most certainly be hanged. And that would, I am sure, be the right decision. But God knows what such a move would do to our relations with the Portuguese.'

Keane spoke slowly, thinking of the sight of Heredia walking back from the fields, his clothes spattered with blood. 'I have good reason to believe that my own Portuguese trooper killed two of their number. He did it to satisfy honour, sir. He of all men knows that this is not the way of his people. Their betters, their officers, will see that. They will not oppose a trial. Sir, I beg of you, will you not try these men? One of them, even? They killed three of the Germans and almost did for one of my own.'

Wellington looked away. 'We cannot risk it, Keane. I am most sorry. Perhaps I have gone too far. But it is the only way to beat the French – deny them all sustenance. The people must understand that. Time is now of greater importance than ever. We cannot delay, Keane. We cannot simply starve out Massena's army. I can see that the people will not stand for it.

'We need to meet him in battle in two months' time, not before, as some would have it. Wait until just as the campaigning season reaches its end and then lure him in to a campaign he cannot win. I need to give the people a victory before they will believe in me again.' He paced the floor for a while and said nothing as the other two men stood silent.

Then he turned. 'When I meet Marshal Massena, I need to meet him in battle on my terms. It must be on my terms, Keane. I am relying upon you to ensure that will happen. Major Grant will give you a new amusement on your way out. Good luck with it.'

'An amusement, sir?'

'A thing which might amuse you, Keane, and that might also help us to win this war. Take my good wishes to Colonel Sanchez and you may tell him that he will have his money just as soon as I can get it. I am sure that I can rely upon you to assist, in any way in which you may be asked.'

This last comment struck Keane as curious, but he made nothing of it. In fact the entire interview had been somewhat odd, with mention of his father and Wellington's obstinacy about the impossibility of sending the Portuguese villagers to trial.

'Good day, Captain Keane. I trust that when we next meet you will be the bearer of better news.'

Keane saluted and went to leave the room, followed by Grant, who closed the door behind them. Once outside, both men walked some distance away from the ADC who was hovering in attendance and a clerk who sat at a large ormolu desk.

Grant took Keane to one side. 'That, I am guessing, was not entirely the meeting you had envisaged.'

'Not entirely, sir. Although in truth I was dreading having to make my report.'

'And I don't blame you, my boy. It's a tricky business, this, and we have to play it with great care. We may be here with the ostensible purpose of defending Portugal against the French, but both of us know, as well as the duke himself, that our real purpose is the interest of Great Britain.'

Keane nodded. 'The duke spoke of an "amusement", sir.'

'His Grace's idea of a joke, Keane. Here it is.' He walked across to a wooden box, which Keane had noticed on entering earlier.

'Sir?'

'Well, open it up, man, go on.'

Cautiously, and thinking that the whole thing might be intended as a curious practical joke, Keane opened the lid of the box, which popped up with a click. Inside were a number of red leather-bound books. Grant walked across beside him, picked one out and closed the box.

'What is it, sir?'

'This, James, is a telegraph code book. Latest thing. We are introducing them into the army. To staff officers and the guides. Do you realize that, using the device with which that book corresponds, we will be able to communicate with troops in the front line within a matter of minutes? We have decided to set up a system of telegraph stations. It pains me to say so, but it is based on a system used by the French for some years with great success.

'Of course, here in the Peninsula the enemy are unable to

use a similar system. It would leave isolated forts exposed to the guerrillas and would be untenable. We, on the other hand, having the friendship of the guerrillas, are at liberty to emulate Bonaparte.'

He chortled to himself at the prospect of using a system perfected by the French against them. 'We have established three lines of communication, with their focal point at Lisbon.'

Perhaps, thought Keane, that might explain Morris's business there. Grant went on. 'The Portuguese engineers – and in fact, Keane, they're not at all bad – under their general Folque managed it. We now have a line stretching from Almeida to Lisbon. Sixteen posts, each of which is visible from the next. They are roughly some twelve miles apart. Another line runs between Barquinha and Abrantes, but that is smaller, with only two posts, and the third is devoted to watching the maritime activity in the Tagus. And then of course we have more in construction, along the defensive lines of which the duke spoke.'

'Yes, sir. I understand the secrecy.'

'Some of the stations have a mast, just like that of a frigate, up which, by a series of ropes and pulleys, it is possible to hoist a number of metal balls. Most are simpler affairs with a single post and a system of numbers indicated by the position of a wooden flag. D'you see?'

Keane nodded.

'Do you realize, you can pass a message to the post at Almeida, and the command, even in Lisbon, may read it within a matter of hours? Hours, Keane, not days. Imagine.'

Keane frowned. 'But sir, what if the French should see the signals? They will know what we intend.'

'Yes, but General Folque has devised a code and that is what I now hold in my hand. A very simple system of numbers relating to commands and messages. He had it put down in a book. This is your copy.'

He handed Keane the small red leather-bound notebook.

'A code, sir?'

'Yes, a cipher which the French will be unable to read. Again, it's something they have been perfecting for years, and here we are beating them with their own weapon. 'And now I have something else for you, James. And I know that it will not please you. The duke has further orders for you.'

Keane looked at him. 'Further orders?'

'Orders that he asked me to relay to you.'

'Tell me what they are, sir.'

'Once you reach Don Sanchez, you are to proceed to Val de Mula, where you will find a unit of Portuguese infantry under the command of a Captain Foote, late of the 69th. With them will be a unit of the local militia, the Ordenanza. You are to take command of this force.'

'To what end, sir? I have sufficient men, more than enough, in fact, for the purpose of intelligence gathering.'

Grant shook his head. 'That's just it, Keane. You are to use them to break up the local flour mills and prevent them falling into enemy hands.'

Keane stared at him. 'I cannot believe it. Sir, this must be wrong. After what has just been said. Even by the duke himself. Are we now to destroy the flour mills? This will surely ruin the country, not just for the French but for generations of Portuguese. It cannot be right.'

'Those are Wellington's precise instructions, and you are the man to do it. I'm sorry.'

'No, sir, I am sorry. I cannot do it.'

Grant grasped him by the arm. 'You must, James, or face the consequences. To refuse such an order would ruin you.'

Keane thought again of Wellington's comment about his father. He stared at the floor. 'How many mills?'

'All that you can find. He is set on it.'

'This is not a job for a British officer. Why can the Portuguese army not do it?'

'You are the man for the job, Keane. That is the duke's perception. Using the Ordenanza to do the dirty work will at least soften the blow to relations with our allies.'

'But under my command?'

'The officers who command the Portuguese regulars cannot do it. It is a diplomatic compromise. And you must at the same time continue to ensure that Colonel Sanchez remains true to our cause. And of course you must ensure that the telegraph can operate fully. You understand?'

Keane nodded. He could see the logic now, and also that there was no way out. He laughed. 'Well, sir, at least it will enlarge my command a little. I'll make colonel yet, before the year is out.'

Grant smiled knowingly. 'That you may, Keane, that you may.'

Grant showed him out, closing the door carefully behind him, but Keane had not gone more than a few paces and was about to descend the staircase when he was startled by a cough from his left. A figure in a red coat came from the shadows.

'Major Keane?' Major Cavanagh smiled at him.

'Captain Keane, sir.'

'Of course. I was forgetting myself. Or should I say, perhaps, anticipating the future.'

Keane was unimpressed by the clumsy manoeuvre, intended to woo him over to the opposition camp.

'You have not had any opportunity as yet to draw the enemy into battle?'

'No, sir. But please be assured that it is paramount in my mind.'

Cavanagh gave him a fatherly pat on the shoulder. 'I shall rest in that knowledge, Captain Keane, just as you may rest in the assurance of advancement when that day comes. We need a battle, Keane. Now.'

With that, Cavanagh turned and walked towards the doors to Wellington's rooms. Keane turned back to the staircase and walked from the building.

He made his way back through the village, his mind in turmoil. Cavanagh had not upset him. The man was a buffoon, and now Keane knew that his future, if he had one, lay with Wellington. Rather, he pondered the situation with the Portuguese. It was bad enough that they could do nothing about the villagers. But now to be told that he must personally supervise further operations against the peasants? It was too much. Of course he deplored anything that would bring innocent people to penury. But that was not his worry. What really concerned him was that it would be British soldiers, his own men included, who would suffer on account of the policy. He did not believe that Wellington or his staff had any real understanding of what was happening out in the countryside. He had seen it. Had seen the expressions on the faces of the villagers. He knew just how desperate they were and what they would do about it; and what revenge meant in this country of saints and shrines and superstition and vendetta. Before long it might lead to a full-scale rebellion, and then where would the army be? Fighting the French on one side and its erstwhile allies on the other.

Other thoughts preyed upon his mind. There was Pritchard.

Of course he had discovered no more about him, and now all the facts seemed to indicate that the man was dead. But Keane was still no clearer as to why, nor who might have killed him. Grant and Wellington seemed to have bought into the story that he had blown himself up, and perhaps that was what Morris had told them. Who knew? He might be right. And why tell them so if he was not certain. Which brought him to Tom Morris.

This was the real worry. More than anything else. He could not dislodge the spark of doubt that was now lit in his mind against the man who for years he had counted as his best friend. But there it was. Nagging away like an old sore. How could Morris be sure that Pritchard had blown himself up? They had not properly discussed it, and that in itself was strange. He wondered if the time he had spent alone had changed his friend. Certainly, he told himself, Morris was no traitor. He was as loyal as he to the Crown and the army. But what did he know that Keane did not. There was something, some secret Morris had not told him and that he knew he must find out.

It struck him that it might have to do with whatever it was he was doing in Lisbon. His friend had never before spoken of having any business interests in Portugal. Keane wondered what it might be.

The evening air was growing cold as he entered the house which had been their billet previously. To his delight he learnt that the men had found it empty and reoccupied it as if it were their own.

They had got a fire going in the grate and were cooking something over it in a huge pot. Whatever it was, it smelt palatable enough and Keane guessed that it might be Gabriella's work. She was sitting close to the fire warming her hands and he noticed, not for the first time in recent days, that her face looked drawn and she did not greet him with her usual smile. He guessed that it must have something to do with recent events. She came from peasant stock and he knew that she had reacted badly to the deaths of the villagers and their taking the prisoners to Celorico for trial. Thinking that perhaps it might change her mood, he spoke to her quietly. 'The villagers will not stand trial.'

'No trial?'

She looked alarmed and Keane realized why. 'No, no, don't worry. They will be set free. Very soon.'

She looked up at him and smiled. 'Thank you. Thank you, captain. I am sorry for this. It is a bad business for us.'

Keane, not wishing to disabuse her of the idea that their freedom had been his doing, merely nodded and placed a hand upon her shoulder. He wondered whether any of the others had heard and hoped they had not. Archer was sitting in a far corner close to Leech, who was lying on a makeshift camp bed, covered with a blanket. Keane walked across.

'I have no wish to offend you or to cast doubt upon your skills as a physician, Archer, but are you sure he would not be better cared for in the hospital?'

'No, sir, I am quite sure. He would only catch a pestilence in going into that place. Believe me. He is better with us. Besides, his fever has just abated and his wounds are clean. Better to be struck with rocks than with ball or shot.'

Keane settled himself down in a chair and placed his boots upon a low table set in front of it. 'I shall need two of you to accompany me to headquarters tomorrow before we leave. I have a package to transport back to the camp.'

Ross spoke. 'Tomorrow, sir? Then we are not staying any longer?'

'No, sarn't, whatever you might have hoped, it's back to Don Sanchez and the hills for us in the morning. That, it seems, is where we do best. We're to collect another command.'

'More men, sir? You'll need another weight of gold at your shoulder before long.'

'I shouldn't get too excited, Ross. My new command is a unit of Ordenanza. The militia. God knows what they'll look like or how they'll fight.' Realizing what he'd said he shot a glance at Gabriella, but she was intent on the cooking.

The others were seated around the large single room that had acted as the principle room of the simple dwelling, whose inhabitants had been a shoemaker and his family.

Silver had discovered the cobbler's tools and his lasts and was busy investigating how they might best be used. He looked up at Keane. 'Need your shoes mending, sir? I'm sure I could manage it. Not really much different from working a wood knife.'

Keane had seen Silver's skill with the wood knife. Before joining the army, he had spent years behind the mast in the Royal Navy, and the long sea journeys had been whiled away in such things. His hands, although they may have looked to most people like shovels, were remarkably sensitive when it came to delicate work.

Keane knew the importance of sound footwear, particularly here in the Peninsula. His own boots he kept in good repair and liked to carry out routine inspection on his men's footwear. In recent weeks, though, not surprisingly, he had been remiss.

'That's a kind offer Horatio, but my own boots are fine. You might ask the others, though. We all need to be well shod.'

Silver called out. 'Garland, how are your shoes?'

Garland looked up from the carbine which he had been

cleaning for a good twenty minutes. 'What? What about my shoes? What do you mean, Silver?'

'How are they?'

'They fit me, don't they?'

'Yes, but how are the soles?'

'Same as the rest. Made from leather.'

Silver shook his head and laughed. 'What about you, Will?'

Will Martin shook his head. 'I had these off a dead man just two weeks back. You recall. That Frenchie we passed lying at the side of the road. You remember. Looked a proper sight. Head half eaten away by crows. Perfect fit they are, and in good fettle.' He wiggled his feet in proof.

Silver was considering whether he should ask Heredia, when he saw that he had crossed the room towards the fire and was talking to Gabriella. For a moment he stopped fiddling with the cobbler's knife and watched the two of them talking in the flickering firelight as she continued to stir the stewpot. Heredia was clearly in the middle of some sort of explanation. He was gesticulating with both hands to impress a point on her. Silver stiffened and Keane glimpsed it.

Gabriella responded and lifted her left hand in emphasis. Then Heredia seemed to make another comment and Gabriella replied with a yell, almost spitting into his face. Silver looked up to see Heredia returning the insult and then she was at him, her hands scratching at his face. The trooper went for her and struck her on the cheek, sending her reeling. She rocked on her seat, missing the fire by inches. But Silver was up now and diving across the room towards Heredia.

Keane was suddenly aware that the man still held the cobbler's razor-sharp tool in his hand. He jumped up and tried to interpose himself between Silver and Heredia, but the latter had already jumped back and was looking for a weapon of his own. He found it in the leg of a chair which one of them had broken up for firewood and brandishing this was ready when Silver struck. The cobbler's knife flicked through the air and caught Heredia on the hand holding the makeshift bludgeon. He yelled and aimed a blow at Silver's head that caught him on the shoulder. Silver staggered and Keane took his chance. As the knife came up again, he pushed between the two men, knocking Heredia to the floor with a blow of his arm while at the same time grasping hold of Silver's rising arm in a vice-like grip. Silver dropped the knife to the floor and Keane could see the fury in his eyes. Heredia pushed himself up from the floor and for a moment Keane thought that he might attack him. But, realizing it was Keane, he stopped himself.

Keane held them apart. 'What the devil's going on? Both of you, stop this, now. Heredia, drop that. Silver, if I see you reaching for that knife, I'll knock you out faster than you can move. What do you think you're doing? Explain yourselves.'

Silver spoke first. 'It's him, sir. He's always staring at me. And at her. You saw, he hit Gabby. On the face. No one does that to my girl and gets away with it. Bastard.'

Heredia replied, 'She deserved it. She called me a murderer. Said I had betrayed my own people. She talks shit. She's from the gutter and she should go back—'

Keane interrupted. 'Heredia, hold your tongue. That's no way to speak of anyone's wife. What did she accuse you of?'

'She said that I had killed those villagers. The ones who went for Leech. That I shouldn't have touched them. They were my people. That we were wrong. I only did what I thought was right. They might have been my countrymen, but what they did was wrong. They stained the honour of our country.'

'So you killed them?'

Heredia nodded.

Keane turned to Silver. 'I can understand your rage, Silver. I might have done the same. But we are a unit. We must act and fight together. If we begin to fight, to argue, with each other, then we cease to be effective. I cannot have this.'

Gabriella was sitting beside the fire, holding her cheek where Heredia had hit her. Still watchful of the two men, Keane turned to her. 'What did you say to him?'

She looked up at him with eyes filled with anger. 'I said that he was a traitor to his country. That he should be ashamed. I know what he was doing in the fields. I saw him return. I know what he did. To do that was wrong. They were poor peasants just trying to defend their rights.'

'But you must see that to have done what they did – to have executed those men and almost killed Leech – it goes beyond human decency. We cannot allow it. However badly they might feel. If they had a grievance, they should have come to us with it. That is the way. Not taken the law into their own hands. If we all did that, then all would be chaos.' He realized as he said the words that he himself had taken the law into his own hands by killing the villager, but watched to see if she had understood. She said nothing.

Keane sighed and shook his head. 'You must resolve this. Now or later. You choose, but the sooner the better. You will not fight a duel. Both of you are too valuable to me to lose one. But you may resolve it by a fight if you wish. Fair and square. A fist fight. Garland can preside. You agree?'

Neither of the men said anything.

'Agree?' It was not a question.

They both nodded. This, thought Keane, was the last thing

that he needed. He had suspected that the relationship between the two men had long been strained. Heredia, despite being only a *sergente* of the Portuguese army, still came from a higher class than Silver's wife, a former prostitute. Such things, Keane knew, from his own background in the class- and religion-ridden mire of Ireland, ran deep. All that it had taken was one event, and the incident at the village had been enough. Now the only way to resolve it and to avoid having one kill the other was to satisfy honour in a fight. He hoped that would suffice.

Silver spoke. 'Can't do it here, sir. We might get picked up by the provosts. Best to wait till we're back at Sanchez's camp, isn't it?'

Keane realized that he was right and also that their fight might provide a spectacle for the guerrillas and show them that the army was about more than uniforms and drill. That his men at least were capable of fighting hand to hand and also that they stood by their principles. He knew of course that, given the stance Sanchez and his men had taken at the village, it would not endear them to Heredia. But in truth he expected Silver to win and knew that the cultural differences between the Portuguese trooper and Sanchez's men were anyway probably too wide to bridge.

'Yes, Silver, I dare say that you're right. Heredia, you agree? When we get back to the camp you may have your fight. Until then I wish to hear no more of this.'

Both men nodded and Silver went to attend to Gabriella, while Heredia slunk away into the shadows to nurse his cut hand.

Keane sat down and took a deep breath. He looked across to Silver and Gabriella and suddenly envied their closeness.

It occurred to him that this too might be something which had affected Heredia. Perhaps the man was simply jealous that Silver had found a companion to share his lot. Heredia had always been quiet about his personal life and kept his thoughts to himself. In Keane's experience those were the ones to watch. The quiet men. The ones who nurtured resentment or whose minds had been addled by what they had seen in battle. He remembered one man when he had been a lieutenant in the Inniskillens. A deeply religious man who would read his prayer book every day. A bible-thumping Ulsterman named Armstrong. He had been a fine fighter in the heat of battle. But when they were out of the line he had retreated into himself.

Then one day, without warning, something had clicked inside the man's restive mind and he had attacked one of his fellow young officers, name of Wright, simply for issuing him an order to clean his boots. Armstrong had gone for the lad with his bayonet and before the men could dragged him off had stuck him like a pig through the belly and the heart. He was hanged of course, in front of the battalion, and Keane had never forgotten it. He wondered now whether Heredia might have anything in common with Armstrong and he prayed that he did not. At least he was not a psalmist, or whatever the Catholic equivalent might be.

He would know soon enough, anyway. After the two men had had their bout. Then he would watch Heredia. He would deal with it day by day. It was the only way.

He called over to Gabriella. 'How's that stew going? I'm starving.'

She looked back at him and managed a smile. That was good, he thought. Perhaps he had managed to cross one of the boundaries she had put up since the affair at the village. Silver turned to him. 'Almost done, sir. Looking as good as it smells.'

'Then get it dished up. All of you– you too, Heredia – get some stew. Archer, will Leech manage any?'

'Yes, sir. I think he will now.'

'Then let's all eat. Will, break out that wine over there. This might be the best meal we all have for some time. Tomorrow we'll be in the hills.'

8

Their return to Don Sanchez's camp was not an easy journey. Keane spent much of the time observing Heredia, wondering whether he might at some point lose his self-control and attack Silver. He suspected that the man was still concerned that with Pritchard's death he would never be cleared and Keane knew that in his world honour was of paramount importance. He had little to lose by killing a comrade, particularly one who had introduced such a woman as Gabriella into their camp.

In many ways it seemed to him that Pritchard was the author of all their misfortune. He had transformed Morris from charming old friend into a man he felt he hardly knew, full of secrecy and mistrust. His death had brought more doubts and left Heredia dissatisfied and reckless.

They found the camp much as they had left it. In their absence Sanchez had taken out a party looking for French transports and had found his prize: a large wooden chest packed with gold objects and precious stones, which had been looted in the course of Massena's march south and was being taken back to the emperor in Paris. He sat with it before him on the ground like some theatrical robber baron, the analogy made all the more telling by the fact that he had draped around his neck a long gold chain hung with a ruby which until recently had belonged to the Bishop of Salamanca.

He greeted Keane with a smile, but remained seated. 'Welcome home, Captain Keane. How was Celorico?'

'As I had expected, colonel.'

'Lord Wellington is well? You saw him? And the prisoners? I trust that you found satisfaction. I had thought that you might wait for their trial.'

Keane showed no emotion. 'They will not be tried.'

Sanchez looked surprised, but Keane thought it sham. 'No? Have they been shot already, without a trial? How very un-British.'

'No. They are to be set free.'

Sanchez smiled. 'A wasted journey then for you, captain. Not at all what you had expected or had in mind. You must be frustrated.'

'No, not entirely, although I prefer to see justice properly done. But no, it was not wasted. I had an interesting interview with the commander-in-chief.'

'You are on good terms with Wellington?'

'I like to think so. I am to take command of a company of the Ordenanza.'

Sanchez's smile grew to a grin and then a laugh. 'The Ordenanza. I don't envy you. They are a rabble. That is indeed a thankless task. Why have you been given such a command? You have your own men and the hussars, and my cooperation is assured. Surely the Ordenanza do not need a man with your skills. They stand in line and get shot. If they stand at all.'

Keane was surprised by the compliment. 'Apparently they need me. It is for a specific purpose.'

'May I know what?'

Keane had not been looking forward to revealing the nature of his task to Sanchez, knowing the reaction it would cause. 'I am to use them to break up the local flour mills. To prevent them falling into the hands of the French.'

Sanchez whistled and shook his head. 'Captain, does Wellington not understand what he is doing here? Is he not content with destroying the crops, knowing what that has done? You took him the prisoners. You showed him. This will surely set the seal on your relations with the people.'

'I am all too aware of that, colonel. But those are my orders. I am sure that the reason Wellington chooses to use Portuguese soldiers, in particular militia, to do this job, is because it will look less damaging.'

'Yes, of course. Well, I don't envy you. Where are the men now?'

'At Val de Mula apparently, near the old fort. I have to take command of them immediately.'

Sanchez took off the gold chain and stood up, buckling on his sword belt. 'It is most interesting, your way of soldiering. You are about to start destroying mills, while others in your army are building.'

'Building?'

'Yes, a wooden towers on a hill.'

He walked with Keane across the village square to a spot looking across the plains to the south-east. 'Look. Over there on the road to Fort Concepcion. Do you see it?'

Keane looked and saw a wooden tower rising on top of the hill. Around it, figures were finishing their work.

'It's a new invention, colonel. A telegraph machine. It can send orders and messages across country by means of signals. The navy have been using something of the sort for some time.'

'Fascinating. Will I see it in operation?'

'Most certainly. I plan to test it at once. You are most welcome to watch.'

Keane left Ross in charge and told him to keep an eye on Heredia and Silver, and then with Sanchez, and accompanied by Archer and two of Sanchez's men, rode across to the hill and up to the summit.

The telegraph station was a tower made from wood rising some twenty feet high at the top of the hill. It had only recently been constructed by the field engineers and still smelt of sweet, unseasoned timber. It was a simple structure, with a staircase leading to a platform at the top on which the telegraph machine had been installed.

As Grant had explained to him, it had a simple mechanism. On a single pole another shorter post had been attached by a screw enabling it to spin freely. A handle at the bottom of this second pole enabled the operator to move the arm through a full circle. At the top of the pole was attached a prominent square of wood, about two feet square and painted bright red, whose position dictated the number. Bottom left would mean 1, left 2, top left 3 and so on. Up to six. When the square was at the top it was simply 'ready'.

Using this system hundreds of number combinations could be transmitted, each of them having a separate meaning, as dictated by Colonel Folque's code book. It had a brilliant simplicity and, thought Keane, seemed infallible, though it all depended on the secrecy of the code book and that, he knew, he would have to guard with his life.

Keane pulled it from his pocket and thought of a message with which to test the apparatus.

Eventually he settled on a simple few lines. 'Message to Almeida station. Good day. Can you read this message? Please reply. San Pedro station.'

He had decided that Archer, who, with his medical background, was the most intelligent and well-read member of his team, would make a good code master and operator, though it was vital to have a replacement should anything happen to him. They stood at the top of the little tower and looked across the plain to where another tower stood on another hill some ten miles distant, near Nava d'Aver. Along with the code book, Grant had provided him with a small map of the locations of the signal towers. Keane drew the eyeglass from his valise and opened it before putting it to his eye.

'I can see figures there. Are we ready, do you think, Archer?'

'I think so, sir. As we'll ever be.'

So Keane found the appropriate numbers in the code book and read them out, and Archer repeated them and carefully moved the arm to the appropriate position.

'391, 276, 400, 661, 325, 391, 243, 281.'

Twenty-four separate movements were required, but it didn't take Archer long to master the system. He finished transmitting and moved the arm back to the 'ready' position.

'How long do you suppose it will take for them to reply, sir?

'If the next station has seen it, then we should, I imagine, receive a response from them. But we want a reply from Almeida. That's two stations away. It might take a few hours.'

Sanchez, who had been watching silently, said, 'It's extraordinary. For hundreds of years these hills have stood here and it has taken generations days to move across them. Now they are being used to make messages travel faster than any man possibly can. Fascinating.'

Again Keane lifted the telescope to his eye and looked at the distant hill station. For a few minutes nothing happened and he wondered if the garrison, four men from soldiers from the Portuguese military telegraph corps, had seen the message. But then the arm moved up. Three separate movements. Separate numbers in groups of three. He spoke them aloud and Archer transcribed.

'391, 276, 400, 391, 461.'

Archer searched the code book: 'Message to San Pedro station. Good day. Message received.'

'It works, sir. What a system.'

Sanchez spoke again. 'Well done, captain, that was most impressive. Now we can tell Wellington where the French are in just hours. An amazing feat.'

Keane nodded. 'Yes, isn't it? Let's see what Almeida tells us. In the meantime I have to find my new command.'

He handed Archer the telescope. 'Stay here and keep watch, and here, take my glass. I'll keep the code book with me.'

Keane rode with Sanchez back to the village and then, taking Heredia and Martin with him, set off in the direction of the town of Val de Mula.

The countryside below them was alive with British soldiers, from small scouting parties of light cavalry and riflemen to an entire battalion on the march. He recognized it from a distance as the 43rd, from Craufurd's division, and realized that they were falling back to regroup at Fort Concepcion, a frontier fortress constructed a century ago which dominated the surrounding countryside.

*

Val de Mula was a small, squalid Portuguese village, although it was hard to tell at a glance whether it had always been so or if the war had been its undoing. It consisted of two streets at right angles, which bisected a square built up on three sides and with a church on the fourth.

He found the Ordenanza gathered in the square, most of them sitting on their packs. A few were stretched out on their backs, apparently asleep.

Their uniform coats were of brown cloth, poorly cut and with green collars and sky-blue facings and on their feet they had a variety of shoes, boots and gaiters. Some of them wore no shoes at all and others a variety of espadrille made from strips of leather. Some had packs of which they had made seats, others did not and a few had rolled blankets of various colours, tied around their bodies from shoulder to waist. They wore hats of two types: some the same shako as the Portuguese regular army, a tall hat similar to the British stovepipe but more tapered; others a low-cut, broad-brimmed black hat. The majority seemed to carry a gun, although even these showed some variety of make and calibre. A few of them had only poleaxes, perhaps, thought Keane, liberated from some ancient castle. Several had pitchforks. Many were unshaven, and it was instantly evident that they had never been regular soldiers. For a start their ages varied between the young and the aged. There were boys of fourteen and old men who Keane thought must have been in their fifties or sixties. There was not much of a military air about them and they wore for the most part expressions of sullen indifference. Keane's heart sank. Even Martin could see the calibre of the men. 'Oh dear, sir. What are we to do with them?'

'Use them, Will. That's all. We don't have to train them and we don't have to drill them and we don't have to fight with them, thank God. They're simply navvies. Muscle power, what they have of it.'

Heredia was scornful. 'They are not soldiers. They're nothing but old men and boys called out by conscription.'

'I wouldn't speak too soon, Heredia, I'm entrusting them to your command as joint *sergente* with their own.'

'Sir?'

'You are Portuguese. You can command them best of us all.'

It was a clever notion, he thought. Put Heredia in direct charge of them and you would give him more responsibility, which in turn would divert him from his argument with Silver and perhaps even give him some purpose.

Their officers, two of them wearing blue coats, and a brown-uniformed *sergente* were standing separate from the rank and file. The *sergente* and one officer, a lieutenant, were swarthy Portuguese. The other man, though, looked distinctly English. Seeing Keane and the others ride into the square, all three turned to greet them.

Captain Aeneas Foote was a tall, wiry man of about Keane's age and he recognized him at once as a fellow officer of the 69th with whom he had served in Egypt. He had not much liked him then and saw no reason now to adjust his judgement. Foote puffed at a cheroot as he watched Keane. Keane seemed to recall that the dislike had been mutual and did not expect a cordial encounter.

Foote smiled at him with what to Keane seemed distinctly like a sneer. 'James Keane, as I live and breathe, it is you. You recall we served together at Alexandria, when you were saved by that sarn't of yours. What was his name?' he thought for a moment. 'McIlroy.'

'Sarn't McIlroy. Yes. You have a damned good memory, Foote.'

Foote looked him up and down and raised an eyebrow. 'I see you're no longer with the Inniskillens. Curious, your new uniform. Portuguese are you?

'No, Foote, I'm not. Unlike you. I might say the same of your own blues. You'll need to be careful you don't get taken for a Frenchman. Might be shot by your own men.'

It might have been taken as a veiled threat, but Foote did not respond.

'So you're the lucky man who's to take over my brave boys, are you?'

'It would seem so, Foote.'

'You'll find them quite unlike any men you may have commanded before. If you take my meaning. You would not call them sharp of eye or quick to respond. They move slow on orders and have a habit of falling out of line when they choose. They own no great discipline, for all my *sergente* has tried. And he has tried, believe me. What will you do with them, Keane?'

'I have my orders. They are to destroy flour mills to keep them from the French.'

'That's engineers' work. I wish you luck of it.'

'Perhaps I can get more out of them than you have managed, Foote. What will you do now?'

'Oh, have you not heard? I'm for a new command. Portuguese regulars. I tell you, Keane, it'll suit me better. You really can't beat a good professional field command and men who will do your bidding. Oh, I am sorry. I quite forgot. But you command others, do you. These two of your men?'

He pointed to Heredia and Martin.

'Yes. Part of my command. We are a mixed force. We take our orders direct from the duke.'

'Do you, by God? So it was he who gave you my men? He must

value you highly, Keane. Highly indeed to rob an officer of his command.'

Keane took the meaning of the comment and tried to ignore it. Heredia had dismounted and, taking his new duties seriously, had walked across to the Ordenanza and had engaged the *sergente* in conversation. The officer, a young man with an extravagant moustache, had remained aloof, smoking his cigar and looking from time to time at Keane and Foote. Keane thought that he might now approach him, but he had hardly begun to do so when Foote's voice came again.

'There was another man, too, apart from McIlroy. An artillery officer, as I recall. Friend of yours, from whom you could never be parted. A little unnatural, some of the men called it.' He smiled to himself. 'What was his name? Hollis? Collins? No, I believe it might have begun with "M".'

'Morris. It was Morris, Foote. Tom Morris, if you must know. And he is still my friend. And I have to say that I find your comment offensive.'

'Still your friend? Really? Last I heard, he was off in Lisbon, having a rare old time with the ladies.'

Suddenly Keane found that he was listening more intently.

Foote went on. 'Or should I say with one lady in particular? A young lady. Miss Blackwood to be precise. Kitty Blackwood. That was it.'

Keane felt as if someone had landed him a sinking blow in the stomach. He felt quite sick. He turned on Foote. 'You are wrong. Quite wrong.'

'No, I think you'll find that I'm far from wrong. I have it on the best authority. Captain Morris is in Lisbon paying his attentions daily to Miss Blackwood.'

Keane stiffened. 'Be careful what you say, Foote.'

Foote stared at him. 'Why, why on earth should I do that? You have no possible claim on Miss Blackwood's hand, do you? How could you?' He paused. 'In fact as I now seem to recollect, did you not fall out with her brother over some matter or other, a duel or some such, before he was killed? Damned shame he was. Should never have happened, should it? Damned fine officer.'

Keane's blood was up. And he did not worry for more than an instant whether by some extraordinary chance Foote knew what he should not and might be alluding to the secret of Keane having killed Blackwood. Foote had gone beyond the mark. Had insulted not only the woman he loved but the man he still considered to be his best friend. He moved closer to Foote.

'You will retract your words, sir, which damn the characters of two of my friends.'

Foote smiled at him. 'So Miss Blackwood too is a friend of yours, as well as Captain Morris. How very interesting. But let me see. Do we think that she might be a better friend of yours than Captain Morris? I wonder. What could we possibly surmise?'

Keane flew at him. But Foote had judged his insults with a nicety and was ready for him. He sidestepped the rush and Keane connected with nothing. Foote turned and waited for Keane to turn before swinging at him. The punch caught him on the left cheek and for a moment he stopped. Then he was on Foote. A punch, his favourite right hook, went in and hit home in Foote's abdomen. The man recoiled and then, coming out of the shock, riposted with a punch to Keane's nose, which opened it up. The blood gushed and Keane staggered. He had forgotten that Foote had been such a good fighter. Although he did not have Keane's instinctive, basic street instinct, his punching was stylish, as if it had been formally taught, which in fact it had. Wiping the blood off his face, his eyes stinging, Keane decided

that the time had come to get serious. He squared up to Foote
as if he was in a ring. Foote naturally did the same. This was
his form of fighting. But just as the dummy punches seemed
to announce a new assault, Keane pulled his masterstroke and
suddenly kicked his right leg out with huge force and drove his
boot hard into Foote's groin. The man collapsed to the ground in
howls of pain and Keane walked across and sank a punch hard
into his face. The blood gushed from his nose. It was enough
for Heredia and Martin, both of whom ran across and pulled
Keane off his brother officer just as he was about to send the
first kick into his kidneys.

Martin spoke. 'No, sir. Not that way. Not now. Not here.'

Keane pulled away from them, managing to free one arm,
and in his fury aimed again for Foote. But he did not connect.
Heredia put out his own right foot, and Keane, concentrating
on the kick, tripped over it and fell sprawling to the ground.
He swore and, getting up, turned on Heredia.

'What the devil do you . . . ?' Keane stopped, realizing with
a start what he had been doing. And, more importantly, what
he had been about to do. Breathless and bloody, he looked at
Heredia. 'Thank you. And you, Will. I'm in your debt, both of
you. Stupid thing to do.'

Foote was still down, clutching at his groin, oblivious to the
blood streaming from his nose. Keane walked a little distance
away from him, flanked by Heredia and Martin. The men of the
Ordenanza were staring as one at him, silent, shocked to see
two British officers lose control and brawl in the street. A few
of them, including the *sergente*, were grinning and nodding at
Keane.

The Portuguese officer, still puffing at his cigar, walked
towards the three men and doffed his cocked hat. 'Sir, I have to

say that I'm a little shocked.' He spoke, as Keane had suspected he would, in English, in the cultured tones of a scion of the nobility. Clearly this was no ordinary officer of militia. 'I did not know that British officers did such things.'

Keane shook his head. 'Ordinarily we do not, lieutenant. But I can only endure insults to a certain degree. I apologize for the display of lack of self-control. I should not have allowed it in front of the men.'

'Oh, I don't think the men minded at all. In fact, you may have done yourself a favour. They had no great love for Captain Foote and they have every respect for a man who can win his battles.'

'It was foolish.'

'You fight well, sir, although not strictly by the rules.'

'Thank you. I'm not proud of it, lieutenant, but it serves a purpose.'

'I would be happy to fight alongside you, sir.'

'Well, it seems that you may have the opportunity ere long. James Keane, Corps of Guides. Stand your men to, if you will, Lieutenant . . . I'm sorry, I do not have your name.'

'Pereira. Don Fernando Forjaz Pereira Pimentel de Menezes e Silva, Count of Feira, at your service.'

He turned and barked an order to the *sergente*, who relayed it to the men. They rose from their positions and within a few minutes were formed up in the square, looking surprisingly better, thought Keane. Meanwhile Foote too had managed to get to his feet, although his face was as white as a sheet. He stared at Keane.

'You're insane, Keane. I'll have you for this, I swear.'

'Do I take that as a challenge, Foote? If so, then I accept. Though where we shall manage it and when, I cannot conceive. I have a war to fight.'

'You accept and then, as quickly, you refuse. You are no gentleman, Keane.'

'I don't think that I ever claimed to be a gentleman. But I will not be known as a cheat and I will not hear my friends slandered. Naturally I accept. Choose your place. I shall choose weapons.'

'I shall get word to you, Keane. And then we shall meet. You have my word on it.' He turned and found his horse, which was tethered to a ring outside the local inn.

Keane, who had cleaned up the blood on his face and shirt and was contriving to look the part of a British officer, stood before the company, flanked by Pereira and the *sergente*. Martin and Heredia fell in on the right. Keane addressed the men in his best Portuguese.

'My name is Captain James Keane and I am your new commanding officer. You are under my command until further notice. You may wonder about my uniform. Although I am British I wear the brown of your own country as do my men. You have already met two of them. The others you will meet very soon. We work with the *partida* of Colonel Julian Sanchez and our orders are to harass the French as much and as often as we can. Lieutenant Pereira will brief you further.'

He hoped that it was enough; that they had, as Pereira had suggested, been impressed rather than repulsed by his brawling with Foote. He thought that they might gain some respect for him, and that, however long they were under his command, he would somehow manage to transmit something of his ideas of soldiering to them. It had not been a good start.

Foote rode past them. Keane ignored him, but Pereira gave him a salute, which he returned before riding on.

Keane watched him go and cursed himself again for having lost his temper. It had taken Heredia to drag him off Foote, and he realized that their roles had been reversed since he had pulled the Portuguese trooper away from Silver in their billet.

Perhaps, he thought, Heredia had understood something. Something that had now occurred to him. The fact that this was a very different form of warfare they were pursuing. Where your friends might so quickly become your enemies, and where you began to doubt not only those about you, friend and foe alike, but at times your own actions. Not for the first time, but now perhaps with more conviction, he began to wonder whether he was really cut out for the job. It had changed him, and it occurred to him that this must surely be what had happened to Heredia and in particular to Morris. He wondered too, once again, about Foote's accusations. And again he dismissed them from his mind.

Right or wrong, he had called out Foote, but they had no date or place set for their meeting. He remembered too that he had given his word that Heredia would fight Silver, and again the parallel struck him as ironic. Why, he wondered were they fighting among themselves, when Marshal Massena was sitting just ten miles away, outside Almeida, with one hundred thousand French troops?

He watched the Portuguese lieutenant speaking to the Ordenanza and wondered if he was aware of the task they had been given or if he believed that he would soon be leading them into battle. He had registered Pereira's title. The young man was a count of the Portuguese nobility and undoubtedly harboured dreams of glory. But to Keane he seemed on first impressions as if he might have a little more to offer than one might expect from an indolent aristocrat.

He walked across as Pereira finished briefing the men. 'Thank you, lieutenant. Follow me to San Pedro.'

9

Archer rode into Sanchez's camp only a few minutes after their return. Keane was watching the Ordenanza filing into the village in what passed for a column of threes. They were hardly the foot guards, he thought, but they had a certain air of confidence that could not be denied. He had, he thought, misjudged their expressions on first acquaintance, and whether it had much to do with Pereira's pep talk or his own spontaneous display of dirty street fighting, they seemed to have improved their temperament.

He counted them into the camp. Apart from Pereira and the *sergente*, who he had learnt went by the name of Dominguez, there were a hundred and forty-eight men in an under-strength company. Still, they augmented his little force considerably, which now numbered his own close group of seven, since Leech's departure, and von Krokenburgh's seventy hussars as well as the detachment from Sanchez's band of fifty lancers and fifty foot, most of them infantry. Sanchez's own force was another four hundred and twenty, so given the need they could muster between them almost eight hundred men with which to meet any enemy.

Archer approached him on horseback, bearing a note.

'The telegraph, sir. We received a message a short while ago, from Almeida. But without the code book, I was unable to translate.'

Keane nodded, took the book from his coat and gave it to Archer. The man scanned the numbers and then thumbed his way through the pages.

'General Cox says that he is short of muskets and equipment. Some of the militia have deserted. They are waiting for Massena, sir.'

'Aren't we all?' Keane shook his head. 'It has the makings of another Ciudad.'

'General Craufurd's men might go to their assistance, sir.'

'I'm afraid, Archer, that General Craufurd will have been ordered by the commander-in-chief that in the case of this happening he is to make only a show of strength. We would not want to sacrifice the Light Division, and General Wellington knows that.'

He knew that Craufurd's men would make a stand beside the town. But he knew too that it would be short-lived and wondered what the conclusion might be. What was the Light Division against the might of a French army?

'Keep in communication with them, Archer. Twice a day if you can. We may yet be able to buy time.'

He took back the code book and, watching as the Ordenanza were ordered by Pereira to stand easy, found Ross staring at them.

'Ah, sarn't, I take it you have seen my new command?'

'If you don't mind my saying so, sir, they're not quite the equal of our lads, are they?'

'No, and nor would I expect them to be. They're conscripts,

sarn't, and look at their ages. They have no great wish to be here. But I wonder how they would do in battle.'

'I didn't think that was why we'd been given them, sir. I mean, I'd not feel happy standing side by side with that.'

He pointed to one of the Portuguese, a man in his late fifties or early sixties, who had sat down in the town square and was mopping the sweat from his brow. He was somewhat overweight and clearly the march had not agreed with him.

'No, I take your point, sarn't, but for every one like that, I would say there's another that has the makings of a soldier. So we have the basis for a seventy-man company in the style of our own army rather than one double that size in the Portuguese fashion.'

'Now you put it that way, sir, I suppose there are enough of them. But I thought they were here to knock down houses.'

'Mills, sarn't. They are here to demolish the mills. And on that count, we cannot lose any time. We must move down to the valley and destroy them before Massena takes the city.'

'Do you think he will manage it, sir? Will Wellington do the same as before and refuse to come to their aid?'

'Without a doubt. He has a strategy and he will stick to it. Just as he has done in the past.'

He called over Pereira. 'Lieutenant, I have orders for your men. We are to advance into the valley of the Turonnes and up into the surrounding hills and break up the mills.'

The Portuguese walked across to him. 'Break up the mills, sir? The flour mills? But that will ruin the people just as much as burning the crops. More so.'

'Nevertheless, that is what we must do. We must prevent them from falling into the hands of the enemy.'

Pereira thought for a moment. 'I can see the logic. But the reality is hardly pleasant. It is all they have.'

'Those are my orders, lieutenant, and your men must carry them out.'

'That will not present a problem, sir. My family may be of the ancient nobility, but me, I am a realist. A man of today. I know what must be done. Even though it will make life hard for my countrymen. They must understand this is the only way to drive the enemy from our land. Perhaps you and I might speak to the men, sir.'

'Perhaps, yes . . . I'm glad that someone can see it for what it is. I hope that your soldiers share your view.'

'They have no choice, sir. They will do what I command.'

Keane saw his chance to broach a subject. 'You have a *sergente*.'

'Sergente Dominguez. Yes. He was in the regular army. The men respect him.'

'I have a mind to offer you another. My man Heredia. He needs men to command. He was a *sergente* in your regular cavalry – dragoons – before he came to join us. Would it be a problem to ask if he might attach himself to you at present?'

'No, sir. That would not be a problem. In fact, it would be a good thing. We have too many men for one *sergente* and I am not inclined to promote any of the men from the ranks. Your man will do very well with us.'

Keane thanked him and was relieved to have engineered Heredia's temporary removal from their company. But he knew that at some point honour would demand that he and Silver fight and he wondered whether it might not be better to get it over and done. First, though, their pressing priority was the destruction of the mills. They were of two types. The water mills that sat in the valleys, and on the hills the tall windmills. Keane thought it best to start with the former.

Down in the valley of the Turrones, where the water flowed fast enough to turn the huge wooden wheels of the mills, they found the first of their objectives. This being their first, Keane had ridden down with a party of two platoons of the Ordenanza, accompanied by Ross, Garland, Heredia in his new role and a half-troop of the hussars as escort. The water mill had been abandoned by its inhabitants in the face of the French advance, for which small mercy at least Keane was thankful. Its location and a few forgotten treasures told of its history as a place of love and laughter. And above all a place of work. For the apparatus was still functioning and the owners had left behind many of their possessions, suggesting that they hoped to return. But it was too late for niceties. Keane took Ross aside.

'Divide up what you can of what's left here, sarn't. Make sure our lads get the better part of it. Shoes, boots, anything usable.'

'Yes, sir.'

Ross began to scour the modest shelves and presses of the mill house and within a matter of minutes had made a pile in the centre of the room. Boots, blankets, old shirts, wine flasks, a few surprisingly full, knives and forks; anything that might come in useful on campaign made its way into the pile.

Keane in the meantime had walked outside and was offering Pereira his wisdom on the best way to demolish a house. 'We need to take it down from the base. So if we remove the door-ways it should fall in on itself.'

Heredia spoke up. 'Sir, surely all that we need to do here is remove the wooden paddles from the wheel. Without those, the mill cannot function. It is useless.'

'Of course, but what if the French manage to construct a replacement. To do the job well, we should take down the house.'

'But, sir. Surely we do not expect the French to sit in this country for months? We expect to meet them in battle. We are hardly going to leave them in possession of half of Portugal.'

Keane, knowing about the defensive lines being constructed by the duke, was fully aware that this was precisely what he expected the French to do. Marshal Massena would be given battle. But after that, as Grant had told him, the duke intended to retreat with the people of Portugal behind his lines and leave the French to the land, a land from which they could not possibly live. That was why the job had to be done properly. So that the French engineers would have no hope of salvaging the ruined mills. But of course for the present all of this had to remain a secret.

'It may seem the easier option, Heredia, but my orders are to demolish the mills, not merely the blades or the sails. So that is what we are to do. However long it might take.'

He thought of Leech, still recovering in Celorico. How he missed his skill with explosives. The man could have had this mill destroyed with powder in an hour. Now they were reduced to breaking it by brute force. Garland took the first blow, wielding a two-handed sledgehammer they had brought down from the camp. He smashed the head into the keystone with little effect. But on the second blow the stone seemed to shift and on his third strike it moved back.

Keane stopped him. 'Wait. The place might come down.' He looked at the wall and tried to estimate where the rubble might fall. 'All of you, move back. Stand away.'

Dominguez shouted at the Ordenanza, who scurried away from the mill.

Keane moved back a few paces with the others and called to Garland, 'One more hit, then run like hell.'

Garland turned and grinned, then, having spat on his huge hands, took up the hammer again. Raising it above his head, he smashed it against the keystone which flew away and into the house, leaving the doorway with a yawning gap. For a few moments nothing happened, and in that instant Garland turned and ran towards them. Then, as they all watched, the sides of the doorway began to move inwards and down, and as they did so the wall above them slipped down. Instinctively they all moved back again. Further now, and it was just as well. For the wall was falling now, stones slipping away from each other as it plummeted earthwards. It hit the ground with an ear-splitting crash, sending up a huge cloud of white dust. They covered their eyes and turned away from the flying rubble. Then all was silence. Peering through the dust, Keane attempted to make out what was left of the mill. Gradually the air began to clear and they could see that while the front wall had collapsed completely, the other three still stood, although that on the left, closest to the apparatus, was leaning in as if it might easily fall at any moment.

'That was well done, Garland. Show them how it's done. Now, all of you, lay in there and get the rest of it down. And take care. Well done. That's a good start.'

Taking Ross with him, he rode back up to San Pedro. The place was quiet and there was no sign of Sanchez. A mist had begun to descend upon the hillside and the air had turned almost tropically humid. It reminded him of evenings in Egypt when the cloth stuck to your back and the neck rag clung to you like a stranglehold. A few of the guerrillas were sitting around a table at the old posada and the remaining half-company of

Ordenanza were being drilled by Pereira. He found Gabriella, Martin and Silver in their part of the encampment engaged in the everyday drudgery that went with being on campaign. Silver was sewing up a tear in a pair of overall trousers while Gabriella sat cooking and singing what sounded like a lullaby. It crossed his mind that she might be pregnant, but he dismissed it. Silver would not be so stupid. Martin was picking lice from his hair with a bone comb he had bought from one of the guerrillas.

Keane did not stay for long. He was impatient to hear whether there had been any word from the forward observers. He had sensed for some time that Massena would make his move soon and had sent word of his fears back to Almeida and Celorico via the telegraph network. He rode fast through the misty afternoon up to the hill station near Nava d'Aver, which as usual was being manned by Archer. Dismounting, he wasted no time.

'Make a signal to the forward station at Alameda. I need a report from them.'

'I have, sir, but there has been no reply. Not for an hour or more. And now this mist's come down, I can't really see.'

Keane put the telescope to his eye and looked towards the distant signal tower, through the haze. For some minutes it seemed he was searching in vain, so thick was the mist. Then, though, there was a gap in the greyness and the tower came into view. But it was no longer there. He could see the pieces of wooden post, lying around the summit, broken up, and by training his glass down the hill and into the valley, he caught sight of three men on horseback, the tower garrison, riding as fast as they were able. Behind them a dust cloud showed pursuers, lots of them, and as he looked the sun's rays struck through the mist and glinted off bronzed helmets.

'Christ. The French. Send a signal to Craufurd's post. I'll give you the numbers.'

He felt in his pocket for the code book, recently retrieved from Archer and, opening it, found the numbers. 'French advancing. About to abandon station. Will ride to join you.'

Archer began to make the signal and within a few minutes it was done. Then, as they had been ordered, Keane and he took down the apparatus and broke the posts in half with the axe provided, before riding away down the hillside. They did not look back and arrived in San Pedro, breathless on sweating horses, just as Don Sanchez was coming in from a routine patrol.

The colonel looked at Keane. 'You look worried, captain.'

'The French are coming. We have to leave.'

'You're sure?'

'They're right behind us, colonel. Dragoons.'

'Captain, are you certain? Did we have a signal?'

'We did not need one. I saw the station destroyed, the garrison chased off. They're probably dead by now. Didn't have a chance. We're pulling back.'

'Pulling back?'

'Unless you want to be slaughtered where you stand. There's at least a regiment of dragoons riding for here, and I dare say the rest of Massena's army not far behind them.'

Without waiting for another word from Sanchez, and still mounted, he found Ross. 'Sarn't Ross, we're pulling out. Have the men bring what they can. Are the others back from the mill?'

'No, sir, haven't seen them.'

'Then I'll go for them.' He glimpsed Sanchez and his patrol. 'Colonel.'

Don Sanchez turned.

'Can you spare those lancers?'

'Yes, of course, but why?'

'The Ordenanza are down in the valley at the mill, directly in the line of the French.'

He turned his horse and, followed by twenty of Sanchez's lancers, made off down the hill. By the time they reached the valley, Heredia and the Portuguese were on the move. Heredia was leading the Ordenanza on foot up the hill from the mill, with Martin and the hussars providing a mounted rearguard, their carbines at the ready. Keane signalled the sergeant of lancers to take his men to join the Germans and sought out Heredia.

'You saw them?'

'Yes. I had a picket posted to watch the road. Just in case. He saw you and Archer and then a crowd of horsemen.'

'You did well.'

'Do you think we'll make it before they catch us?'

'It may be better to stand here. Form square.'

Heredia looked doubtful. 'What? Do you really think we can do it, sir? With these men?'

'What choice do we have. If they catch us on the run, we're done for. It's our best hope.'

Keane surveyed the ground. The mill was some four hundred yards below them now and they were struggling in loose formation up the open side of a gentle hill. There was light cover on the ground, of no use against cavalry. But away to the left at about thirty yards stood a coppice of trees.

Keane shouted to the cornet of the German hussars who was standing with his men further down the slope. 'Mister von Cramm, to me.' The young officer trotted up. 'Sir?'

'Lieutenant, I want you to take your men with those lancers

over there and hide them in that wood. Stay close to the edge.'

'Sir?'

'We're going to make a stand. Here. Right here. We'll drive off the French and then get back to the camp as if the devil were on our tail. The infantry will form a square, and once we've let off a couple of volleys and they come to a halt, you will come out of the trees and have at them. That should send them running.'

Von Cramm smiled, confident in Keane's experience, and rode off, and Keane watched as he ordered the hussars and dragoons to wheel away and up the hill towards the little wood.

He rode down to Pereira, who was with the Ordenanza. 'Lieutenant, have your men form square. Do you think you can do it?'

Pereira nodded. 'We have practised it in drill, sir. We will do our best.'

'It had better be your best, lieutenant. You won't have another chance.'

He watched as Pereira shouted the command in Portuguese to form square. Aided and prodded by Dominguez and Heredia, the militia began to form what looked like a line, two deep and thirty-five men wide. Dominguez took position eight men in from the left while Heredia walked in to the sixteenth man from the right. Pereira gave another command and pushed by each of the *sergentes*, the man facing each of them turned, one to the left, one to the right, followed, somewhat haphazardly by his comrades until two sides of what would be the square stood at right angle to a third. Finally, Heredia came round to the halfway point of the longest side and directed the man there to walk to their rear. Keane was impressed. They had completed the square and it had not taken as long as he had expected. Of course on a field of battle it would have been a different story and they would not have stood a chance, but here they had managed it. He trotted across and, creating a gap, walked his horse through to the centre to find Pereira and the others.

'Well done. Not quite parade-ground stuff, but well done all the same. Right, have them fix bayonets.'

'Sir, some of them have no bayonets.'

'Well, have them use whatever edged weapon they have. The front rank at least can manage it.'

Within a few minutes each of the front ranks of the four sides of the tiny square presented something of an obstacle of steel. From bayonets to pikes and the occasional sword, all manner of sharp weapons projected beyond the wall of men.

Keane gave the order to load. And it was taken up by Pereira and his two *sergentes*. The men fumbled into cartridge boxes, haversacks and pockets and, bringing out cartridges, bit off the ends and poured ball and powder into their barrels before ramming them home. They primed their pans and stood ready to receive the enemy. Well, thought Keane, as ready as they might ever be. He wondered if they would stand when the assault came. He did not have long to wait. They heard the dragoons first. They came with a great rumble in the earth and then a jingle of harness and the whinnying of horses. Commands in French drifted across the stillness and then they were in sight. A ragged, galloping mass of green-coated horsemen, emerging on the opposite ridge and sweeping down towards the abandoned mill. Keane tried to count them and reckoned there must be two squadrons. The Portuguese were hopelessly outnumbered and he hoped that a bloody nose from the Ordenanza, followed by the surprise of the hussars and lancers in the wood, might be enough to drive off the dragoons and buy time for their escape.

The French galloped up from the mill, huzza-ing and whirling their sabres as they saw the tiny Portuguese square. Keane could almost smell the elation and disbelief in their minds as they increased their pace, eager to destroy this ludicrous enemy.

But they had not counted on the new fire in the spirit of the militiamen.

Dominguez and Heredia gave the order. 'Present. Make ready.'

Keane growled in Portuguese from inside the square. 'Wait for it. Hold your fire. Wait . . . wait.'

The dragoons were close now, too close perhaps.

'Fire!'

The first volley brought down four. It was not enough to stop them, thought Keane, but it slowed the onslaught.

'Fire!'

The second rank fired and more of the French fell. This time the front rank of dragoons reared up, the horses reluctant to attack the wall of bayonets and spikes. They wheeled and turned, for the most part slashing in vain, too far away from the men in square. Two of the dragoons managed to make contact, and three of the Portuguese fell with sabre cuts to their heads. But then, as the dragoons stood and it seemed for a moment as if they might break into the square while the second rank fumbled to reload, there was a yell from the left and the hussars and the lancers broke their cover and poured out on to the hillside and into the right flank of the milling dragoons. The lancers came first, driving their weapons into the French, pig-sticking one man after another before dropping their lances to leave them hanging and drawing their swords. The hussars slashed down, cutting deep into flesh and severing limbs. And the French were unable to respond. Turning, trying to pull round, they seemed to Keane to be floating in maelstrom of carnage in front of the Portuguese lines. Heredia called out, 'Steady. Don't move.

Steady.' And the Ordenanza did not move. Most of them. One youngster threw down his pike and ran back into the square, but Keane stopped him with his hand and grabbed the front of his tunic.

'Don't run now, boy. One gap in the ranks and they'll come through. Stay with your friends. They need you.'

He looked up at Keane with wild eyes and then, seeing that there was no way out, turned and found his weapon.

The cavalry carried on, pushing the French along the line of the square and back down the hill. They gave no quarter, but the French fought back and Keane saw two hussars go down as well as a number of Sanchez's men. Then, as fast as they had come, the dragoons had turned and were fleeing back into the valley and away up the hill. Von Cramm gave the order not to pursue and his men stopped where they were. The only cavalry, thought Keane, that he had ever seen do so. As the duke always said, once their blood was up there was generally no stopping them.

Led by Pereira, the Portuguese gave a cheer while the lancers walked across the French dead and wounded, sticking their lance points into the side or chest of any man they could see was still alive. It was not as Keane would have wished, but this time he thought it best to let it go. Besides, the last thing they wanted was wounded prisoners.

He turned to Pereira. 'Well done. You managed that better than I could have hoped.'

'Me also, sir, if the truth be known. It was you, sir. You inspire the men. They would not have done it but for you.'

Keane laughed and wondered if it had been his brawl with Foote that had endeared him to them so much.

He watched as some of the Portuguese walked out of the

line to gather up a souvenir from one of the dead dragoons. One man took a helmet, another an enamel cross pinned to an officer's coat. All of them were grinning and seemed almost in disbelief at what they had done. Bt Keane knew that this was no time for trophy hunting.

He turned to Pereira. 'Those would only have been the advance guard. There will be more where they came from, and worse. And their blood'll be up now, when they hear about this. Come on. We need to move fast.'

With no great regard for formation, with the lancers to their front and the hussars once again forming a makeshift rear-guard, the four of them herded the Ordenanza further up the hill and on towards the village. Don Sanchez had not been idle.

'I heard the firing. We thought you must be killed.'

'No. I don't die that easily, and nor do these men, it seems.'

10

They went as quickly as they could away from San Pedro, in the direction of Almeida, hoping to find Craufurd's force as they went. Keane presumed that they would have abandoned the position at Fort Concepcion and be making for the river.

There was no time to harness carts that would only delay them and so, much to Keane's shame, there was no alternative but to leave behind a dozen or so men too badly wounded or sick to march or ride. They left supplies for those who might live and notes attesting to the fact that they were soldiers, not guerrillas, and deserved to be treated according to the articles of war. Keane very much doubted, though, whether such rhetoric would make any difference to their chances of not being shot, which he rated low.

They formed up as a column of march, with Keane and the guides at their head, accompanied by Don Sanchez. Von Krokenburgh and a half-troop of the hussars came next, and then the Ordenanza in two half-companies. Behind them came Sanchez's infantry, whose ability to form column of march made the Portuguese look, in Keane's eyes, like professional soldiers. The rearguard was found by another half-troop of hussars, under cornet von Cramm. Sanchez's cavalry provided the flanking screen, moving alongside the column but at some fifty yards distant, keeping an active watch through the mist for the enemy.

They went by the road, snaking down from the hilltop to the plain and then on towards Almeida.

With every step Keane thought they must be caught, but there was no sight of their pursuers and at length, after an hour's march, one of the outriders approached him.

'Captain, we can see a large force. Over to our right.'

'What are they? French or British?'

'I do not know, sir. It's hard to tell.'

Keane rode across to the picket line and, taking his glass from his saddlebag, put it to his eye. The man was right that there was a considerable force to the south. He strained to make them out and then caught sight of a British colour, the Union Jack, flapping in the breeze as they marched. He counted two red-coated battalions, some others in brown, and ahead and on the flanks light cavalry and green-jacketed infantry, moving fast. The Light Division. 'They're ours, by God. That's Craufurd.'

He was certainly abandoning Concepcion, and it looked to Keane as if he might be making to cross the river Côa. He wondered if he intended to stop by Almeida at all. It was perfectly possible that he would not. After all, he had approved Wellington's abandonment of Ciudad.

Keane decided, however, that he would not share his thoughts with Sanchez. He turned and rode back to the Spaniard. 'We've found Craufurd, colonel. He's just down there, in the north valley.'

He was about to add 'and another thing', when there was a huge explosion. It came from away to their right, the north-east, and it shook the earth around them. The air seemed to echo with the blast.

Sanchez looked at Keane. 'What was that? More of your mills coming down?'

'No,' said Keane. 'I would wager that was Craufurd's engineers blowing up Fort Concepcion before Massena gets there.'

'And now he's making for Almeida? Do you suppose he will blow that fort to pieces too? Or will he just cross the river and leave the town to its fate, like Ciudad?'

Keane did not rise to the challenge. 'No, I would say that he plans to draw a battle line beside the town.'

'He will be crushed. How can he hope to stop Massena?'

'Of course he cannot do that alone. But he can fight a holding action. That is my guess. For the last three months he has managed to hold off an entire French army with a division that is no larger than brigade strength. I don't think he'll give it up now, whatever Wellington might have ordered. We must join him.'

'Must?'

'Colonel, if your men would join us, that is where I am heading.'

'Is that in your orders, captain?'

'No, colonel, but at this moment I don't think my orders count for much. I am ordered to send back information, but the telegraph posts have been taken. I am ordered to break down the mills, but I cannot do so with the French on our tail. I am ordered to liaise with the *partidas* and in particular with yourself. It would seem most prudent, given that we have sixty thousand Frenchmen at our heels, to throw in my lot and that of the troops under my command with General Craufurd. May I count on your support?'

'You may take your portion of my force. A half-troop of lancers.

I do not intend to stand in a set battle against the French army. I have better things to attend to.'

'Where will you go?'

'The hills. Where else? We are not made for set-piece battles, Captain Keane. And neither are you. Be careful, captain. I will keep a watch on what you do and I will find you again if you survive your battle with Massena.'

With that he raised his hand and called away his escort. Then riding down the column he found his infantry and within seconds they had broken ranks and were scrambling up the hillsides, followed by those of his lancers who had been scouting on the right of the column. Those on the left remained behind, as if nothing had occurred. Within a few minutes Keane had lost almost half of his force.

He turned to Ross, who was riding beside him. 'Damn him, that man infuriates me. He operates in the name of no one but himself. To remove half of our force in such a way, just as we most have need of it.'

'In truth, sir, they were never hardly our force, were they not?'

'You're right, sarn't, but I was hoping that I might count on him.'

'Oh, I shouldn't do that, sir. Not never. Not on that one. Now the lieutenant back there, he's a proper gentleman.'

It was curious, thought Keane, how such men as Ross recognized the nobility, and although they would not suffer fools, deferred to them when it was right, from instinct.

He gave a command and moved the column off down the hillside, on a dust road, in the direction of Craufurd's men. He doubted whether the French would pursue them now. They would have seen the clouds of dust put up by the Light

Division and be uncertain as to their strength. To see Keane's small command coming in on them would have confused their scouts even further.

They were over the river Seco now and in a plain well below the hills. Keane looked to his right and was surprised to see cavalry closing in on his flank as they descended. He shouted to von Krokenburgh.

'What's that there? French?'

On their captain's command, six of the hussars turned and rode towards the advancing troops, then returned and found their commander.

'No, they're Craufurd's pickets. But the French have turned them. They're pulling back to the river.'

They had all come down now, and as they did so the retiring British cavalry caught up with them.

Keane found a cornet of horse. 'Any idea what's happening?'

'The French, sir. Coming on in some force. More than we can manage. We're falling back. Who are you?'

'The general knows us. Keane and the guides and a troop of the German hussars.'

The young officer rode off and Keane watched him go, followed at a pace by his men, Light Dragoons in helmets like their own, and then the remainder of von Krokenburgh's parent regiment.

He turned to Silver. 'We had better get a move on or we shall certainly be caught by the French.' Looking towards the infantry he saw Pereira. 'Lieutenant, double the men for a while, if they'll take it.'

The Portuguese officer looked at him quizzically, but Heredia explained his meaning and soon the Ordenanza were moving faster, although the older members were obviously having some difficulty.

Martin spoke. 'We could try them at the way the Rifles march, sir. You know – twenty paces at a walk, then twenty at a run.'

'Good thinking, Will, but perhaps it might be better to make it ten in each case. Go and tell Heredia.'

And so that was how they advanced across the plain towards Almeida, just as the Rifles would have done. They crossed another river, the Alvercas, and once over, Keane rode to find Pereira.

'Lieutenant, take your men as close to the river as you can. If you can, find one of the two battalions of cacadores and attach yourself to it. Take position to its rear. We might call on you as a reserve.'

Having issued the order, he left the infantry in the valley and escorted by the hussars and lancers, moving steadily westwards, Keane, with Ross, Archer and Silver beside him, climbed his horse up towards the crest of a ridge, from where he might afford himself a better view.

He could see the ramparts of Almeida as clear as day from here. It was a huge place, a star fort in the old style that had been perfected by the French under Vauban. It looked benign, with its grassed-over mounds, but Keane knew that within them lurked dozens of cleverly devised defensive enfilades which could rip a company to shreds as it was caught in crossfire of grape and canister. He had seen similar constructions many years ago when still a youth, fighting in the northern French campaign with the Duke of York. And a fine fiasco that had turned into for the British army. Almeida looked as if it could hold out for days if not months, and that, he thought, must surely be what Wellington had intended. The whole campaign, it seemed, was about buying more time in which to outwit the French.

Turning to the left he had a fine view across Craufurd's lines. He had deployed his five battalions on the hills that ran westwards of the road. First came the hussars and Light Dragoons closest to the town, then the 43rd, by a small mill, a *pombal*, as the locals called them. The 95th were next, followed by the two battalions of brown-coated rifle-armed cacadores and finally, on the extreme right, Craufurd's strongest regiment, the 52nd, under its notorious, fire-breathing Colonel Beckwith.

Beyond them all, on the road, lay the stone bridge over the Côa. Aside from that, Keane could see no other means of escape from Massena's army. And that lay in all its threatening blue-black mass beyond the bridge.

He could see the Ordenanza too now. As they neared the lines, passing by the newly set skirmishers of the 43rd and the 95th, they moved further down the road until they reached the rear of their countrymen, Craufurd's two battalions of cacadores, who had behaved with such valour at Alameda. Keane watched as Pereira formed them up as best he could.

Ross looked on with him. 'That's the 52nd there, sir, their yellow colour.'

Keane saw it flying in the breeze and noticed that as they were the closest of Craufurd's battalions to the bridge, this might imply that they might form any rearguard that might be required. He had placed the cavalry on his left, by the town.

'It's damned lucky, sarn't, that he has our hussars and lancers with the Ordenanza, or he'd have no cavalry at all on his right flank.'

There was the crack of gunfire and with it a louder noise, the rumble of artillery as the allied guns on the ramparts of Almeida opened up. Their targets were the French columns on the far side of the field, nearest to the town. Closer to where Keane and the others stood, though, white powder smoke was visible and he heard the crack of more gunshots and saw a number of riflemen of the 95th in their distinctive bottle green, running and engaging the enemy in the lee of a tall mill building. One of those that had they made more progress, he thought, would have already been destroyed.

As he watched, Keane saw the French come on. A single battalion of infantry at first. They moved fast towards the mill and, though harassed by the riflemen, had soon closed on them and pushed them out.

The green-coated figures ran towards the lines, followed by a stream of redcoats. Looking at the field it seemed to Keane as if at any moment, through sheer number, the French might outflank Craufurd's men. But no one seemed to be aware of it save him. Turning, he looked for Craufurd and found him as usual on a rock, surveying the scene with admirable sangfroid.

Keane moved fast towards him. 'General, sir, I know it is not my place to tell you your business, but might it not be prudent to fall back beyond the Côa before the French outflank you?'

He pointed to the right flank where as plain as day they were able to make out a large body of dragoons and chasseurs.

Craufurd glared at him with searing black eyes. 'No, captain, indeed you are right; it is not your place. I do not intend to retreat, not at once, without giving a good account of myself.'

'Of course, sir.'

Keane wondered whether Craufurd could know that he was privy to Wellington's express instructions that he should not engage the French on the east side of the Côa, lest he be trapped and lose part of his command. Clearly he was now ignoring those orders. It was a brave gesture but ultimately, surely, doomed.

As if to confirm Keane's worries, as they watched the Rifles still falling back from their encounter at the mill, Keane noticed a group of horsemen off to their left. Suddenly the horse were upon them. Keane put his glass to his eye and saw scarlet and sky-blue uniforms. French hussars. They were cutting at the riflemen as they ran while behind them fresh dragoons were coming in to join the fray.

Craufurd had seen them too. He pointed and asked an ADC, 'Over there, on the right flank. What's that?'

'French horse, sir. They've got in among the Rifles.'

'Good God. Have they any assistance?'

Keane scanned the area and to his relief saw a body of redcoats fire a volley into the oncoming dragoons. 'Yes, sir. They have support.'

The redcoats fired again and he could see riflemen reaching the safety of the lines.

They could see the French marching into formation now. Craufurd turned to Keane. 'Who are they? Do we know? You should know, Keane.'

'They're from Ney's corps. That's Massena's vanguard. We had news on the telegraph four days ago. It's General Loison's division. Twelve battalions in all, in two brigades under Ferey and Simon.

'He has the French Hanoverians with him too, sir. Of course, they may run. And only one battalion of light infantry. The remainder are line. And some cavalry. Dragoons and chasseurs. He won't have had time to get all of them here, though. One brigade, I would say, and I'm willing to wager, two thousand horse.'

Craufurd nodded. 'You're good, Keane. Damned good. At least we know what we're facing. Obliged.'

The French continued to form up and Keane remained with Craufurd, giving him occasional further briefings as the regiments came into view. It had been an orderly affair thus far with, apart from the skirmish with the Rifles, a strange silence hanging over the field. But this was now broken by the sudden beat of drums from the French right flank.

Both men turned their heads at once to the noise and saw, on the extreme left of Craufurd's line, next to the ruins of the old walls of ancient Almeida, three columns of French infantry advancing straight towards them.

The guns in Almeida opened up with greater force now, but their ranging was not good. Craufurd and Keane could see the cannonballs flying over the heads of the advancing French infantry, who came on in three blocks of blue, one darker than the others.

Keane spoke. 'That's his light battalion, sir.'

Craufurd nodded, watching as the French passed by the walls of Almeida, almost unscathed.

The 43rd at last opened up from their stone enclosure with a great volley that brought the advancing light infantry to a stop. Craufurd smiled. 'Good, that's good.' But before they had time to get another in, the French were charging at them, yelling as they came. Bayonet met bayonet as column collided with line and Keane knew that now there would be only one outcome. The whole idea of deploying in line against column was to stop the French with musketry. If the British line allowed French column to close, the sheer weight of the latter was almost certainly bound to break the former. The two men, along with Craufurd's staff, watched it unfold before them.

The French were unremitting, dogged. They would fall back under fire, their bayonets miraculously beaten back, only to come on again, supported this time by the hussars, who rode down an entire company of the 43rd, sabring more than Keane could count. And then he realized Ney's plan. It was not just to attack the British and push them back. It was clearly to isolate Craufurd's force from Almeida.

'Sir, do you see how they're doing it?'

'Yes, Keane. He's damned clever. He's dividing us from Almeida. He intends to surround us and then to take the fortress. If his cavalry get round our right flank, we are lost. The only thing we can do is to get across the river.'

Keane said nothing, but thought to himself that if only Craufurd had taken his advice earlier, they might have been able to save the lives of those men down there being trampled to death beneath the steel-shod hooves of the hussars' mounts.

Craufurd summoned an ADC. 'Ramsay, take a note to Colonel Beckwith. Have him pull back the cacadores in his brigade and take up a position overlooking the Côa. The rest of the infantry will cover the road to allow the artillery and wagons to cross the river. That is paramount. I want an orderly withdrawal, not a retreat. Make that clear, Ramsay: this is not a retreat.

'Keane, you and your men had better do the same.'

Keane and the others wheeled away from Craufurd and headed towards the Ordenanza. They were drawn up in two ranks behind the cacadores and he soon found Pereira and Heredia.

'We're pulling back. You're to go with the cacadores, over the bridge and up the hill.'

The French artillery had opened up now, and as he spoke two rounds came in from their front and struck the ground just behind the rear rank of the militia.

'That was lucky. You had better get moving. Your luck won't hold forever.'

Heredia spoke. 'What about you, sir, and the others? Where will you be? And what of the hussars?'

'We will take our chances with the staff, I think. The hussars will cover your retreat. We need all the cavalry we can get, as far as I can see. And Sanchez's lancers.'

As Pereira went to give the orders to Sergente Dominguez, Keane took Heredia to one side. 'How are they in the field? Will they make it? They look a little uneasy.'

Heredia replied in his usual direct manner. 'It's funny. They are actually fine under fire. I don't think they mind it. Two or three of them look as if they might leave. But no more. But they're still not soldiers, sir.'

'Well, just get them across the river, if you can. Make sure the guns and wagons cross before you do.'

The order from Craufurd had evidently reached the cacadores now and the first regiment were already pulling back out of the line. They moved in an orderly way, led by their officers, towards the bridge. Keane could see the artillery teams limbering up to the front of the infantry and soon they were galloping towards the river. The cacadores halted to allow them to pass and then moved on fast again, anxious to get across the river and away from the blades of the French horsemen.

Keane was not sure what had sparked it, but the reaction of the 1st Cacadores was very different from that of their comrades. He and the men were moving off towards Craufurd's command post when the second Portuguese battalion came running down the road before them, hell for leather.

He looked for their officer and found a mounted colonel, himself struggling to keep up with his disordered men. Keane spurred across to him. 'Colonel, stop them. You must order them to stop, sir. They must stop.'

The colonel looked at him wide-eyed, and Keane could see that he too had lost his nerve. He shouted to the cacadores in Portuguese. 'Stop. Go back. Form ranks.'

But it was too little, too late. They were in blind panic. All they could hear was the cannonballs. All they could see were the French. They paid him no heed.

It was, he thought, bizarre that while one unit of light infantry could behave so impeccably, its identical twin should reduced to no more than a rabble, but such was battle.

All across the field now the terrain, which consisted largely of vineyards and walls, had caused battalions to fragment into company units, and under their company officers they now began to fight independently in individual combats.

Realizing that the order was now to withdraw, some of the companies began to pull back and, as Keane watched, four companies of the 43rd and some of the 95th fell back together in good order and formed a defensive screen on the hill overlooking the Côa which would provide covering fire and protection for the ammunition train and the other units to pass across the bridge.

The hussars were going across now, and Keane's own men with Sanchez's lancers. The French still came on but gradually the units in the hills were beaten back. It was then that Keane looked across to the south and saw what looked like a battalion of redcoats. He called to Archer. 'Here, your eyesight's better than mine. Look over there and tell me what colour those coats are.'

'They're red, sir. Red with yellow facings.'

'I thought as much. But if they're our men, who the devil are they and why aren't they over the bridge?'

Archer looked again. 'They might be Swiss, sir. I heard Colonel Sanchez say there is at least one regiment of Swiss with Massena, and you know the Swiss that fight for the Frenchies wear scarlet coats.'

'Look at their shakos then. Can you tell what shape they are?'

'They're black, sir.'

'I know they're black, Archer. The shape, man, the shape. Are they British or Swiss?'

'They're straight hats, sir, straight up and down, like stovepipes. Like ours. If you want my opinion, those men over there are our infantry. And they look as if they need help.'

'It's the 52nd, by God. They'll be cut to pieces.'

Keane rode across to where Craufurd was standing on a vantage point, surveying the field. 'Sir, with respect, may I ask what you intend to do about the 52nd?'

Craufurd stared at him. 'Captain Keane.' He shook his head. 'Again you come to me. What is the problem? Are the 52nd not across the Côa?'

'They are not, sir. They have not moved from their position.'

Craufurd put a telescope to his eye and looked towards the south. 'Christ almighty. Ramsay, take a message down to Colonel Beckwith and the 52nd. Over there. Tell him to disengage and pull back. Before he's overrun.'

The ADC galloped off and Craufurd turned to Keane. 'Thank you, captain. Indebted to you. They'll need covering fire. A screen.'

He surveyed the hill above the Côa.

'Keane, take a message to the 95th. They've just cleared off that hillside there. But they will have to retake it immediately. You won't be the most popular messenger. But it has to be done. Find their colonel if you can. I did hear he'd been hit. They must do it, Keane, and swiftly, or we shall lose the 52nd. Tell them the order is directly from me.'

With Silver, Ross, Garland, Martin and Archer riding behind him, Keane pushed his horse down the hill and then, taking off across the plain, spurred her on fast towards the 95th on the slope above the river. The Rifles were lying down, their weapons at the ready as always, scattered about the hillside. He found an officer, a captain, he thought, though it was always hard to tell with the greenjackets.

'Where's your commander?'

'Can't say. He was hit coming up here. He may be dead. He was with number-one company. Who are you?'

A musket round came zinging in and just missed Keane's head before lodging in the rock behind him.

'Christ, it's a bit hot here. Keane, Corps of Guides. I've come from the general.'

'From Black Bob?'

'Yes. Orders from him: you're to take back that hill.' He pointed in the direction from which the Rifles had just pulled back.

'Are you quite sure? We've only just come from there.'

'Quite sure, captain. Those are the general's orders. You must take it back in order to allow the 52nd to get away. If you do not, they are sure to be caught and cut to pieces.'

He pointed down into the valley where the 52nd were fighting for their lives. The captain followed his direction and in an instant understood.

'Yes, I see. Right.'

He called across to one of his men. 'Sarn't Jones?'

'Sah.'

'Get the men together. We're going back up that hill.'

Keane and the others moved away, riding back towards

Craufurd, but as they went, Archer called out, 'Sir. Over there. Look.'

Keane turned to see the line on the hill that had been formed by the 43rd and 95th was under attack from a great column of the French. A swarm of men pushing up the hillside. As he watched, he saw the redcoats fire and then, rather than standing their ground, pull back as the mass of Frenchmen came on. There was no stopping them. Below them, the bridge was still full of traffic: wagons, guns and men squeezed into a tiny funnel were trying to get through and across the river and the French could see it. Massena was determined not to let them escape. Again the French infantry came on and again, after a volley, the 43rd fell back another few yards.

Keane did not wait. He turned to Ross, called, 'Follow me,' and rode hard across to the red-coated companies. A captain of the regiment, mounted on a handsome bay horse, was behind them urging them to stand as best he could. Keane pulled up hard beside him. 'Come on, come with me, sir.' Keane drew his sword. Then, riding directly in front of the British line and followed by the captain, he halted and stood up in his stirrups. Taking off his helmet he waved it three times in the air.

'Forty-third, follow me. Send these buggers back to Paris.'

The captain had taken off his cocked hat now and waved it in the air before riding with Keane beside him down towards the French. In front of them lay a mass of blue-coated infantry, their muskets at the present, advancing steadily up the hill. Keane did not look behind him but hoped to God that they were being followed. He yelled to Ross, who with the others had come round before the redcoats. 'Are they with us, sarn't?'

'Yes, sir, they're coming. Don't worry.'

There was a huge cheer from their rear as the British infantry poured down the hill with charged bayonets pointed towards the French. Keane found himself looking at a thousand Frenchmen and wondered for a moment what he was doing. But it was clear that the French were even more dumbfounded by what they saw before them.

In an instant their triumphant and irresistible attack which had been pushing back the redcoat line came to a halt, as the enemy inexplicably made a mad charge towards them led by a man in a brown coat and a British officer. Their own officers, equally bewildered, tried to make them advance, but could not. As the men of the 43rd increased their pace behind him, Keane led the others and the captain off to the left of the line.

But before the lines met, the French broke. It began with the skirmishers, the *voltigeurs*, out in front, who began to turn and run back into the ranks. And once that happened, there was no hope. The whole French column just seemed to implode, turning in on itself in panic and scrambling back down the hill and away from the redcoats. It was over in a matter of minutes and Keane and his men stood their ground, as the redcoat came to a halt and presented a firing line, letting off a volley after the departing French.

The captain turned to Keane. 'Napier, William Napier. Thank you for that. I was almost there myself. But thank you, Captain . . .'

'James Keane. And these are my men.'

'Obliged to all of you, I'm sure.'

He winced and Keane noticed blood on his breeches. 'You've been hit.'

'Yes, in my hip. Think I'll live.'

'I'll have my man look at it.'

'You have your own physician?'

'Yes, Archer's first class. Medical school.'

As they watched, the 52nd came hurrying back towards the river and now, safe from threat from the advancing French, crossed the bridge quickly and with no loss.

Keane replied. 'I think it may be our turn to cross now. Captain Napier, after you.'

Once on the far bank of the Côa, Keane found the Ordenanza and regrouped his own command. 'Sarn't Ross, what's the butcher's bill?'

'No one hit, sir. Though we seem to have lost three of the Portuguese, sir, missing.'

'Something of a miracle, sarn't, I'd say.'

'Yes, sir, given what we've just seen and done. By rights you should be dead, sir. Bloody brave, though.'

'Thank you, sarn't. Enough, I think.'

Archer, who had been attending to Napier's wound, returned in triumph. He held up a misshapen musket ball. 'Got the little bugger out. The captain was very grateful. Gave me a guinea for my trouble. Told me he couldn't fathom, though, how a medical man might have ended up with you, sir.'

Keane smiled. 'We seem to have got away.'

'By the skin of our teeth, sir.'

'Yes, Silver. That wasn't an easy one.'

'Are they ever easy, sir?'

Archer pointed down the hill. 'It's not over yet, sir. Look.'

The last of the redcoats had barely crossed to the other side of the bridge when with a great roar a column of French infantry approached it. Led by a colonel on a magnificent white charger and with the regimental eagle, the French pushed on to the little bridge three abreast and began to cross.

From all around them musketry and rifle fire began to open

up. Keane looked but did not see a single one of the Frenchmen fall. The bullets were missing them by a mile.

'It's the trajectory. They can't get the angle right.' Of course the muskets had little chance of hitting, but the riflemen and cacadores would have a good chance if only they could work out the angle. The French continued relentlessly across the bridge and for a moment Keane thought that all the bullets in Hell would not stop them. And then it happened. One of the riflemen hit the colonel and he stopped for an instant, then fell off the white horse, slumped on to the parapet of the bridge and disappeared over the edge into the ravine below. There was a cheer from the hillside and the French came on, an officer dragging the colonel's horse back. Now, though, the Rifles had found their mark. In what was almost a volley both the 95th and the cacadores opened up and a score of Frenchman fell.

Still the French pushed on. Their artillery had set up a little way back and were firing up into the hills, making the occasional hit on the allied lines.

Silver spoke up. 'It's a little too hot here, sir, don't you think?'

Keane kept watching the French. Again the rifles fired and more Frenchmen fell. The front rank of the column walked over the dead and dying, intent on gaining the other side. At last they were there and half a dozen *voltigeurs* peeled off to find cover on the hillside. But the rifle fire was relentless and within a few moments the head of the column just disintegrated. The enemy stopped on the bridge, pinned down and decimated. The bodies piled up until they were parapet-high and then the *voltigeurs* decided that they should retreat. But that was now impossible. Men poured down the hill as the riflemen continued their massacre.

Ross turned to Keane. 'This is murder, sir. Just plain bloody murder, what we're doing.'

Keane shook his head. 'It may well be murder. But never criticize that which saves your life, sarn't.'

Cut off from the column by their own dead, three of the *voltigeurs* met their ends on British bayonets, two more with a bullet. The last of them, climbing up the wall of the dead, reached the top, only to be shot down by a Portuguese marksman. He fell, Christ-like, his arms outspread, to join his dead colonel in the valley below. And then the column retreated, leaving the bridge to the dead and the dying.

The British and the Portuguese gave a huge cheer and Keane saw Craufurd, standing high among them, waving his hat in the air for his victory.

He might claim his victory, thought Keane. It was not much though. In fact, he had very nearly lost his command. The Light Division. Not that anyone would ever know that.

Somehow, they had all come through it alive. But Keane knew that this was not the end. That the French would clear the bridge in a day's time, or two days at the most, and that they would cross it, and that before that happened Craufurd would have taken them all thirty miles back. And Keane and his men would go with him and find a new position to defend, until the French came again.

11

Keane sighed and, staring down at his dust-covered boots, spat into the dirt the wad of bitter tobacco on which he had been chewing. And then, looking up, wondered if by some miracle he might see Wellington and his staff come cantering over the crest of the hill at the head of the army. But he knew it to be a wish that would never be fulfilled.

Late July had given way to August, and all through the searing summer heat the town of Almeida had lain under siege.

The French guns blasted away at her ramparts, without much impression, while her people cowered in their bomb-proof case-mates and shelters and her garrison replied with shot and shell, with which they were amply supplied. And through all that time Craufurd's men stood by near the little hilltop town of Castello Mendo and watched and waited, and with them stood Keane.

They had pulled back some ten miles immediately after the action on the Côa, along the lower road towards Guarda and Celorico. Keane had, as ordered, maintained a presence at the rear of the division and after a few days had begun to send out patrols.

It had been almost three weeks earlier that the first reports had come in that the French were beginning siege trenches. Using the remaining telegraph hills that lay between Almeida and the coast, he had signalled his findings to Celorico. Clearly this was the way Massena intended to attack Portugal. He would take Almeida first and then turn on Wellington's army. The question was, which road would he take. The southern route following the British withdrawal or the northern through Pinhel and Fornos?

There was nothing for them to do but sit back and wait. Keane, though, had unfinished business. Every day Craufurd received a fresh update from the citadel by telegraph. To date the fortifications had held up under the French bombardment and Governor Cox was satisfied that they had more than enough food, supplies and ammunition to hold out for some time, two months at least. Marshal Massena would have a long wait on his hands.

And when, thought Keane, he finally did take the town and march into the countryside into Portugal, the good marshal was in for an unwelcome surprise. For his army of more than one hundred thousand men would be without food or supplies or any means of finding them.

Keane had lost count in his head of the number of mills they had managed to destroy in just two weeks. He had made a note of it, but always it seemed less on paper than it was in his mind. They had grown accustomed to abuse from the peasants, although there had been no opportunity for a repeat of the incident at Nava d'Aver. Besides, Keane now travelled in some force, if not for fear of revenge attacks by the peasants, then on account of the French cavalry patrols that were becoming more audacious by the day.

The escort for the Ordenanza on these expeditions would

generally consist of a party of Sanchez's lancers, who he knew would have no qualms about pig-sticking the peasants. Heredia of course went with them, and Keane had no doubt about his feelings on the matter.

The Ordenanza, surprisingly perhaps, had risen to their onerous task and developed an aptitude for demolition. But best of all was the fact that Leech had returned, his wounds healed, and taken command of the operation, as Keane had known he would. He had detached a selected party from the Portuguese and trained them up in how it was possible to use just a small amount of powder to destabilize a building and bring it down.

Keane had expressed his fascination, and as he wound his way up to the hilltop windmill that Leech had selected for a demonstration of the art, he was surprised by a feeling of guilt.

After twenty years of soldiering there was not much that made him feel guilty. It went with the job. You were being paid by the king to do everything required of you to defend the nation. Everything and anything. That was it, wasn't it? There was surely no question of blame. But there it was, for the first time perhaps, he had felt that he might be doing something wrong.

But of course they had done it. It had been a dreadful fortnight, although not unusual for a soldier's life. Periods of sheer boredom alleviated only by patrols which had yielded no real information. There had been no special intelligence to transmit back to Wellington. No information gleaned from the guerrillas and he could also sense the impatience in Celorico.

He had hardly seen Sanchez. All that he had managed to do was, as his new orders had instructed him, stick close to Craufurd's division.

Still convinced of his victory, Black Bob had pulled back from the Côa before the French had had a chance to regroup. But regroup they had, and now the two armies had been sitting apart from each other for the best part of a fortnight.

The camp was restless. All soldiers, given a time of inactivity, will revert to type. Those who had in a previous life been felons will begin to thieve, the gambler will turn a card or roll dice and cheat if he can, and the murderer will make his own plans and await an opportunity. Keane's camp was no different and he knew it, and he was well aware that Heredia and Silver were still looking for the chance to settle their score.

After recovering from the shock of the battle at the Côa, he had allowed them all two days of indolence. But that was enough. He had to get them moving. The Ordenanza were easy enough to handle and that at least separated Heredia from Silver, whom he took out with the others on patrols that had no real objective.

Finally, though, after two weeks, and with no battlefield encounter with the enemy in prospect, he had agreed to let the two men have it out, under his supervision and according to his rules. They would fight. And since early morning when the word had got out, the camp had been alive with speculation.

He had found Gilpin taking bets.

'Who'll take a guinea against Heredia? Come on, lads. Guinea 'gainst the Portuguese.'

Keane stopped him. 'I'll take two, if I may.'

Gilpin stopped, surprised. 'Yes, sir. On who, may I ask?'

'On you, Gilpin. I'll wager a guinea that you are flogged within an inch of your life by next week for taking a wager from your comrades.'

Gilpin stared at him. unsure as to whether he might be in earnest. 'Sir?'

'Gilpin, I will not lay any bets, and I advise you not to take any. This is a private matter. The men may gamble on it if they will, but do not forget that you are one of their own. Just be discreet.'

The fight was scheduled for that afternoon. It would be refereed fair and square by Garland, the seasoned prizefighter, and the contest would be stopped by a knockout or when a man stayed down for a count of ten. That way, Keane reckoned, he would not lose either of two valuable men. He would just have time, he thought, to view Leech's demonstration at the mill before heading back to the camp for the bout, which would, he hoped, clear the air once and for all.

He urged his bay mare on up the hill and turned to Archer, who was riding alongside him.

'I've been thinking, Archer, about the general's code book. You know it is really very simplistic. Anyone who might spend time studying our signals would eventually decode them. It can be done, I'm sure.'

'Yes, sir. I was trying to calculate the probabilities.'

'You can do that?'

'Yes, sir, mathematics was one of the subjects that I studied when a student.'

Keane thought for a few moments. 'Could a new code be created, do you think? A better one. More secure.'

'Certainly, sir. In fact I had been considering just such a thing.'

'Had you now? We should talk more on this matter. I have a feeling that this war will be won and lost on intelligence, and that a great part of that intelligence will be based around codes. The French have long used them and no doubt will do so again here, whenever they can, despite the guerrillas. We would do best to be prepared and to outwit them before we start.'

They had reached the top of the hill now on which stood a

small *pombal*, a flour mill, on top of which was the apparatus, a series of four huge sails, turning slowly in the gentle summer breeze. It was a good vantage point and higher than Keane had thought from his map. But then, as he continued to discover, the maps with which he had been furnished by Scovell sometimes bore little relation to reality and required continual redrawing.

They stopped the horses to the left of the mill and Keane trotted forward a little. There before him lay the plain of the river Côa and over to the left the fortress of Almeida. Beyond it he could see the French entrenchments, dug as parallels, and from them there now came red-orange flashes indicating that a bombardment was under way. He watched as the shells exploded in the town, and listened, trying to name the calibre of the ordnance. It seemed to him that these might be larger guns than the French had used before and he wondered whether the siege might be becoming hotter. He was about to pull his sketching book from his valise and make a drawing of the view, when Archer called to him and he remembered his purpose. They made their way further up the hill and through the screen of Spanish lancers. Then, at length, at the top of the hill they saw a wagon containing two barrels of powder and guarded by three men of the Ordenanza. Beside it, ready to welcome them, like a proud father showing off a favourite child, stood Leech.

'Good morning, sir. We're ready for the demonstration if you've a mind to watch.'

'Good day, Leech. Please continue.'

Behind Leech stood his party of Ordenanza, some thirty of them, hand-picked by Leech himself for their better intelligence.

He continued. 'You will observe, sir, that I have set a single barrel of powder with a trail of black powder leading back to a place of safety. Behind the mill is another barrel. When the small barrel explodes it will trigger the other, larger barrel. The combination of the two and their positions will serve to bring down the mill entirely.'

'Fascinating, Leech. One thing before you blow it.' Keane dismounted and walked with Leech and Archer across to the point from which they could see Almeida some eight miles away. 'Look down there. You're a gunner, Leech. Tell me what's happening. Something's changed, hasn't it?'

Leech studied the town and the French lines, watching the artillery and counting the seconds it took for the shells to fall and observing the explosion. 'Howitzers, sir. They're using howitzers. And pretty big ones by the look of it. That's what's changed. They mean business, sir.'

Massena was becoming impatient and he had managed to bring up the heavier French siege guns and the howitzers, guns with truncated barrels, Bonaparte's favourites, that would throw a case-shot incendiary bomb overhead and into a fortification.

'We must send word back to the duke. I'm sorry, Leech. We have to do this now. Can you wait?'

The man looked crestfallen. 'Aye, sir. I can wait. Though it's dangerous, once the charges are set, you see. Anything could disturb them.'

'Well, do as you think. You may have to blow them without me. I'm truly sorry, but this must be done now.'

They left the gunner and rode fast down the hill and north towards the telegraph station located on the hill close to Castello Mendo, five miles away. This had been Archer's home twice a day, every day for the past two weeks, either with or without Keane, and as usual now they found it attended by its permanent crew of three Portuguese telegraphists. Here it was that they had transmitted news from Almeida back to Celorico. But aside from those daily reports, there had been little else to report, as surprisingly, aside from their assault on Almeida, the French had been completely inactive. It was almost as if their previous exertions might have exhausted them.

They reached it quickly and, racing up to the summit, found the Portuguese already receiving a message from Almeida.

As it came in, Archer made a note of the numbers and in turn Keane looked them up in the code book.

'Under very heavy fire. Many casualties. Enemy using howitzers. Explosive shells starting fires.'

He showed it to Archer. 'It is as we thought. They have increased the bombardment. I wonder how long Cox can now hold out. Make a signal to Celorico. "News from Almeida. Enemy using howitzers. Many casualties. Fires started. Have observed from above. Situation grave." Sign it from me.'

Archer began to create the code numbers and was writing them down to hand to the Portuguese signallers when there was a huge explosion and the very earth seemed to rumble and shake beneath them.

Keane looked aghast at Archer. 'Did you feel that? That was the devil of a bang. Good God. Leech.'

'Christ, sir. Those charges must have gone off. I wondered if he'd set too much explosive. You know that he tried to destroy that mill three days ago? It hadn't fallen and he was determined to make it do so.'

Keane's stomach felt suddenly hollow. He imagined that Leech would have set another, larger charge and that it might have gone off prematurely.

'Come on. You have your physician's equipment?'

'Carry it always, sir. Though I wonder if there will be anything I can do.'

They rode as fast as they could back towards the mill. The road snaked its way down the hillside and up again, back the way they had so recently come. Nearing the top of the hill, Keane fully expected to find debris from the mill scattered in all directions and whatever might be left of Leech and the Ordenanza. But there was none to be seen. Nor was there any smell of explosive or burning.

The wagon stood where it had been, but the lancers and the picket of the Ordenanza had gone. Keane thought it strange and was hugely relieved to see Leech, carefully picking up a barrel of gunpowder that seemed to have slipped over inside the tailboard.

'Leech? Thank God you're all right.'

Leech turned. 'Sir?

'Christ man, we thought you must be dead. That explosion.' It was only then that he noticed that the mill was still standing. 'If it wasn't the mill, what the devil was it?'

Leech looked at him and shook his head. 'Don't you know, sir? Look.'

He pointed to the vantage point on the hill from which they had so recently observed Almeida. Keane dismounted and, with Archer, hurried over. The lancers and the Ordenanza were standing there already, silent, spellbound, aghast.

For, on looking down on Almeida now, Keane saw a huge column of smoke rising from the centre of the town. Fires were burning everywhere, it seemed, but principally on the left and on that part closest to them.

Leech was standing at his side now. 'It's the town, sir. Bloody great blast. Whole magazine must have gone up. Poor bastards.'

Keane just stared at the shattered fortress. 'It's incredible. How the devil did it happen?'

'I would suppose that a shell must have landed in the powder magazine when it was standing open. Like while they were moving the barrels. That's all I can think must have happened. Damned bad luck, sir, ain't it?'

The smoke was starting to clear now and, looking down, Keane could see that huge blocks of masonry had been hurled far outside the ramparts, together with cannon and parts of equipment. He sought out the huge medieval castle with its four massive towers, which had stood in the centre, and the cathedral which had been nearby and, with its huge crypt, had acted as powder magazine for the town. Both had simply disappeared.

'I'm going to take a closer look. Archer, with me.'

They made their way cautiously down the hillside closest to the enemy lines. Here was a similar path leading down, but they were careful to stick to cover. For even though Keane knew that the French would have been stunned by the explosion, he could not be sure where their pickets and reconnaissance patrols might be. They came out of the trees and then rode on to a plateau and looked towards the city.

From the centre of Almeida a thick plume of grey smoke was curling into the sky. Below it, all seemed to be a sea of flame.

'Christ, the whole place is destroyed.'

Archer pointed. 'No, look, sir. It's only on one side that it's gone. See to the right there, the east side seems fine.'

He was right. But anyone could see that the place was now indefensible. The shock wave must, he thought, have hit the French trenches with some force. Even from where they stood he could see some damage to the siege works. There would have been men thrown off their feet, concussed, wounded and perhaps even killed. An image of utter confusion entered his mind.

As they rode back up to the hill Leech waved at them. 'Go, sir. Get on your way now. I'm going to blow the mill.'

Keane nodded. They would not wait to watch this time either. The man could not be diverted from his task. And Keane was mulling over other things in his mind.

So, carefully, Leech set his fuses and within a half-hour the mill was blown.

The noise and the vibration made their horses jittery and once again he thought of the French and the huge impact of the blast in Almeida. And he realized at once that here was an opportunity that would not come again.

He turned to Archer. 'That's it. We must use the moment. We need to act now. Find the others. There's no time to waste. No time.'

He increased his pace and together they rode back towards the camp and in through the lines.

It was late in the day that they arrived. As they passed the 43rd, Napier approached him. 'Keane, what on earth was that bang? Sounded as if half the world had gone up.'

'You might say it has for some poor people. That was Almeida. Powder magazine must have taken a hit. The whole place is blown to pieces. Well, the castle and the church. Part of the walls has gone too. Once the French recover their wits, they'll take the place in hours.'

Napier whistled and shook his head. 'That's it then. Portugal open to Massena. This is not what the duke wanted at all, is it?'

'No,' mused Keane, 'not at all.'

Keane's bivouac lay close to those of the cacadores and to his relief all of his men seemed to have assembled there.

Keane turned to Ross and Silver. 'Thank God you're all here. You felt that explosion?'

Ross replied for them all. 'Yes, sir. What the hell was it?

'You don't know then? That was Almeida. The magazine blew up, we think. Half the place is gone – the castle, the cathedral too, and I imagine half the people and the garrison. All the country round about is crevassed. Think what the French must have felt in their trenches.'

Garland laughed. 'They'll be stone deaf, sir.'

Martin shuddered. 'And shaking. Out of their wits.'

Keane looked thoughtful. For a few moments he said nothing, and then. 'That they will, Martin, and we can use that to our advantage.'

'We can, sir?'

Keane smiled. 'Don't you see? The French will be as shocked as we are. More so, being closer. They will have been taken unawares and some of them will have been actually physically injured. Others will be so shaken they won't be able to fight. So we can take our chance and go in and take one of them.'

Gilpin asked, 'A prisoner, sir?'

'Yes, but think what we might do. If we succeed in getting as far as possible into their lines, as, say, a forward command position, who might we find there?'

Martin answered. 'An officer, sir. Maybe a colonel.'

Keane shook his head. 'What if I were to say a general, perhaps? What of that? Think big, lads.'

Silver shook his head. 'Are you serious, sir? You can't be. Surely.'

'Quite serious, Silver. We can do it, if anyone can. But we need to act instantly. Get your kit, all of you, and come with me. We leave in five minutes. No more.'

It did not take long for them to assemble and soon, leaving just Heredia and Leech with the Ordenanza, they were off and back down the hill, travelling towards Almeida and the French lines.

As they rode, Silver turned to Ross and spoke quietly. 'He's finally gone one step too far. Don't you think? This is mad.'

'It may be mad, lad, but we're doing it all the same.'

'But to take a general! He must have lost his mind, sarn't.'

'He lost his mind a good long while ago, Silver. Didn't you know that. That's what he's doing with all of us.'

It was dark as they rode down through the vineyards and emerged back at the bridge over the Côa. It shone pale in the moonlight and for a moment Keane thought that he could make out figures on it. But it was only shadows. Perhaps because they had lost so many men there the French had not posted a guard, and certainly it had a curious atmosphere about it, as all battlefields do after nightfall. A chill in the air.

They rode fast over the river.

The flames curled upward from the city and it seemed to Keane as if the very ground around him still bore the shock of the explosion.

Archer, whose opinion he had come to value increasingly as that of an educated man, was riding a few paces behind him.

Keane pulled back a little and spoke as they rode. 'If you were a French general, where would you place your forward command post?'

'Somewhere from where I could see the objective but which was not excessively close to the enemy so as to make it hazardous.'

'So we are looking for somewhere on high ground just within artillery range.'

He pulled out his sketchbook from his valise and began to draw a simple plan. 'Here's the town and here the ramparts.

And here are the French trenches. Their forward positions. They follow the ramparts in a semicircle, so. I would put myself, just . . . here.'

He stabbed with the pencil a little off to the left of the French position and to the ear of the trenches and siege-works. 'Now where would you say we are now?'

'By my reckoning, sir, if our camp is here –' he pointed – 'then we must be around here.'

Keane nodded. 'Yes, I think you're right. So, in theory, if we take ourselves as close as we can safely get to the French lines and then say three hundred yards to the north and strike in here, we should find our general.'

They set off at a slow trot, strung out in single file. After a hundred yards, Keane signalled them to dismount. They left the horses with Garland and set off again on foot, swords drawn, fanned out in an arc, all of them vaguely aware of Keane's hastily drawn plan. After about another hundred yards they heard voices. They sounded agitated and they were speaking in French.

Keane signalled his men to halt and listened. From what he could gather there were two men. Presumably standing guard. One said something along the lines of, 'I have ringing in my ears.' The other that he was half deaf too and still shaking. Then the first man said, 'The poor general. To be thrown from his horse like that. He is shaken. The blast got him too. You know it knocked some of the gunners clean off their feet.'

This was it. Precisely the opportunity for which Keane had been looking. There was no finesse required. No trickery to lie their way in. What was needed here was to be swift, silent and deadly.

He made another signal across to Silver and then, in time

with one another, the two men began to move forward up the slight incline, towards the sentries.

Near the top, both men dropped to the ground and began to crawl. Keane could hear his own breathing, and his heartbeat sounded like a drum. But he knew that both were audible only to him. Reaching the top, they peered over and saw the two sentries. They were still talking, standing almost with their backs to them. A little way off a blue-and-white striped campaign tent suggested that Keane might have been right to suppose this to be a command post.

He looked at Silver and nodded. Then, slowly, each man crept round to the side, Keane to the left, Silver to the right. It took them a long minute to get within striking distance of the sentries. But once they were there, they did not delay.

Keane launched himself at the man on the left, knocking him down and in almost the same instant slitting his throat with the edge of his knife. He was aware of Silver doing the same. Then silence. There had been a clatter of arms, that was all.

Keane looked around. He could hear more voices off to the left and listened again. More French, but they did not seem to have heard and their conversation was all of the explosion. He nodded to Silver and motioned that he should remain standing over the bodies. Then sheathing his knife, he drew a pistol from his belt and, having pre-loaded it, cocked it before walking slowly towards the tent.

Keane paused only for a moment at the flap and then, with a flick of his hand, flipped it open. Inside stood a tall campaign chest and beside it a table on which was spread a map, weighted down by two carafes of wine, one empty, one full. And beyond the table, over in the corner, on a field bed, lay a French officer, in his forties, his eyes tight shut. Keane moved quickly. For although the man seemed to be asleep, he could not be sure. He stood over the Frenchman and, noticing the cross of the Légion d'Honneur pinned to his chest, whispered, in French, '*Mon général*, how are you feeling?'

Without opening his eyes, the man muttered something, then said more audibly. 'Go away, Auguste. I have had a nervous shock. My head is ringing with the noise and I ache all over.'

Keane replied, quietly, 'I'm sorry, sir. But you must come with me.'

The general opened his eyes and seeing Keane closed them again before opening them a second time, this time in horror.

'Who are you? Where is my servant? And the guards?'

'They're dead. I am a British officer and you are now my prisoner. That's all you need to know, general. And now we must leave.'

'If you think I'm going anywhere, young man, you're wrong.'

'No, general, you are wrong.'

'I will call the guards.'

He opened his mouth to shout, and as he did so Keane nudged the muzzle of the pistol into his stomach. 'One sound, just one, and I'll pull the trigger. It makes no difference to me. The guards will come anyway. But either way, you'll be dead. Unless you come.'

The general shut his mouth, then looked up. 'May I at least take my sword?'

Keane shook his head. 'Please, general. Credit me with more intelligence.'

The general smiled and, with Keane holding the pistol at the small of his back, walked from the tent. Outside, Silver was still standing over the bodies. On seeing them, the general stopped and stiffened. Keane pressed the gun into his back. 'Not a sound. Keep walking, sir, if you please.'

It took them less time to reach the horses than when crawling. And they found the others gathered there.

Keane kept the gun pressed hard in the man's back.

'Gentlemen, may I present to you. General . . . Oh, I'm sorry, sir, we were not properly introduced. I am Captain James Keane of the British army and you are . . . ?'

'Général de Brigade Mathieu de Labassee.'

'There we are. I present General Labassee.'

Fully expecting the expedition to be a success, they had thoughtfully brought an extra mount and the general mounted before Keane had Garland tie his hands to the pommel of his saddle. Then they set off, in single file, back to the camp.

Archer spoke to him as they left the hill station. 'A general, sir. That'll surely please the commander-in-chief.'

'Yes, Archer. But I'm not going to let them have him all to themselves.'

'Sir?'

'I intend to get my own information from him before he is taken before Wellington. We need to know certain things, and I think it might be best to strike when the iron's still hot. When the man is still in a daze from the explosion and his abduction. Now's our chance to get some real information, and I think I know the way to get it.'

They had put their high-ranking guest in a tent of his own, close to that of Black Bob himself, albeit under armed guard and with no recourse to any weapons. Taking with him Archer and one of Don Sanchez's lancers, Keane chose his moment carefully, timing his visit to the prisoner to shortly after Craufurd himself had had an interview. He met Craufurd and an ADC as they emerged from General Labassee's tent.

'Ah, Keane. Clever thing you did. Damned clever. A brigade general. The duke will be pleased. Don't see those every day.'

'Did he tell you anything, sir?'

'No, not much. Leastways nothing that we didn't already know. He's General de Brigade Labassee, veteran of Marengo and Friedland, Commander of the Légion d'Honneur, commander of the second brigade of infantry in Marshal Ney's 6th Corps.'

'Let's hope that I can do better.'

'Do you think you will? Good luck.'

And with that he was gone. Keane pushed open the tent flap. The general was sitting at a campaign table with a glass of wine. He did not look happy.

'You.'

'Sir, it is good to see you again, and my sincere apologies for transporting you here in such an inglorious manner. You have met my colleague, trooper Archer. But I don't think you have made the acquaintance of our friend Miguel Carrera. He's one of Don Sanchez's men. You have heard of Don Julian Sanchez, perhaps?'

The general's face looked pale and he took a sip of wine. 'Yes, I know of Sanchez. He is a constant trouble to us. What business does this rogue have in my tent? Get him out.'

'This rogue, sir, has every right to be in your tent. In fact, you owe him an apology.'

'I do? The devil I do.'

'It was your men killed his wife and children last year as they passed through his village. He would like an apology and he would like to know why.'

Labassee stared at the lancer, who gave him a smile that chilled his blood.

'My men killed his family? You are wrong, captain. If they did, there must have been a reason. They were insurgents. Armed insurgents.'

'Armed insurgents consisting of a heavily pregnant girl and two boys of two and four?'

The general had begun to sweat now. 'I refuse to apologize for something that was not my doing.'

'You do?'

'I do. Where is General Craufurd?'

'Oh, we passed him as we came in. He said that he knew you would apologize. Particularly when you knew the alternative.'

'Alternative?' Labassee took another sip of wine.

'Yes. You see, I would like a little more than an apology, general. I would like some information. It is my job to find information. And recently I have not been doing my job very well, which is where you come in.'

'I am sorry, captain, you have me at a disadvantage. I fail to understand.'

'Perhaps this will make you understand better. Carrera here wants an apology and I want information, and if we don't get what we want, I am quite sure that he will be happy to escort you to his commander's camp in the hills, not so very far from here. When you get there his friends will strip you naked and string you up by your arms and then they will begin to get the information in the best way they know. And believe me, general, after just a few minutes of that, you will be only too happy to tell them. But of course by then it will be too late for you. You will survive for a little longer – a day if you are unlucky – and when they cut you down maimed and bleeding and crying out for mercy, you will be thankful when they kill you.'

He paused, letting the general's now trembling hand grasp the goblet and bring it to his dry throat for another gulp of wine.

Keane went on. 'Or of course you could give us both what we want now and save a great deal of trouble and unpleasantness all round. Although I'm sure that my friend here would be most disappointed.'

The general stared into space and finished his wine. He set the goblet down on the table. 'What is it that you want to know?'

It took half an hour, and by the end General Labassee had loosened his collar and had a fresh glass of wine and Keane had the information he wanted. Only the lancer, Carrera, was left wanting, for he had not been given a French general to torture. But Keane gave him two guineas from his own purse instead, and so even the Spaniard went away happy.

Silver quizzed him. 'What did he say, sir? Did he tell you anything?'

'Yes, Silver. He talked. Who wouldn't, given the choice. He told me a great deal. The French have a new spy in our army. He's an officer. Portuguese apparently, or attached to the Portuguese. He was not sure which. There were other things too. It was very useful. You did well. All of you did well.

'Will, where's that brandy I was saving? Break it out. We all deserve something.'

While Martin opened the bottle that Keane had managed to carry away from Celorico on his last visit, Keane mulled over what Labassee had actually told them. Yes, he had admitted that there was a new spy in the camp. He knew about Pritchard, he said, and that he had died in an explosion. The new man was, he thought, a Scotsman and wore a Portuguese uniform. He was attached to the division that they had fought on the banks of the river Côa. Had masqueraded as a new arrival from headquarters. He did not have his name, he said, and Keane believed him. The threat of torture at the hands of the guerrillas was still in place, and Keane did not think the general would lie with the Spaniard standing so close by.

The other information was perhaps even more important. The French apparently knew about the code book. They had no idea how the code worked, the actual numbers and their meanings, but they knew of the book and were doing everything they possibly could to get hold of a copy.

With that the general had thought that Keane might have enough. But he wanted more. Keane had asked him for any information regarding Massena himself.

The general had thought for a while. Had described his commander, his appearance, his weight and height and character, his likes and dislikes. Still Keane quizzed him. Oh, there was one other thing. He had his mistress with him in Ciudad. Henriette was a real beauty. All the way from Paris. He was besotted with her and would do anything she asked of him. In reality, though, the general had it on good authority, although she loved the good life, she loathed Massena, who was a boor and a lecher, and longed to be rid of him. That, thought Keane, might prove a most useful piece of information.

He was thinking about the conversation, as they sat about the campfire, taking swigs of the liberated brandy, when Craufurd approached them.

'Captain Keane, did you have any luck with our friend the general?'

Keane got to his feet and the others followed, making a

semblance of standing to attention. 'Oh yes, sir. He was most obliging.'

'Really? You must let me in on your secret.'

'It was quite simple really, sir. I just showed him Sanchez's man and told him that if he did not tell me what I wanted to know, then he would be handed over to the guerrillas. Then I gave him a detailed account of what they would do to him. That appeared to do the trick very well.'

Craufurd raised an eyebrow. 'That was completely immoral, captain. To terrify a senior officer into divulging his army's secrets with threats of torture? It was quite inappropriate.' He paused. 'Well done, Keane. Brilliant.'

As dawn rose, Keane lost no time in telegraphing the news back to Celorico. Here at last was something positive to report to Wellington. He asked for an escort for the general back to headquarters and was told by reply that he would have one by the end of the day.

The general's escort, consisting of a squadron of the Horse Guards, arrived the following afternoon and Keane was surprised and, if he admitted it, not a little pleased to see Major Grant riding at their head. Grant dismounted outside Craufurd's tent and was just being greeted by him when Keane strode over.

'Major Grant.'

'Captain Keane, I hear that you have found us a prize. A *général de brigade*, no less.'

'Yes, sir. He was a little unnerved by the explosion.'

'Yes. What a catastrophe. Your own news was doubly welcome on account of the previous messages. We understand from Almeida itself that a French shell fell into the walls of the castle just as the gunners were moving powder to the bastions.

It would seem that something in the region of one hundred and fifty thousand pounds of black powder were ignited along with close on a million musket rounds. Amazingly General Cox survives and most of the garrison. But perhaps one thousand people were killed and many more have been gravely wounded. Much of the town has been reduced to a single storey. Cox has very little powder left him. He has been signalling to us, but of course what can we do? Wellington will send no more help to Cox than he did to Ciudad. How can he? It is the same problem again. It is merely that he had expected that Almeida would hold out for a long time. I believe that Cox will surrender tomorrow.'

'That is grave news indeed, sir.'

'Yes, the duke is devastated. It was not in his plan.' He turned to Craufurd. 'My dear general, the duke is keen that I should speak with you about the state of the division and impress the need that you keep it at its best. You are the absolute rearguard of the army and the first point of contact.'

He addressed Keane. 'Captain, I should be obliged if you would remain here while I speak with General Craufurd.' Then, leaving Keane outside, he accompanied Craufurd into his tent, emerging half an hour later. Keane had not moved and Grant acknowledged his presence.

'Captain Keane, thank you for waiting. I would have another word with you.'

He bade farewell to Craufurd and, with the Horse Guards now escorting Labassee, turned to Keane and took him aside.

'James, we need a few moments to talk. You will realize that the loss of Almeida is a disaster. The duke is now more than aware that he must play for the time in which to complete the defences for Portugal and he knows that the French will advance against him forthwith unless he does something. He is resolved on drawing in Massena to ground of his choosing for a wholly destructive battle.

'And now, after the loss of Almeida, we will be again on the retreat. The duke is most insistent, James, that I should impress upon you the need of delaying the French and also for some means of persuading them somehow to come into Portugal on a route of our choosing.

'You must falsify information and have them believe it to be true. No one must suspect otherwise. '

Keane thought for a moment. 'We may be able to delay them a little by harrying actions, sir. But to persuade them to take a certain road will be hard.'

'We both have full confidence in your skills, Keane. It is not every captain who can capture a *général de brigade*. In particular one as renowned and respected as Labassee. I do look forward to speaking with him. I am sure that we have much to talk about. Did you manage to get anything from him yourself?'

Keane paused, unsure, for once even with Grant, how much he should give away. 'Well, sir, yes, in fact. I have ascertained that Marshal Massena has his mistress travelling with him, all the way from Paris.'

Grant smiled. 'Really? How fascinating. And what can we deduce from that?'

'Apparently he will do anything she asks and in reality she hates him.'

'Really. She must have a way about her. Perhaps she will tell him to travel by the high road through Guarda and Viseu?'

'I hardly think that she will do so, sir. Unless she is in your pay also.'

Grant laughed. 'Sadly, James, my finances and those of the duke combined, I suspect, don't stretch to suborning a French general's mistress, much as I would love to do so. Anything else?'

'Yes. The French have another spy in our ranks.'

'You have a name?'

'No name. But I am told he is a Scot and wears Portuguese uniform.'

Grant scratched his chin. 'Could be any number of men. Still, it's a start.'

'Oh, and sir, the French know of the code book and want to get their hands on it.'

'Of course they do. That is not news to me, I'm afraid. But it does confirm what I thought to be the case. Still, you have done well. Let's see what else you can come up with now. I shall give your news to the duke. Thank you, Keane. Most obliged to you.'

He turned and rode off with his prize safely under escort, and back in Celorico that evening, after they had entertained Général de Brigade Labassee to a dinner of guinea fowl and local cheese and fruit, washed down with a passable Rioja, Grant talked with Wellington deep into the night and assured him that somehow the French would come by the high road to ground of his choosing, that Keane would see to it and that he should go ahead with his plans. They would get the French to the place he wanted them to be and then they would give them more than a bloody nose.

And the following day an officer of the recently formed corps of engineers, based in Coimbra, received an order from the high command instructing him to begin work on the creating of a new road that would run the length of a hill some sixty miles away from Almeida, along the reverse side of a long ridge that was known locally as the Serra do Bussaco.

12

Keane sat in his tent in the camp. It was early the next morning and Ross had only recently brought him a mug of tea. Of course it wasn't proper tea. It was made with some sort of a leaf , but it was warm and wet and served with milk, and it served its purpose. He was shaving in a bowl of cold water and the blade of his razor being somewhat blunt, he kept nicking himself under the chin.

The events of the previous day and his conversation with Grant had been going through his mind throughout the night and he had sent Ross off to find Archer. He had an idea in his head and wanted to run it past him. His men were a talented bunch. Rogues and cutpurses and frauds, but some of them stood out for their wit and wisdom. Martin was that sort and Keane was aware that in Archer they had acquired another: someone with a more than average intelligence, who in other circumstances would have become an eminent physician, but who now, thanks to his own misfortune and momentary stupidity, had provided the British army with a man who could provide something more than medical expertise. A man who might just help them win the war.

He was drying his face and dabbing at the cuts when Archer entered.

'You asked for me, sir?' He saw the blood. 'Nasty.'

'Yes. Just stupid.' He buttoned his shirt and tied the stock, which was mercifully black, tight around his neck before pulling on his coat.

'Archer, I have a plan. Say nothing until I have finished explaining it to you.' Archer looked attentive and Keane began, knowing full well the effect of his next few words. 'We're going to give the code book to the French.'

'What? I mean what, sir?' Archer laughed. 'What do you mean? Why on earth would we do that?'

Keane stopped him. 'I said, say nothing. Right. We have a French spy among us. An officer on the Portuguese staff. What we're going to do is have someone befriend that man, whoever he might be, and allow him to take the code book.'

'Yes, but I still don't see why, sir. And how will we do it?'

'In time, Archer. Give me time to explain. If you think about it, it's quite simple. There cannot be that many Scottish officers in the Portuguese army now, attached to this division. So, what I want you to do first, Archer, through the good offices of General Craufurd's ADC, Captain Ramsay, is to find the potential candidates. That part is easy enough.'

'Me, sir?'

'You, sir. Bear in mind that there may be more than one. You'll want the names of all the officers in the Portuguese service who have joined the division since the end of June. Then find out which of them are Scots. And when you have found out who he might be, then make sure that you fall in with him.'

'How do you suggest I do that, sir? I'm a mere private soldier and he is sure to be a major at the very least. He'd hardly speak to the likes of me.'

'Yes, I have to admit that had me worried for a while. But here's an idea. You're a physician, yes? And I'm willing to bet that whoever he is, whatever his rank, he will have some sort of ailment. We all have them, don't we? From sores on our feet, to the ague, the pox, worms or worse. It's up to you to find out what his problem is and then cure it.'

Archer shook his head. 'Oh yes, sir, that seems very simple.'

'Archer, if I didn't know better I would think that you were being facetious and put you on a charge. I'm in deadly earnest.'

'Sorry, sir. Yes. I will do my best, of course.'

'You'll have to act quickly. Later today, I think. I will provide you with drink, a good bottle of brandy from my personal store. You won't get him drunk, of course; he'll be on his guard. But be hospitable. And in the course of your, how can I put it, friendly conversation, let slip that you are involved in the use of the telegraph and that you have a copy of the code book.'

Archer began to look uncertain.

'You can do it, man. Come on. Simply be a good doctor, explain your background, win him over, then play the friend and choose your moment. Appear as if you have taken too much brandy. Take your leave and put your valise somewhere where it might simply have been mislaid. Let him find it and take the book. And there you are.'

Archer looked at him. 'You said it was simple, sir.'

'Yes, glad you see that too. It is just so. Exactly. So that's your part played out. Then what happens is: he copies it, discovers your book and returns it to you and meantime sends the copy back to his generals and they begin to read our signals. But what he won't know is that you and I will then be sending out signals that are utterly incorrect.'

Archer began to smile.

'The French will read our signals and decipher them and follow them up. And in that way we will lure them to ground of Wellington's choosing.'

Archer grinned. 'It is brilliant, sir. Quite brilliant. And really very simple.'

'Good. The most important thing is that we don't reveal any of this to the commander-in-chief until the French have hold of the book. He would almost certainly forbid it. In fact he'd be aghast.'

Archer frowned. 'And with good reason, sir. The problem as far as I can see it, is that once the book is gone, it's gone. The French will have the whole code. They will understand the nature of the army's secret weapon. My God, sir – the duke will have you shot.'

Keane smiled. 'That had occurred to me also. The answer of course is to devise another, better code.'

'That would be a good answer, sir. But who will create a new code?'

'I, or rather, you, Archer, with your eminent mathematical and medical mind. You will devise another code book.'

Archer looked at him. 'You want me to create a cipher, sir?'

'That's exactly what I want you to do.'

'I don't know.'

'Archer, if you can accomplish the first part of this task, then to create a new cipher will be child's play.'

It was late that night that Archer returned to Keane's biv-ouac. Craufurd's Light Division was to move again at dawn, back towards the main body of the army, and as Keane's men, the lancers and the hussars included, were not part of that regrouping, the men had spent the past two hours making sure that gambling debts had been settled and any other business with friends in other units taken care of.

Keane was writing his daily report. He sat at the campaign table that Silver had bought for him from the servant of a dead captain of the 43rd killed at the Côa. It was a splendid piece of kit, made from box, with folding legs and a hinged top, which packed away to the size of a small folio and was easily carried on the flanks of Silver's horse. It had only cost him a guinea, and a drink in it for Silver of course. The man was making a name for himself as a scrounger and their small part of the camp had blossomed recently with all manner of items, from silver candlesticks to a large embroidered cloth, which had previously been an altar cloth in the convent by the Côa. Keane's tent had come to resemble a cross between a grand country house and a gypsy caravan.

Normally the reports Keane wrote to be passed back to head-quarters, in the usual, tedious way, for the few men under his immediate command, would have been a simple affair, com-pared to the chore it had been as a company commander with his old regiment. But, with the Ordenanza and the lancers still effectively in his command, he had to include accounts of their behaviour, their misdemeanours and their movements.

The lancers he had sent out that morning on picket duty, but they had had no run-ins with the French. The hussars like-wise, although in a different direction. Leech's detachment of Ordenanza had, as usual, been engaged in demolition duties. One of the lancers had been wounded in a brief exchange with French dragoons. Another had been put under guard for three days for going missing for two. Nine more of the Ordenanza had deserted, though they had been mostly old and infirm and unwanted. The hussars had, as was to be expected, kept themselves to themselves, and every morning Captain von Krokenburgh held a formal inspection.

He included in his notes a comment about Heredia rising to his role as an NCO. He praised Leech for his success in blowing the mills and was just in the process of tallying up the expenditure and costs for the day and the week when Archer appeared.

'Sir. I think I may have found him.'

Keane looked up. 'Really? Have you? Can you tell me?'

'There is a Scot, a major by the name of Macnab, who appeared two weeks ago at Craufurd's headquarters, claiming to have been sent from General Beresford. He had papers, which seemed to be in order, though no one had seen him before.'

'Ramsay knows nothing of your purpose?'

'No, sir, nothing at all. I told him I was simply looking for a cousin of mine from Edinburgh whom we believed to be with the Portuguese.'

'Where is this Macnab now?'

'He was on Craufurd's staff, but is now attached to the command of the Portuguese brigade with General Barclay. They are pulling out tomorrow, towards Guarda.'

'Damn. What do you intend to do?'

'They're billeted in an inn at Monte Peroblio, to the south. I'm on my way there now. I thought the confusion of their move tomorrow might be a good opportunity to pretend to leave my valise.'

Keane smiled. 'Good work, Archer. Very good work.'

It was shortly after noon on the following day that Archer

returned to their camp. He found Keane in a clearing in the rocks that served as a parade ground. He and Heredia were attempting, with varying degrees of success, to drill the Ordenanza. The others were away on one of their regular morning patrols to the east. Keane, knowing the importance to discipline of routine, had instituted the timetable over the past week. Seeing Archer, he handed over to Heredia. 'Drill them for another ten minutes. Then see what you can do about their musketry.' He did not aspire to much, but it was better to make an effort than live in hope.

He hurried over to Archer, who looked exhausted. 'Well? Did you find him? Macnab?'

Archer nodded. 'Yes, sir, he was with another British officer in the Portuguese service. Name of Foote.' Archer waited for the name to sink home.

'Foote?'

'Yes, sir. You know him. You remember. The Ordenanza.'

Keane snapped. 'Yes. I'm aware that I know him, man. I could hardly forget.'

So Foote had rejoined the Portuguese and was now friendly with this man Macnab who might be the spy. Perhaps that would give him occasion to call out Keane as he had sworn he would. Realizing his over-reaction, he apologized to Archer. 'I'm sorry. It was just . . . the name. It took me by surprise.'

'Yes, sir, I understand.'

'Foote – you're sure it was the same man? Did he recognize you?'

'I'm quite sure of it. We are distinctive in our uniform, sir. As you say yourself.'

Keane hoped that Foote would not have wondered what Archer was up to, that he might not suspect that he had been sent on some mission. Keane did not for one minute suspect Foote himself of being a knowing accomplice of a spy. He was, to be frank, far too stupid. But he might easily be taken in by Macnab and that would be worrying. The best way to deal with a spy was to isolate him. Now that opportunity seemed to have gone. But Keane was contented in that the agent here should be a buffoon such as Foote.

'Did Macnab take the code book? How did you manage it?'

Archer nodded and smiled. 'Yes, sir. I reached the inn and managed to persuade the billeting sergeant that I was lost and on my way back to the front after delivering a message to Celorico. He found me a bed and it was then that I spotted a group of Portuguese officers at a table. But they were not Portuguese at all, but very much British. I observed them all evening and gradually their number dwindled. By degrees I brought myself closer to them until I was near enough to overhear their conversation. There were but the two of them remaining now, and the one I took to be Macnab spoke from time to time in a pronouncedly Scottish accent about his gout and how it would flare up and how he wished he had a scarifier to bleed himself.

'It was then that I settled on the plan. I approached them and said that I had overheard their chatter and that I was a physician and might be able to help him. I then produced a scarifying tool from my bag, one I have had for some years, and the man's face lit up. He asked to buy it and of course I played that it was not for sale.

'The other man goaded him on and he attempted to offer money for it. Still I refused. Naturally, not wanting to lose the tool, Macnab invited me to drink with them. He could tell, I suppose, that I was not an ordinary private soldier. I explained over a glass how I had come to be with the army and that I now worked with the guides. At this point he became quite animated in his interest and I could tell it was him. The spy. It was then that I produced the brandy.

'I made out that it had been purchased on your account but that I preferred their company.'

Keane nodded. 'That was a clever turn. To allow them to suppose that you disliked me.'

'I offered both a drink and of course they accepted. I did as you had advised and you were quite right, sir. Macnab may have made out that he was blind drunk, but he did not drink, or hardly at all. He did buy the scarifier from me, though.'

Keane laughed. 'Never one to miss a trick, Archer, are you?'

'If you say so, sir. Anyway, when I awoke this morning my valise had vanished. The whole thing. It was most definitely Macnab. Either him or Foote at least. I made a noise about it, of course, but Macnab and the others were gone.'

Keane smiled and patted Archer on the back. 'Excellent. Well done indeed. Our trout has taken the fly. Now it is up to us to reel him in.'

It did not take long for Archer's valise to reappear. In fact it was a matter of two days. They were still encamped in the same place near Castello Mendo, although with the rest of the division now some distance away to the west, they themselves were now close to leaving, believing that the French might commence their advance into Portugal at any day. Keane, though, was reluctant to move until he had ensured that Massena would advance by the route he wanted him to take.

The lancers had provided the pickets overnight and it was one of them who sounded the alarm. The man shouted and the camp sprang into life.

Keane was dressed already but buckled on his sword and found Ross. 'What is it?'

'A party of horsemen coming in from the south-west.'

'South-west? That's our army. Who are they?'

'No idea, sir. One of the Spaniards called us out.'

Martin walked up. 'We can stand down. It's a party of Portuguese cavalry.'

Keane swore and cursed the lancer, but supposed that it was better to be alert than dead in their beds. He walked across to the group of horsemen who had dismounted and were watering their horses.

Their officer, a lanky lieutenant, saluted him. 'Sir. We come with something belonging to one of your men. A saddlebag. With Major Macnab's compliments and his thanks for a good evening.'

Archer was with them now. 'Ah, thank you, sir. How very kind of the major.' He took the saddlebag and deliberately did not look inside but simply walked away.

Keane continued to talk to the lieutenant. 'I do not know Major Macnab. Is he recently arrived?'

'Yes, sir, came out from Britain some five weeks ago. Attached to the general's staff. He is at brigade headquarters.'

'Where was he before? His name seems familiar.'

'I believe he was with a Scottish regiment, sir. I am sorry, I do not know the name or the number.'

'I wonder if he's the same Macnab I knew. Can you describe him? His height, his hair, his eyes.'

The lieutenant shrugged. 'I suppose he is of medium height, blue-eyed with reddish fair hair.'

'No, no, that doesn't sound like my man. Shame. Well, thank you, lieutenant. That was good of you.'

He was about to say goodbye but the lieutenant delayed. 'There is one more thing, sir.'

'Yes, lieutenant?'

'Another of the officers, a Captain Foote, asked me personally to send his regards to you. And he said that he was looking forward to remaking your acquaintance very soon.'

'Thank you, lieutenant. Will you take my reply to Captain Foote? Will you tell him please that I am as eager as he to see him again and that I will leave no stone unturned until I do. Thank you.'

The lieutenant saluted again and then rode off with his men back the way they had come. Keane turned and walked after Archer. 'Well, is it in there?'

'Yes, sir, safe and sound and not a page of it missing.'

'Well, I think we can deduce that Macnab, or whoever he really is, has had a good look at it. I'll wager a month's pay he's copied it complete.'

'Yes, sir. In fact I can prove that to be true.'

He pulled out the book and opened it at a page. 'Here, you see this page, sir. I had inserted a small flower in here. And here it is. But it was most certainly the other way up when I left it. And on this page I left a rose petal, very small. Now gone.'

'That's it then. How long do you think it will take him to begin using it?'

'If I were Macnab, sir, I would start straight away.'

'Yes, I should do likewise. Tomorrow morning. Well then, let's give him some meat to get his teeth into, shall we?'

The following morning Keane and Archer rode out to the closest telegraph station to Castello Mendo. It had been abandoned in the withdrawal of the division, but the Portuguese telegraphists had been specifically instructed by Keane not to destroy the apparatus. He and his men would do that when they cleared out. They had decided on the wording of the first message. Firstly, they had agreed, they should send some word of the position of the French and this they did, commenting on the fact that a scouting party of *chasseurs à cheval* had been encountered by the lancers and driven off and that they had observed light infantry occupying a hill to the south of the destroyed fortress across the Côa, whom they believed to be the 2nd Light from General Reynier's 2nd Corps.

Those parts of the message had been quite genuine. The next few lines, though, contained the essential misinformation:

'Expect French to move soon. Information indicates they will take lower road. Ensure fortifications in place on Celorico road.'

Keane read out the numbers to Archer from Folque's code book.

'451, 637, 786, 521, 964, 236, 846, 642 . . .'

The sequence went on and the arms of the telegraph moved up and down and round, transmitting the spurious message to the next hill station, from where, Keane prayed, it would reach Macnab.

He hoped it would be enough to begin to entice the spy into believing in them. Time was everything now. If Grant's schedule was to be adhered to, by which the duke must face Massena in a pitched battle and deflect him away from marching deep into Portugal before the lines were completed, they had perhaps a week, in which to persuade Macnab that the northern route would be the best for Massena to follow. It was early September, and with the two armies but a few days' march apart, every move had to be carefully calculated.

The following day, Keane sent out the lancers and hussars in a screen towards Almeida, hoping that they would spot the first signs of any French movement. At the same time he and Archer rode out again to the hill station and sent the second message. There was the usual round-up of overnight information. The fact that the light infantry had remained static and cavalry had been observed in the valley. And then, once again, the key phrases. This time they read:

'North road looking increasingly vulnerable. Bad terrain and poor road make this unlikely attack route.'

On the third day the message was even more insistent.

'The allied army will make a stand on the southern road near Ponte Murcella. We do not believe that the French will come by the north route. The south is the obvious way. Therefore we will position our forces in the south and fortify that road as best we can.'

Keane thought it might be enough. He prayed that it was.

It was Archer, though, who articulated the thought that was preying on his mind.

'Sir, has it occurred to you that the signallers and not least those who translate the signals back in Celorico might not be wondering what the devil we are doing sending these messages?'

'Yes, it had crossed my mind. I expect that we shall get a response ere long. Most probably today.'

They had had no response to their previous messages apart from the general standing acknowledgement provided by the Portuguese telegraph corps. It was all that Keane had expected from an army on the move, in retreat, whose main purpose was to receive intelligence rather than provide it. Sure enough, though, today there was something more.

'Information received regarding north route. This is known to us already. Please advise.'

Keane was relieved. 'Thank God. I was worried that they might ask us what the hell we thought we were doing? That would have given the game away.'

'We're lucky they didn't, sir. Do you think he'll have taken the messages as real?'

'I have a feeling he will, Archer. He will be desperate to please his masters, not just Massena but those back in Paris, not least the Corsican himself.'

And Keane was right not to worry, for in his tent in the Portuguese camp near Celorico, a certain Major Macnab had just finished writing an encrypted message addressed to Marshal Massena. He sealed it and then folded it into a small square and tucked it into his pocket. Then he donned his topcoat and hat and, with a word to the sergeant of the guard, went out to visit his forward positions. But after half a mile Macnab turned his horse and rode away from the Portuguese lines and, after an hour's hard riding, when he was about halfway to Almeida, he stopped in a clearing containing the ruins of what had once been a small border castle. He dismounted and, making sure that he was not being observed, he walked quickly to one of the walls, dislodged a loose stone and placed the square of paper behind it before replacing it neatly just as it had been. Then, remounting, he turned and rode back to the Portuguese lines. And sometime later that day, when the French had pushed forward their reconnaissance parties to form a screen beyond the Côa, another horseman rode into the same clearing and, lifting the same stone, withdrew the paper. Then, reading the name written on it, he tucked it away and rode off. But this time the rider wore a dark green coat and the white enamel cross of the order of the Légion d'Honneur and was accompanied by a colonel's escort of a squadron of *chasseurs à cheval*.

That evening Keane sat with his men around the small fire they allowed themselves, in a rocky clearing which through a quirk of the land shielded the flame from any observers to the east. Martin had discovered it a week before. Silver, with Gabriella resting her head in his lap, was humming a shanty, as he often did. Something about the Spanish Main, while whittling away at yet another of his pieces of scrimshaw; this time using a piece of pine he had created a clever likeness of Wellington himself. As usual, Heredia was messing with the Ordenanza, although Keane realized that he could not again postpone their match and that it must happen soon. Martin got up and turned the improvised spit of a bayonet which held a rabbit he had shot that day. Garland and Gilpin were playing dice with Leech, while Ross, Archer and Keane sat together.

Ross spoke. 'We still have no real idea if Marshal Massena will come by the route we want him to come, do we, sir?'

Keane had to admit the truth of it. 'No, we don't. We've done our best. But if only we had some means of verifying it. We don't even know for certain that Macnab fell for it.'

Archer nodded. 'I'm sure he will have, sir. Sure of it.'

'Well, even if that is the case, Ross is right. How do we know that's the way Massena will come?'

Ross laughed. 'The only way you'd ever really know that, sir, is to talk to Massena himself.'

Archer grinned. 'You're right there.'

Keane nodded and then was silent for a while as sparks flew up from the fire and faded in the night. He reached for another wineskin and filled his cup before speaking again. 'That's it then. That's just it. I will hear it from Massena himself.'

Ross shook his head in disbelief.

Archer spoke. 'How, sir? How will you do that?'

'I can speak Portuguese and Spanish, and French for that matter. What if I were to contrive to get myself into Massena's headquarters in Almeida before they leave – in disguise – and listen to his plans?'

Archer laughed. 'Really, sir, capturing a general is one thing, and letting the French have our code – for which you're sure to get a roasting. But this is the best yet. I'm sorry, sir. For once you're going too far. How do you expect to do it?'

'In disguise, as I said. Gilpin managed it in that bastard Morillo's camp, didn't you, Gilpin?'

Gilpin nodded. 'Yes, sir. I can't say as I'd want to do the same again, though.'

'Well, that's it. Whatever anyone might say. I'm resolved to do it. It is the only way.'

Silver looked at him. 'Not wishing to be disrespectful, but you're bloody mad, sir.'

Keane smiled and shook his head. 'Think so? You haven't heard the half of it.'

He poured another large glass from the wineskin and offered it around. 'I have another idea. Massena's mistress is with him. We know that from Labassee. We also know that he will do anything for her.'

'Well, sir . . .' Martin was at him now. 'She won't persuade him to take his army down a suicide road.'

'No, but, given that he will almost certainly be coming by the northern road anyway, what is our second most important task?'

Archer answered. 'To delay him as long as we can, sir.'

'Exactly. And what is the easiest way in the world in which to delay a man?'

Silver smiled. 'To use a woman to do it for you. Clever, sir, damned clever.'

'So what say we pay her to keep him there? The longer we can delay him, the better. The duke intends to bring him to battle, but if we can win more time before that happens, then it is surely to the good.'

Martin shook his head. 'Now that really is mad, sir. She will be loyal to him. Devoted. Why would she take money?'

'You are still young, but in my experience, Will, any lady who is a man's mistress is only too happy to accept money to betray him. It goes with the territory. After all, isn't a mistress just one big lie? I have money. What's left from Soult's hoard.'

'But that's yours, sir, same as we had our shares.'

Gilpin whispered to Silver, 'Not that you've any left of yours, Horatio, eh? Gambled it all with Craufurd's buckos.'

'Shut your trap, Gilpin. I lost it fair and square.'

'Does your Gabby know how much?'

He nodded towads Gabriella who had got up and walked across to the rocks to answer a call of nature.

'No, and nor she will neither. For you won't tell her, will you? If you know what's good for you.'

Keane turned to them. 'That's enough. You all had your share and I had mine and what I do with it is my concern. If it benefits the war and our brave commander, that will be recompense enough.'

He paused. 'Of course, if it benefits the common good and all of us in particular, then so much the better. Besides, an investment now might just pay off in the long run.'

'Sir? What do you mean?'

'What I mean is just that if we can do this and if we should delay Massena, then there is bound to be a moment when a part of this benighted country, with at least one large town, will be empty of any troops.'

Silver looked at him. 'Sir, are you suggesting . . . ?'

'I am suggesting nothing. I am merely reminding you that none of us has been paid by the army for a very long time and that there is a town on their route by the name of Fournos. It has a big cathedral and a number of very grand houses. I passed through it earlier this year. We have no troops there at present, nor ever will have. The duke is moving his entire army south, through Celorico. Also, the inhabitants of Viseu, the great and the good at least, will not be there. They will all have left in the face of Massena's advance. But if Massena is delayed, he will not be there either. Which is where we come in.'

Gilpin smiled. 'With empty saddlebags and rucksacks and fast horses.'

'Yes, Gilpin, I think you have my meaning. We go in and out, and whatever is found to be missing when Massena is beaten and the owners return will be blamed on the French. Now, who's behind me with this plan?'

They all nodded and Silver muttered an expletive under his breath.

Archer was the first to speak. 'How do we get in, sir? The French will have sentries posted everywhere, won't they?'

'I very much doubt it. They know the place cannot be defended and that, save for the guerrillas, nothing really can trouble them in there. And if they consider it they will soon realize that the guerrillas would actually not think of raiding such a large French encampment, the command centre of an entire army. No, we should not have any great problem in getting in. Getting back out may be a different case.'

He took another drink and smiled at them. 'Of course, there is another thing. For this to succeed, at least two of us will have to wear civilian dress. We've done it before, but you know that it means we can be shot as spies.'

He looked at them all and they wondered whom he could have in mind. But they were quickly put at ease, all save one man. Keane poured the unlucky volunteer another cup of wine. 'I'm very much afraid that's you and me, Gilpin.'

Gilpin managed a thin smile. 'I see, sir. That's just the way of it. And if I can survive a camp full of murderous heathen dagos, then I'm sure I can survive the French.'

13

It took a day to do everything necessary. While Keane tended to unfinished business and sent another message with Archer to confuse the French, Gilpin took Martin and the pair rode as fast as they could back to the division, as ever on the scrounge.

Keane did not tell Lieutenant Pereira nor the lancers about what they really intended to do. This was to be a final long-range patrol before they pulled back. But having taken the natural decision to leave Captain von Krokenburgh in overall command while he was absent, Keane alerted the German as to the true nature of his mission and gave him his orders. They would be back in five days' time at most. Von Krokenburgh was to move the men westwards every day. Only a couple of miles. If after five days Keane had not returned he was to march as fast as he could to rejoin Craufurd.

Von Krokenburgh was amazed. 'You really think you can do this thing? It would be extraordinary.'

Keane shrugged. 'I don't know if we can manage it. But nothing ventured, nothing gained. We have to know if our deceit has worked. Otherwise I cannot tell Wellington that he is safe to assume Massena will fight on his ground.'

Von Krokenburgh saluted him with some formality and wished him well, although in his heart he thought that he had never in his life witnessed any gesture equally as mad and as brave. In truth he did not think that he would ever see Keane or his men again.

Keane did not take all of his direct command. Heredia, Ross and Leech were to remain with the Ordenanza, along with Gabriella. Silver had not been happy about such a situation, and Keane himself had felt somewhat uneasy about leaving two such enemies together in the camp, but Silver had relented when Keane had suggested that Gabriella be placed under the personal protection of Lieutenant Pereira.

The lieutenant for his part had taken Keane's request to take care of her with good grace and shown himself once again to be a true gentleman.

By the early evening, as the light grew dim and the sky turned red, they were ready.

It was twenty miles to Almeida, but Keane had devised a plan which would provide them with support posts in stages on their return journey. Only he and Gilpin would go into the town. They would leave two men at each of two halts on the route to act as support if they were pursued and as a means of getting word back should they not return.

As the sun finally set, the depleted company rode out from the bivouac and on to the road to Almeida, taking with them a cart packed with sufficient supplies for five days, procured by Gilpin, who also drove the vehicle.

More importantly, the cart held wine, packed neatly into stamped wooden boxes lined with straw.

This too had been 'found' by Gilpin, and even now at General

Craufurd's headquarters one of the aides was being reprimanded for having misplaced four dozen bottles of the finest Rioja and the sutler was on a charge. And so a present that had been on its way to General Wellington, having been liberated by guerrillas from a French convoy, was now being returned to Marshal Massena.

Keane had thought that it would be better to ride through the night. He looked about at the others and hoped that he was not taking them to their deaths. They were all, he told himself, volunteers of a sort. Most of them rescued from the hangman's noose and the firing squad to serve at his side. Besides, if they came through this, he had promised them the reward of booty.

He had decided that he and Gilpin should retain their uniforms until the last minute, and for the present at least they had the appearance of nothing more than a routine patrol and would not, if captured by the French, be subject to the laws of war that stated that anyone caught out of uniform in enemyheld territory must be considered a spy and shot out of hand. The cart of course would be a problem to explain away. But by then it would probably be too late anyway. They would address that hurdle if they came to it.

They rode in silence, or as close as they could get to it, with their swords wrapped in leather covers and no noise save for the rattle of the cartwheels, the jangle of the harness and the sound of the horses.

Up in a tree a night owl hooted and Martin looked up, reminded not for the first time of his home on the family farm in County Down. A home he had left after getting a maid pregnant. It had been his choice to leave. His father had said that it was of no great consequence. That many of his friends' sons had made the same mistake. That the girl could marry their gardener, who was keen enough to have her. And Martin had agreed. But his conscience was pricked. He was not like those others. Never had been and, waking one morning, he had decided that if he were to live a life that was not a lie, he must leave. And so he had taken his dearest possessions and crept out of the house, not looking back.

He thought now of his father out on the estate. Of partridge shooting and the talks on nature and farming which had fuelled his boyhood imagination and he wondered how the old man was. He had not written since breaking the news of his enlisting. Perhaps one day, he thought, he would return. When all this was over and old Boney dead and buried.

The owl flew off, beating the night air with its wings, its silhouette a black shape against black. Garland, edgy and unhappy to be out in the jet-black darkness of the country at night, jumped. 'What was that?'

Martin laughed. 'An owl, you doxie. Just an owl.'

Midnight came and went and by four in the morning they had reached Alvesco and Keane was impatient to be off. But first he donned his disguise. Gilpin, the brilliant scrounger, had done them proud and Keane had opted for a broad-brimmed hat with a red handkerchief tied beneath it, a waistcoat and a pair of red trousers and short boots. He had not shaved and his face, already weather-beaten from campaigning, looked as leathery as any swarthy Spaniard. Gilpin himself wore a straw hat, a waistcoat and cropped trousers over espadrilles. Having the same swarthy look but lacking Keane's massive frame and stature, looked a natural for his assistant in the roles they were about to play.

Garland had guffawed at them. 'You look even better than you did at Oporto, sir.' Even Archer had managed a quip. 'If I didn't know better, sir, I'd take you for one of Sanchez's men.'

They left Garland and Martin in a coppice outside the village before setting off again, Keane riding on the cart with Archer, Silver and Gilpin.

They knew this road well, having retreated along the same route just five weeks before and the wreckage of that withdrawal lay all around them on either side: packs, hats, a broken cart and the other detritus of an army on the move, papers, ruined shoes, bottles, cups and broken clay pipes.

They entered the gorge of the Côa and climbed up the road towards the bridge, whose high arc spanned the ravine.

He had half expected a French picket to be posted there. But there was none and he realized that Massena must now feel completely confident in his possession of this hard-fought territory.

As they crossed the bridge Keane recalled the French assault: the colonel shot, falling arms outstretched into the gorge. He supposed his body might yet be down there or had been swept into the river to be washed out into the Atlantic.

Two hours more and dawn was coming up now, scouring the sky of darkness. The little group rattled along the dust road towards the entrance to the town and Keane felt helplessly exposed. He hoped that their disguise, which had seemed so convincing to the others, would actually persuade the French that they were who they pretended to be. But he was not reassured.

He knew that there would be no cover from now on, as for around a mile around the ramparts which surrounded the town the trees had been cleared in all directions centuries earlier, another defensive measure.

The second support post was the deserted convent at Barca and here Archer and Silver settled themselves in the bell tower, from where they could survey the surrounding countryside without fear of being seen. The horses they hid with Keane's own mare in the old refectory and barred the door from within before climbing the tower. Silver watched the little cart shudder off down the road towards Almeida, which lay before them like some star that had fallen to earth, illuminated by the first rays of the morning sun.

He spoke low, though no one could have heard them in their eyrie.

'I hope Mister Keane knows what he's doing. Right into the lion's lair he's going. He's a bold one.'

Now Keane and Gilpin sat together on the long seat at the front of the cart as Gilpin urged the horse on with his whip and spoke gently to her in Spanish.

They were coming in from the west side of the town and Gilpin turned to Keane. 'Sir, just a thought, if I may. Shouldn't we go round the ramparts and come in from the north. We're meant to be travelling down from Madrid. Won't they think it strange, sir?'

Keane shook his head. 'I had thought that, but the fact of the matter is, if we come in from this side, where the explosion did its worst, then we probably won't encounter much of a sentry post. Once we're in it won't matter which direction we've come from.'

To their right and left lay the French army, the occasional campfire lit for the sentries, stretched out across the plain, awaiting the order to advance. Keane felt their brooding presence like a great leviathan ready to spring from sleep and strike.

Almeida loomed before them, huge and forbidding. As they approached the ramparts Keane looked up at their sheer scale and thanked God that he would not be leading a forlorn hope or a storming party up their steeply angled stone walls. A voice inside him, though, reminded him that this was a foolish thought. That if they survived this mad undertaking it would certainly be to fight again, and that part of that fighting, if they were to finally push the French from Spain, would surely involve just such an attack on such a fortress. He shuddered.

He was aware too now of the debris surrounding the ramparts that had been thrown from the citadel by the force of the explosion. Gun carriages lay strewn like children's toys, with their great bronze cannon ripped from their mountings. Huge blocks of stone lay everywhere, blackened with scorch marks and among them piles of nameless, shapeless things which might just once have been parts of a human being.

The French, however, had improvised road blocks at the places where gates and guard posts had been blown away.

As they came within sight of any watchers on the walls, Keane turned to Gilpin. 'Just act naturally.' Their story was simple. They were two wine sellers. Keane the boss, delivering wine for the marshal, sent from Madrid by King Joseph, the brother of the emperor himself. They were also, though, searching for a loved one who had met his end in the explosion. Keane's character's brother a servant for the British when they had been here. In Keane's mind his character had no love for the British, blamed them for all that was wrong in the peninsula and would offer his services to the French if they paid him.

Gilpin nodded, 'Yes, sir.'

'And for heavens sake don't call me sir again. I'm Alfonso. Remember, you're Manuel? And you are my assistant in the wine trade.'

They arrived at the outer ravelins and made their way up the scarred and pockmarked entrance drive which only a few weeks before would have been impassable for being under cannon fire. Now it was silent and all around it was evidence of the effect of the huge blast. They passed more of the wreckage of huge siege guns that had been tossed from their bastions, the metal of the barrels twisted by the force into unimaginable shapes. The earth was cracked and burnt and raw, and stones of all sizes and varieties lay scattered at random. Trotting the cart slowly up the incline, they found themselves rising until they were on top of the outer bastions. Before them they saw all that remained of the west gate. Two ragged stumps of stone. As Keane had predicted, the old permanent guard house had gone with the gate, but the French had rigged a temporary structure with trees and stones and at this stood two infantrymen, their muskets at the high porte.

Keane whispered to Gilpin, 'Steady. Remember: Manuel and Alfonso. From Madrid.'

They reached the sentries and Keane went first, explaining in his best Spanish that they were wine sellers from Madrid and came with a present for the marshal, from His Highness King Joseph himself.

The sentries walked round to the rear of the cart and looked at the boxes. He prodded one and pointed to it. 'Open up. Let us see.'

Keane jumped down from the cart and, using a bar that was in the cart for this purpose, levered off the lid of one of the boxes. To his relief inside was a layer of three bottles of wine. The sentry picked up one of the bottles and looked at it. He shouted to his colleague, 'Looks like the right stuff. He's telling the truth. Let them in.'

Gilpin had said nothing but now, in impeccable Spanish muttered a thank you. The guard smiled at him and nodded him on his way as Keane leapt back up on to the seat. The little cart rattled over the grille that was all that remained of the gate and into the town.

Keane turned to Gilpin once they were out of earshot of the sentries. 'Well done. Nice touch. We should be on the London stage.'

'At least we're in, sir.'

They continued along the main street from the west, just as if they knew exactly where they were headed, an old escape technique that Gilpin had taught Keane, learned in his days as a petty thief and housebreaker in London.

They found themselves on a wide street which before the blast would have been the main thoroughfare at the west end of the town and a fashionable district. Now, though, it was no more than two rows of empty and shattered single-storey houses, their upper floors having been sliced off like the top layer of a cake. Looking in as they rumbled past, Keane was aware of the poignant rubbish, a tumbled jumble of desks and wardrobes, beds, chairs, clothes, papers and ornaments. It was the stuff of life. The possessions that had once meant something to someone. And occasionally he would glimpse something more horrific. Some physical trace of the people who had owned them. An arm or a leg, seared to the bone, an immolated carcass and, once at least, a grinning skull. Nothing or very little seemed to have been done to get rid of the corpses and as they walked on further the stench became oppressive.

Gilpin turned to Keane. 'Blimey, sir – sorry, Alfonso. This place gives me the willies. I don't like it.'

Keane could not help but agree. The town was far worse than he had imagined it might be. Although the terrible explosion had happened more than two weeks before, the place still held the stench of death. 'Yes, I know. It's not good. You would have thought that the French would have buried the dead. It will breed disease ere long.'

They were passing the castle now or all that remained of it. The foundations were still there in the plan of the towers that had stood for so long. But of the rest of it there was nothing. Here surely must have been the epicentre of the blast. And he realized that the powder had been stored in the crypts beneath the cathedral. It must have been as Leech had said. In carrying powder out of the magazine, something, perhaps a lucky shot, had ignited a barrel and that had sparked the chain reaction which had resulted in the explosion. Simple and deadly.

As they drew closer to the centre of the town and away from the blast zone, they began to see more evidence of human life. There were people on the streets and shops and cantinas. But there was little of the gaiety or bonhomie they had come to expect from a Spanish town. The townspeople looked sullen and preoccupied, as if something was preying upon their minds. The place was full of French soldiers. All types, from hussars to common infantrymen, had been admitted on passes from the surrounding camps to drink and whore. As Keane and Gilpin drove the cart further into the town they tried to avoid eye contact with anyone, but soon, Keane knew, some drunken private or sergeant would spot them and cut up rough.

He spoke quietly to Gilpin. 'We need to find Massena's headquarters. Any bright ideas?'

'If I was a French marshal, I'd make my billet where the British general had his.' He was about to add 'sir' but managed to bite his tongue.

'Good thinking. And Governor Cox's house would be where, do you suppose?'

'Somewhere salubrious. Keep driving, as if we know where we're going.'

'I'll do my best.'

'I suppose we could follow some of the French. I'll look for the highest-ranking officers I can see.'

Gilpin shook his head. 'Yes, but what then? What do we do to get in and then to get to him?'

'Something will present itself.'

They took the cart further in, constantly changing direction as the road became too narrow. Generally, though, they managed to head to what they took to be the direction of the centre and eventually found themselves in a large plaza.

This surely, thought Keane, would be their opportunity to find the calibre of officer he wanted. He searched for a French staff officer and eventually found what he was looking for.

Two French officers, both of them with long moustaches and smoking cheroots, stood talking outside a cantina. Keane recognized the uniform of the general staff. Navy blue coats with a light blue front.

He muttered to Gilpin, 'There, over there, look.' They both stared. 'Staff officers. They're sure to be heading towards the HQ, eventually.'

They stopped the cart and Keane prayed that the officers would move off before anyone came to ask what was in the cart and what they were doing there. Keane jumped down, bought a piece of meat from a passing vendor and ate it, pretending to pass the time in much the same way as a number of other peasants who were in the square. Secretly, of course, he was keeping an eye on the officers.

At length, when they had finished their cigars, they left, by the north corner of the square, and he and Gilpin followed.

The men walked fast and with some purpose and eventually emerged into another plaza. An entire side of the square was occupied by a single building, a huge palace of a place which had been hung with tricolour flags. Keane took it to be the headquarters building. When the two officers entered, it confirmed his hunch.

The next question was, how could they get inside?

'That it, then, sir?'

'What did I tell you?'

'Sorry. How are we going to get in?'

'Bold as brass. Shoulders back. That's how we get in. Bluff and balls.'

Keane had Gilpin take the cart round to the rear of the headquarters, and sure enough there they found a service entrance, an archway in seven-foot-high walls enclosing a courtyard. The place was alive with servants, scrubbing, washing, cleaning and attending to a dozen other duties. As luck would have it, a fruit supplier had just made a delivery and was pushing his handcart away from the archway as they rolled up.

Keane jumped down and ran through the arch across to the man he had just seen take delivery. 'Excuse me, señor.'

The man turned and Keane could see he was not a local. He was elegantly dressed in a green coat with gold trim and white breeches. 'Yes. Can I help you?' He spoke with a distinct French accent.

'We have a delivery, your honour.' It was always better to flatter them with an inflated title, thought Keane.

'A delivery. Do we know about this?'

'Not sure, your honour. Bit of a surprise, you might say.'

'What is it you have?'

'Wine. For the marshal. From Madrid.

'From Madrid? How do you come from Madrid?'

'The wine is a gift from King Joseph, the emperor's own brother. We have travelled far, sir.'

'Indeed you have. And you are . . . exactly?'

'My name is Alfonso Jesus Maria Dominguez, wine merchant of Madrid. This is my assistant, Manuel Ibanez.'

While they had been talking, Gilpin had driven the cart through the archway and stopped beside Keane. The steward looked them both up and down and Keane kept his nerve as he walked round to the back of the cart. The steward had seen the boxes and the one which had been opened.

'You have an open box here.'

'Yes, sir. The guard at the gate.'

The steward reached in and picked out one of the bottles. He handled it gently and looked at it carefully, the label, the seal, with the eye of a man who knew what it was he was examining.

'This is the good stuff. Very nice. The marshal is a lucky man. And not for the first time. You may proceed, Dominguez. Take it to the kitchens. The large door on the left of the courtyard. I will tell the marshal's valet to expect you. Take one bottle and go alone.'

Keane remounted the cart and they drove on through the arch and stopped outside the kitchen door. He turned to Gilpin. 'You'll have to wait down here while I see him. Wish me luck.'

They entered the kitchen and unloaded the wine under the direction of another servant. As they finished, a French officer appeared at the doorway leading from the kitchens to the rest of the house. His moustache, plaited side whiskers and pigtail identified him as a hussar.

'Which one of you is Dominguez?'

Keane walked over to him. 'I am Alfonso Dominguez.'

'You're to come with me. And bring one of those bottles.'

Keane followed the officer into the house and along an empty corridor to a staircase. They ascended two floors and emerged into another corridor, hung with tapestries, at the end of which were two tall doors. The officer knocked and a voice from within called to enter.

Massena was standing with his back to them, gazing out of the window at the town below.

'So tragic. Such destruction. So unnecessary.' He turned and saw Keane. 'Who's this?'

The officer spoke. 'This man has come from Madrid with wine. A gift from the emperor's brother.'

'Ah, yes. The wine merchant.'

Turning to Keane, the Marshal spoke in Spanish, fluent but with a southern French twang. 'Show me what you have.'

Keane walked across to him. Massena was less imposing than he had expected. He was of medium height with a shock of greying dark brown hair and a tanned complexion. Most noticeably, his right eye was sightless and remained fixed in one position. He wore the uniform of a marshal of France, with its lavish gold embroidery and decorations and a scarlet sash.

Massena took the bottle from Keane and held it up close to his one good eye, reading the label. 'This is very fine wine.'

'Only the best for your honour, sir.' Keane hoped that his own Spanish would pass with the Frenchman.

Massena lowered the bottle and stared at Keane, looking at him carefully. 'Well, this is most welcome. Welcome indeed. It was a long way for you to travel, was it not?'

'Your honour, I have other business here. It was in fact most timely.'

'Other business?'

'My brother lives here but we have heard nothing of him. He works as a servant. I am worried. I heard about the big explosion and we have seen the damage. It is terrible. Horrible.'

'Yes, terrible. You say your brother is a servant. Who for?'

Keane looked down. 'He was a servant for the British, sir.'

Massena raised an eyebrow. 'Really, the British? And are you also a servant of the British, Dominguez?'

Keane froze. Had Massena seen through his disguise so easily? Could this be the end? Quickly he scanned the room for a means of escape but could see none. They were two storeys up and the windows were bolted. There was an armed hussar officer by the door and all that Keane had was a dagger in his boot. There was no hope. He blundered on. 'Oh no, Your Majesty. I hate the British. That is my problem. Me and my brother, we have not spoken for a long time and now I fear I may not see him again.'

'You hate the British?'

Keane nodded. 'Oh yes, sir. They have ruined our country with this war. You are the future, sir. You, France, the Empire, that is the modern world. My brother is stuck in the old ways. In the Church and all the saints. I do not believe in this. I am a man of commerce. I buy, I sell. The world continues and money grows. That is the way we must be. That is the French way. The French can bring prosperity – there has to be pain with every revolution.' He stopped and then thought he might as well say what was in his mind. '*Vive l'empereur.*'

Massena on hearing the words raised his hand in the air and repeated them. '*Vive l'empereur.* It is good to see someone so enlightened. I insist that you join me for a drink. Did you know my own father was a wine seller?'

'No, sir, and thank you. What a great honour.'

Massena signalled to the hussar, who motioned to the valet

to bring glasses and a bottle. Keane noted that it was not the wine that he had brought, that was far too special, but one already in a carafe.

Playing his advantage, Keane went on. 'It may amuse you to know, Your Highness, that this wine, this very vintage, is in fact the same wine that my brother had asked for the British governor here, and I know that the Duke of Wellington himself has drunk it.'

Massena laughed. 'Wellington's wine, eh? That's good. That's damned good. Here, have a glass with me, wine merchant.'

Again Keane could not help but wonder whether the marshal had seen through his disguise, but he put the thought aside.

The marshal seemed intrigued. Keane supposed that he might be wondering that a man should travel from Madrid with no escort, carrying wine that his servant might have taken, just to deliver it to Massena and with the purpose of finding a brother who might be dead. Perhaps, he thought, the story had touched him.

It seemed clear too that what amused him more than anything was the fact that Dominguez's brother had worked for the English and the revelation that the Duke of Wellington himself had drunk the same wine. Suddenly a light came into the marshal's eyes.

'You say you hate the British. That you admire French ways and the way of the emperor?'

'Oh yes, your honour. I am a Frenchman through and through.'

'Then I have a proposition for you. Will you work for me?'

'With pleasure. But how? What should I do? I know nothing of the court or of wars.'

'No, not here. I need someone who can be my eyes and ears. I have need of a spy.'

Keane stifled a smile. 'A spy? But I am no spy, sir.'

Massena looked hard at him. 'You are a man. A businessman, you say. Well, I have a proposition. I will pay you to spy for me. You can get into Wellington's camp with your wine, can you not?'

'Perhaps, sir, but it was really my brother who—'

Massena cut him short. 'No buts. You can do it, can't you?'

'Yes, sir . . . although, my business needs me.'

Massena laughed. 'Your business? If you provide us with good information, my friend, we shall pay you handsomely. You will not lack funds. So. What do you know of the British?'

Keane was warming to his role. 'Of course, I travel around. The guerrillas do not stop me. They know me. But they don't know the real Alfonso Dominguez. I know where the British are going and what they are doing.'

'Tell me.'

'They are retreating all the way back.'

'Which way? Which way are they going?'

'They are going by the south, but the guerrillas say they are building great blocks to stop an army. They are planning for the guerrillas to ambush you on that road. The way to the south. They do not think you will come from the north. That road is too rocky. It's not good.'

Massena smiled. It was as he had thought. The signals from the spy had been right. 'Dominguez, have some more wine. You are most interesting company.'

He raised his glass. 'To a bright future and to the Empire.'

Keane raised his glass. 'The Empire.'

Massena spoke again. 'Wellington is breaking the mills and burning crops. Is the town of Viseu big enough to supply an army?'

'Quite big enough, sir, and the British have not cleared that way yet. My cousin who lives there says it is the only place not emptied by the British.'

Massena nodded. It was decided.

'This has been most useful. I have enjoyed our chat. Why don't you stay here for the night. Go to the kitchens and you will be given some food and can then enjoy the town. Cavalet here will give you something for your trouble. For carrying the wine and for the information you have given me. I will see you again in the morning, Dominguez. And we will talk more. I need information from the British and I believe that you are the man to provide me with it. You will be my spy.'

Keane rose and bowed low. Massena got up and walked with him to the door, which was opened by the hussar. 'Until tomorrow, Dominguez. You have been most helpful.'

Keane nodded. 'Thank you, your honour.'

He was about to leave, following the hussar, when Massena grabbed him by the shoulder and he felt the strength of the grip. The marshal spoke in a half-whisper, almost spitting the words. 'Do what I ask of you, Dominguez, and I will make you a rich man. Betray me and I will cut out your heart before your own eyes.'

It was said with such icy coldness that Keane knew it was in deadly earnest.

Outside, in the corridor, the hussar officer opened his sabre-tache and taking out some coins gave them to Keane with a smile before going back into Massena's rooms.

Keane opened his palm and counted. Sixteen silver livres. He whistled, as Dominguez might have done and walked away from the marshal's quarters, elated and terrified. He was amazed at what he had achieved. He had spoken to Massena, the great hero of Essling. He had even made a deal with him. But he had one more thing yet to do.

He found Gilpin in the kitchens and the two of them passed several hours in the town, avoiding the French patrols and sticking to the smaller side streets and darkest corners of the cantinas. When it was safe to do so, Keane briefed Gilpin on his interview with Massena and before long, had devised a plan.

The kitchen was much as they had left it that morning, save for a huge pot of rice and chicken cooking slowly on the range. Gilpin introduced Keane to the cook, Maria, a homely matron who, if she did recognize their fraudulent accents, was content or intrigued enough not to give them away.

They sat at the long kitchen table and were each presented with a huge plate of rice and chicken. A carafe of wine was placed on the table and the cook sat down beside them.

'With the compliments of the marshal himself. He must think a lot of you.'

She went off to attend to her other pans and Gilpin smiled. 'She's all right when you get to know her. Not bad actually. Makes a good stew.'

'I'm not after her for her stew, Manuel. Remember.' He called across to the cook, 'Hey, Maria. This is delicious. Give me the recipe.'

She came over, eyelids a-flutter, flattered by Keane's attention. 'Señor. It is very simple. Anyone can make it.'

'Not like you, though. My man here tells me you have a special ingredient.'

'Oh no, sir. Nothing special.' She sat down with them. 'You're making fun of me. Both of you. And here I am rushed off my feet cooking for the marshal and his lady.'

'Yes, you must be very busy. But what an honour. Still I'm sure you manage to get some time off.'

'Oh yes, sir, sometimes.'

'Manuel here was wondering when you might be free, weren't you, Manuel?'

Gilpin tried to look bashful. Keane went on. 'When does the marshal let you rest? Is he at you all the time?'

She blushed. 'Oh no, sir. Not all the time. He takes his dinner at three o'clock and then he has a rest. If you can call it that, as his lady's always with him. Or didn't you know that? Then he's on parade and then he comes back and has his supper.'

'How long do you have off while he's at his parade?'

'Oh, he's very punctual. As you might expect. He's out on parade every night at six. It lasts for an hour exactly and then he drinks with his officers before retiring for supper at eight.'

'Well, Manuel, there you are, your question is answered. Maria would love you to call on her between six and seven.'

Gilpin nodded and looked across at the reddening cook.

A bell tolled five times and Keane sprang up.

'But look, what's the time now? It's almost five o'clock. We're holding you back. We'll see you later. After eight. Once the marshal's finished. How would that be? We could have a nice evening. Four of us, perhaps. Have you any friends?'

She smiled at him. 'I can find you a friend.'

'That would be nice, Maria. Till then.'

They left the kitchen and doubled back into the marshal's private quarters, where Keane had noted a small dark recess below the stairs. It was in that space that they now hid.

The two men waited in the shadows for almost an hour until, as a clock chimed six, Keane urged Gilpin to his feet and the two of them raced up the back service stairs to the marshal's apartments. Keane edged his face around the corner of the wall to the corridor and, just as the cook had said, the marshal's door opened and he left, attended by the hussar officer, who turned to close the door behind him.

Keane whispered to Gilpin. 'Right. I'll go in on my own and try to find some sort of written evidence that he's taking the north route. Give me an hour and keep watch. We have two hours at the most, but if I'm not out within the hour come and get me.

Keane moved silently along the passage and once outside Massena's doors put his hand on the handle of that on the right. He pushed down and the door began to open. He pushed hard and was inside, closing the door behind him. He was alone in the room and listened for any signs of life but heard none.

Feeling confident, he walked across to the large desk that dominated the window recess and which presumably had belonged to the British governor, General Cox. He began by opening the drawers and had just reached the second when he became aware that the handle on the door on the wall opposite that through which he had entered had begun to move. Instinctively he felt for his sword but of course found nothing there. The door handle moved again and Keane, deciding it would be best to stand his ground, reached down into his boot and found the dagger, holding it so that the blade was hidden within his palm.

At last the door opened and he found himself face to face with one of the most beautiful women he had ever seen. He congratulated the marshal on his exquisite taste.

She was small, of perfect height in a woman as far as he was concerned, with a shock of auburn hair that fell in ringlets about her shoulders. Her light blue eyes flashed across the room and met his while he took in her beauty. Her narrow shoulders framed an ample bosom which gave way to a neatly tapered waist and legs which seemed impossible, given her height. But the most surprising thing about her was that she was clad in the uniform of a French hussar.

She looked at Keane with alarm, but he could tell that it was not total surprise and he wondered how long she might have been regarding him through some unseen spyhole in the panelling.

She spoke in a voice that was at once afraid and self-assured. 'Who the hell are you?'

'I'm no one, madame. No one really. An acquaintance of the marshal's. I delivered this wine earlier.'

'You're lying and I'm going to call the guard.'

'Why would you want to do that?'

'I think you're an insurgent. A guerrilla. Be warned. I am armed.'

'Of course you are. And so am I.'

She stared at him, trying to puzzle out his presence there. Wondering if he was a guerrilla, an assassin or merely a thief. If so, then he had surely come to the wrong place. For Massena was one of the most avaricious and possessive men she had ever met.

'Who are you?' she asked. And there was not a trace of panic in her voice.

'The truth?'

'The truth will do, if you've nothing better.'

'I'm a British officer.'

She raised an eyebrow. 'You are?'

He removed the hat and the handkerchief and smiled at her and this time he spoke in French. 'James Keane, ma'am. Captain.'

'You really are, aren't you? I should call the guard.'

'You'd be lucky. They're all on parade with your man and then they'll go and get pissed and then he'll come back to you stinking of hooch and tup you till you're red raw. That's the sort of man he is, isn't it? The good marshal.'

She stared at him wide-eyed. No one had ever been so blunt, so unforgiving. 'Yes. Yes, that is just what he's like.'

'And you hate him for it.'

She looked at him again. How could a man she had just met know so much about her? She nodded.

She looked so strange, standing there dressed as a cavalryman in a uniform which fitted her form so well that it accentuated every perfect contour. The effect was more erotic by far than if she had been naked. Although at that moment that was precisely what Keane was wishing for.

He moved closer to her and gently inhaled. He had forgotten the smell of a woman, musky and heady. He felt intoxicated by her and was suddenly conscious of where they were. What his purpose was and what he had to do. She was very young, twenty-one at the most, and he wondered what she was doing with Massena, a man in his fifties. There must be a tale behind their relationship and he was willing to bet it was a tragedy.

He had a hunch, and on a whim suddenly tore at her tunic and exposed her back.

She gasped and gathered the cloth as it fell around her bosom. But Keane turned her hard so that he could see her shoulders. And sure enough there it was. On her left shoulder blade a small but distinctive mark. A mark in the shape of a dagger, made with a branding iron many years before and that might easily be mistaken for a birthmark or other blemish.

He smiled. 'I thought so. You're a cathouse whore.'

She covered herself and stared at him.

'How dare you? I am a respectable woman. My husband is an officer of dragoons. A major.'

'That sign says otherwise.'

'What do you know about it? I was a dancer.'

'A dancer? I know enough. Enough to have visited one of those establishments in Paris myself a few years ago. All you tarts, you're all owned by your madames and that's when you get branded. How old were you? Fifteen? Sixteen?'

She looked away. 'I was fourteen. My father needed the money. We were very poor.'

'And so he sold you. The bastard. Sold his own daughter to a meat house. Christ.'

'Stop!' The tears were welling in her eyes now. Keane thought he was doing rather well. She went on. 'He couldn't help it. He was my father. My family had to live.'

Keane stopped. 'You've done well, haven't you? Done all right. Mistress of the Prince of Essling. Not bad. Mind you, he was only a guttersnipe, wasn't he? Perhaps you're well suited. Did Massena buy you too?'

'Don't be ridiculous. You disgust me. Get out. I'll call the guard.'

'I told you, they're all away playing soldiers.'

He walked over to the sideboard and, picking up the flask of wine, poured himself a glass before going on. 'I think he did. He bought you. You're his slave, Henriette. Am I right? You might look the part, but you're more his whore than his mistress. I'll wager he's a bit rough with you. Though maybe you like them that way. No, I think you've had enough of the marshal, or the prince or whatever he calls himself when you're alone. I bet you're just dying to get away.'

'What if I am?'

'Perhaps I can help.'

'How? What do you know?'

'I know about you.'

She stopped. 'Who are you?'

'I told you. I am a British officer.'

'Not like any I have ever seen.'

'That's because I'm not like any other British officer. For one thing, I'm Irish. For another, I play by my own rules, not the army's.'

'What? Who are you really?'

'Why don't you ask yourself that question?'

She began to sob. He held her to him and she let herself go, losing herself in his arms.

He whispered gently. 'Tell me your name.'

'Henriette. Henriette Lebreton.'

He repeated the name. As if he needed to remind himself who it was he was holding in his arms. It felt unreal and he wondered how he had managed to find himself here. Then she looked up and instinctively he kissed her. Her eyes were open now and she kept them open, wanting to see what he would do. He felt her return the kiss and he knew that his instinct had not been wrong. Danger made a man do such things.

She could feel him against her now, and pulling her face away from his, but without letting go of his arm, she led him through the doors from where she had appeared and laid him down on a huge canopied bed that smelt exactly like she did.

Then, as her ripped uniform fell away, she lay down beside him, unbuttoning his tunic, whispered in his ear, 'Can you kill him?'

And Keane knew that this was not a dream. It was real and he wanted her.

'Yes,' he answered. 'But not now. Not here. Yes, I can kill him. I will kill him, when I have the chance, for you. But I want something in return.'

She pulled him towards her. And outside in the courtyard the servants came and went, and down the hill on the parade ground Massena inspected his troops and the drums played their evening tattoo.

And Keane wondered what he had done.

14

They rode at breakneck speed back towards the old convent, leaving the soaring, looming ramparts of Almeida behind them. Gilpin had saddled the carthorse and Keane had found a likely-looking mare tethered in the marshal's stable yard. It was only after they had left the town and were about to quit the city walls that Gilpin, who was riding to the rear of Keane, had commented on the horse.

'Sir, have you seen what's on your nag's rump?'

Keane looked down to his left and past the navy-blue and gold saddlecloth noticed a brand. It was a monogram in the shape of an ornate letter 'E', surmounted by a crown.

'What's that for, d'you think, sir? Espagne?'

'No,' said Keane. 'That 'E' stands for Essling, and the crown is that of a prince. This is one of Massena's own horses.' He patted the beast's neck and smiled to himself. Two of the marshal's prized possessions, each of them branded, and he had had them both.

They had moved fast and had been out of the archway before the groom and the kitchen staff had known they were gone.

Now his mind was full of Henriette and her smell lingered in his nostrils and on his fingers and his clothes. Events had not gone quite as he had planned, but the result had been all that he had hoped, and more.

In his pocket he carried a note copied with care by himself from an identical one in Massena's hand. It was, he thought, perhaps the most precious piece of paper with which he had ever been entrusted. It contained an order written to Marshal Ney to take the army up to pursue the allies by the northern route, through Viseu and then down to Coimbra by way of Bussaco.

Henriette had found the original for him when he had asked, left where she had seen Massena write it earlier that day, and had pressed it into his hand. It had not taken long to copy and he had even forged the signature, such was his skill as a draughtsman.

And he for his part had promised to return. Or at least to find her, wherever she might be, and to rescue her from Massena, if not to kill the man. He would do his utmost to find her. As Keane knew well, promises made in the heat of passion are seldom kept.

But this was more than a promise and they had sworn to one another that if they could not meet again in Spain then they would contrive to find each other somehow in Paris, her home town. Keane knew a place. A place with which she was familiar. A little cafe on the rue du petit Temple, close to the Place des Vosges in the old Jewish quarter. That would be their rendezvous. If ever he could manage it and if both of them were still alive.

He could not quite believe how fast it had happened. It had just felt right. There was nothing more to it. How could there be? He knew that he did not feel the same for Henriette as he did for Kitty Blackwood. But then he caught her scent again and for a moment or two began to doubt himself.

He wondered how long it would be before someone raised the alarm in Almeida. Of course he and Gilpin would not be there to meet Maria and her friend that evening, nor would he be on hand to see Massena in the morning to resume their talk of spying. And he wondered how long it would be before the marshal would discover that there was something missing from his rooms. A silver snuffbox embossed with a gold eagle and the initial 'E'. Perhaps he would not notice it at all. He would blame one of the servants. Or maybe Dominguez. Keane felt his saddlebag to reassure himself that the box was still inside and smiled as he thought of the marshal's expression. He prayed that Massena would not suspect Henriette of involvement, nor that he would question why the hussar's uniform which he had had tailored for her had been torn before she had time to have it mended.

She had given Keane useful information. The number of men in each of Massena's corps and what she had heard said of their abilities. But one thing had been puzzling him. She had known of the presence of the British spy in Wellington's army, but had not thought his name to be Macnab. What it was, though, she could not recall.

She had also promised to delay Massena for as long as she could and Keane thought she was in earnest. At first, when he went to leave, she had begged him to take her with him and it had been all he could do to stop her clinging to him. She was desperate for some way out from the hell of being at Massena's whim and Keane seemed to be her only means of escape. He had to trust her.

Gilpin called to Keane as they rode, 'There's the convent now, sir.'

Keane looked, but in the dusk could see no sign of life in the darkened building and hoped that Silver and Archer were still there and had not been killed or taken by the French. There was no point in subtlety now and the two men carried on riding until they were close to the convent walls. At fifty yards, they were hailed from the top of the bell tower.

It was Silver's voice, calling down as he might have done many times from a topgallant, 'Thought you'd never get here. sir.'

Archer was standing at the door. 'Were you followed, sir?'

'Not as far as we know, but let's not delay. We need to get across the river.'

'Did you get what you wanted, sir?'

Keane smiled and exchanged glances with Gilpin. 'Oh yes. We got exactly what we wanted, thank you, Archer, and a good deal more.'

They rode through the night from the convent at Barca, not stopping, across the Côa and back to Alvesco where, collecting the others, they had continued on to Celorico, now abandoned by the allies. Keane had told von Krokenburgh they would be absent five days and to meet them at Mortágua on the sixth day, but in truth he had never expected the mission to Almeida to take that long. Keane had something else in mind.

The route from Celorico to Viseu climbed steadily upward. They left behind the flat lands of the plain around the Côa and within five miles the terrain had become mountainous and inhospitable. The road led across country and he was aware that, according to Massena's orders, this was one of the routes that the French must take. It gave him great hope, for the surface was surely the worst he had ever seen.

Keane's horse stumbled on a loose rock, sending shards of

stone spinning down the hillside. He called back to the others, 'Watch your step. The road's unstable. Take it easy.'

The road was every bit as bad as he had imagined it to be. In fact it was little more than a rocky path and there would be little or no hope for the French to move their baggage carts and wagons over such a route. The artillery park would be in chaos. All that the French would be able to do would be to actually rebuild the road. It would be a nightmare for them.

They entered the hilltop town of Viseu up a winding road. The road continued upward and into the centre where behind a high crenellated wall stood the ancient cathedral. It was a pretty place, thought Keane. But as he had suspected, it was empty of life.

Silver was by his side. 'Sir, how big is this place?'

'How big? You mean, how many people live here?'

'Yes, sir.'

'I was told about nine thousand souls.'

'Then, excuse me, sir, but where the bleeding hell are they all?'

The people had gone from Viseu. Terrified of being taken by the French and only too aware of what had befallen their compatriots in Oporto the year before and Ciudad Rodrigo a few months ago, all had fled.

Soon, Keane knew, the French would come and the place would be ruined, its churches wrecked, the crucifixes and sepulchres blighted and broken, private houses ransacked and anything of value taken. Well, he was damned if the French were going to have it all their way.

'We'll have to be quick. I have a report to make at Coimbra. I have a few words of caution. Remember, first of all, this is not

usual. Be considerate in what you take. Try not to take anything of purely personal value, and nothing too big or ornate.
Remember, we're not supposed to be here, and if the provosts
find out then you'll hang and I'll be cashiered. Got it? And
remember, when you're done we'll split it evenly, and that
includes a share for Heredia and Leech too.'

They all nodded.

'Now go, and be back here in the hour.'

They were as good as their word. An hour later and they were
back at the plaza, laden with booty. Keane walked from man to
man looking at the piles of loot that lay at their feet. There was
gold plate from the cathedral, and goblets and other objects
which could be melted down.

Martin had brought down a large gold altar cross from the
cathedral. Keane shook his head. 'I told you, Will. Too big.'

They were just loading the last of the silver plate into the large
fodder bags that hung from the horses' flanks when there was
a clatter of hooves on cobbles in the distance, down in the lower
part of the town. Martin rushed across to the parapet.

'Cavalry, sir. Lancers.'

Keane spun round and ran across. 'All of you check your
weapons and ammunition. Christ, the French shouldn't be here
for days.'

He peered over the edge down to the lower town and saw
them, But it was not the French that Martin had seen. The pen-
nants carried by these lancers displayed the national colours of
Spain. Sanchez had found him.

In a matter of minutes the upper plaza was filled with Sanchez's men and the don himself.

He rode towards Keane and dismounted. 'Captain Keane. I thought that you were heading for Celorico.'

Keane shook his head. 'No, colonel. We had a change of orders. Diverted here.'

'So I see. But I ask myself, what is it that you are doing here, with all this plunder?'

Keane smiled at him. 'Plunder? Oh, you have the wrong impression, colonel. This is not plunder.'

'It looks very much like plunder to me, captain. What would you like me to call it?'

'This is part of the duke's scorched-earth policy. We are denying any means of subsistence to the enemy.'

'Do you think that the French eat gold now? I know they are monsters, but even they would find that difficult.'

Keane laughed. 'You misunderstand me. We are taking this abandoned gold and silver back to Coimbra to provide Wellington with the means to sustain his army. Sold or melted down, it will provide pay for the men and buy supplies. If we leave it here it will fall into the hands of the French and simply be sent back to Bonaparte.'

Sanchez raised an eyebrow. 'You expect me to believe that?'

'Believe what you want, colonel. It is of no matter to me. We are taking this back to Coimbra, to the Duke of Wellington.'

'I don't think so.'

'What?'

'I think that we both know your plans, Captain Keane. And I think that you will now agree for us both to enjoy a share of the booty.'

'And if I say no?'

'I have sixty lancers here who will help me get what I want and later we will ride into Coimbra and sadly report to your general the deaths of six of his guides, caught by the French on their way back from a patrol.'

'That's blackmail.'

Sanchez nodded. 'I suppose you could call it that. Just as I could call what you have here plunder.'

Keane knew when he was beaten. 'Very well, we will divide up what we have with you, fifty–fifty. But I would advise you to take another look. You may find things that we did not and you have more hands to carry it.'

Sanchez nodded. 'Yes, that would be a wise decision.' He shouted a command and his lancers dismounted and split into search parties, scouring the town for riches.

Eventually, after another half an hour, the men returned. Throughout the wait Keane had said nothing to the colonel, but as they returned he said merely, 'Would you really have done as you threatened? Killed us all in cold blood?'

Sanchez shrugged and laughed. 'Of course not, captain. What do you take me for? Surely I am allowed my little joke? After all, we are friends, are we not?'

Keane smiled, but was not sure whether he believed the man. One thing had been troubling him these past few weeks when they had been parted from Sanchez. And now that worry had been resolved. For there, strapped to the guerrilla colonel's saddle was his own gun, lost in the wager by Martin.

And he was resolved, how he did not yet know, to get it back.

'Captain Keane, you have been looking after my men. They tell me only good things about you. They all have full bellies, which is also very good. But they have not had much sport with the French.'

'No, we have been waiting for the French to attack. You know how it is.'

Sanchez looked at him. 'No, I don't know. I take the war to my enemies. Since we last met, I have had the chance to kill many more of them. Some with your very own gun.' He patted the saddle holster.

Keane smiled. 'Nice to see it being used so well.'

'Of course now there is no need for that.'

Keane looked at him. 'It's begun?'

'This morning. At dawn, the French 2nd and 6th Corps crossed the Mondego. By now they will be across the Côa.'

'Forty miles away.' Keane looked thoughtful. 'They're heading for Celorico. Then they'll cross the Mondego and head here. It took us the whole of a long day. With the artillery and baggage train, it will take them four. And they'll have no food or supplies.'

Sanchez interjected. 'And they will think that when they reach here they can resupply. But everything is gone. People, animals, food, drink. And now they won't even have any booty. Massena will not be happy.'

'Almost as unhappy as he must have been when he realized that I had taken his horse. Did you see her?'

Sanchez looked across at where Keane's horses were tethered. He was suddenly animated. 'Which one, the grey?'

Keane nodded. 'She's a beauty, don't you think? Sensitive to the touch, strong and goes like the wind. What a prize.'

Sanchez walked slowly across to the horse and patted her on the nose, to which she responded and nuzzled towards him. He moved around her, taking in every measure of her form, running his hand over the brand. He lifted her tail then moved round to the head once again, gently opened her mouth and looked at her teeth.

'Fantastic. What a horse! How much will you take for her?'

Keane shook his head. 'She's not for sale. I'm sorry, colonel.'

'No, seriously, Keane. We all have our price. How much?'

Keane thought for a moment, as if the idea had just come to him. 'I'll take my gun in exchange.'

Sanchez raised an eyebrow. 'Of course, I could still just kill you all.'

'But you won't, colonel, will you?'

Sanchez laughed and shook his head, then walked across to his horse and, unstrapping the carbine holster, extracted Keane's gun. 'It's a real pity. She's a beauty.'

'So's the horse. And she's Massena's own. Think of that, colonel, to ride against the French on Massena's own favourite horse.'

Sanchez handed him the gun. 'Done.'

Keane took it, opened the lock and snapped it shut. 'Seems to be in working order. Thank you for taking care of her. Of course, I'll need a mount myself now.'

Sanchez laughed. 'Don't think for a minute that you are having mine, captain. I'll exchange with one of my men. His nag will do for you. You have the gun. That was our deal.'

Yes, thought Keane, he had the gun and Sanchez had Massena's horse and the men were still dividing up the booty and Keane took care to make sure that it was done even-handedly.

There was just one last thing. One thing which he could not resist. He turned to Sanchez. 'That would appear to be everything. If you are agreed, colonel, we will pack up and leave.' He paused. 'Colonel Sanchez, I have a final favour to ask of you.'

'I will listen. Go on.'

'I would be greatly honoured if you would ride with us down to Coimbra, so that I may introduce you to Wellington. So that he can at last meet a man who has done so much to further the efforts of his army.'

Sanchez pondered the idea for a moment. 'Yes, of course we will ride with you. In fact, we will all come down. There will be a big battle soon and I want my men to be a part of that victory. We need a victory, captain, and Wellington will give us one. Before the winter. So we will come.'

So together they rode out of the ghost town of Viseu, Keane with his gun and Sanchez with his horse, and Keane realized that in many ways Sanchez and he were alike. Two men, battling the odds, taking opportunities as they arose, always quick to spot a chance. Always ready with an answer and, for all their unorthodox ways, at heart, men of honour.

The road down from Viseu was better than that on the way up, but it was still tortuous. Close on forty miles of twisting mountain dust-road, whose surface of baked, scorpion-infested rocks would sometimes be no wider than the thinnest ridge, capable of taking just one man at a time.

Sanchez's men had joined him where the Mondego met the Criz at Fosado. Five hundred infantry and another hundred horse to swell the ranks of Wellington's army.

They marched on, through the fertile valley of the Criz, where normally the crops would have been standing chest high and cattle would have been grazing by the water. But the guerrillas and the Ordenanza had clearly been as busy as Keane's own command. The place was now transformed into a wilderness, the towns deserted, the livestock driven off down to the south.

Even when they left the barren hills, thought Keane, there would be no solace for the French down here.

*

Crossing the river at Mortágua, Keane was relieved to find that his plan had worked and that von Krokenburgh, the hussars, Sanchez's remaining lancers and the Ordenanza were all already there, along with Leech, Ross, Heredia and Gabriella.

The Hanoverian grinned widely. 'Welcome, Keane, how good to see you. We did not know how it had gone.'

'Thank you, captain. I did all that I set out to do. The French are fooled and will fall into Wellington's trap.'

Leech found him. 'Sir, you're all safe, thank God.'

'How are the mills?'

'Less of them standing now, sir, I'm happy to report, than there were when you left.'

Keane laughed. 'And no casualties?'

'No, sir, but I don't think my hearing will be the same again.'

Silver sought out Gabriella. Pereira had been as good as his word and Heredia had not troubled her, nor she him, so she said.

They fell in together and slowly the swollen column, now comprising almost eight hundred men, began to climb again out of the valley and up into the hills. After some five miles, Keane stopped to consult his map. It was a desolate spot. A long ridge, running for some seven miles at almost two thousand feet. As he had predicted, they emerged on to the ridge of the Serra do Bussaco, about ten miles north-east of Coimbra.

He rode back down the column, towards Sanchez. 'This is where the duke will fight his battle, colonel. This is his chosen ground. Look down there.'

He pointed down behind the ridge, where the reverse slope of the hill angled gently down to a new road. Men, some in red coats, most in shirtsleeves and grey overalls, were working on it even as they looked.

'Down there's the duke's road. He's planned to bring the

French here all along, and that road behind this position will enable him to move battalions at will, out of sight of the enemy.'

Sanchez stared. 'He planned all this?'

'Yes, that's what I've been doing, colonel. Laying a trap which would bring the French here. Right to this place.'

They had crested the top of the ridge now and Keane could see what a perfect position it was. It was flat in some places. Ideal for troop formations. Perfect for hiding an entire army. It was dominated on the left by a large building which Keane had marked down as a convent, surrounded by an extensive wood. On either slope of the ridge stood several small villages, all of which Keane presumed would now be deserted.

Sanchez stood and stared at the position the British army would soon occupy. 'It's extraordinary. Such planning. Such care. Genius.'

They did not pause for long on the ridge, but as they descended on the road to Coimbra, Keane realized how everything he had done, all he had accomplished over the past two months, had suddenly come together.

Sanchez was right. Wellington was a genius. If by some miracle the French did come to Bussaco, if the British and Portuguese did meet them on that ridge, then he was certain the allies would prevail. The telegraphs, the deception, the kidnapped general, the captured couriers, the codes, the smashed mills and the ruined peasants. All of it. All of it would be worthwhile. Battle would be joined on Wellington's terms and, God willing, the British and their allies would prevail. And Massena would lick his wounds and the defensive lines would be finished and they would retire into Portugal and the French would again be confounded. Genius indeed.

At last, he thought, it all made sense. All, that was, save one thing. Pritchard's death. Who had killed him and why? Was it Macnab? And where was the spy now?

Coimbra was as it had always been and it was almost as if there was no war being waged not thirty miles away. The town seemed to go about its workaday life, just as if it might have been in an English shire. Of course, he knew that all this might change in an instant. That if the French showed themselves over the ridge, then the town would simply cease to exist. People would flee to Lisbon and the town would become another Viseu.

For today, though, Coimbra was their solace. They trotted in through its high arched gate to find streets flanked with market stalls. Keane knew the route to the headquarters building that had been occupied by Wellington in the previous campaigning season and led the column to a part of the town where they would be able to make camp without causing too much of a commotion: a patch of open land on the south side, where an olive grove provided shelter and a small stream gave running water. It was all that they could have wished for.

He rode across to Ross. 'Sarn't Ross, I need to report to the duke. Find billets for everyone, will you? Captain von Krokenburgh will want his own rooms. Might as well put him in with me. Colonel Sanchez too, if he's of a mind to do so. Find yourselves somewhere tight and warm. The rest can do as they please.'

He dug into his haversack and pulled out a small purse, which he threw to Ross, who caught it. 'Buy wine and provisions for all our men. Just our men, mind. I'll see you in the hour.'

*

Together with Sanchez, Keane trudged up the curving path of cobbles that led through the narrow streets of Coimbra towards Wellington's headquarters.

His mind was filled with the spirit of the coming battle. Though he wondered, as always, how Wellington would receive him. Knocking at the door, he was admitted by the duke's unctuous ADC, Captain Ayles. 'His Grace will see you now, captain.'

Keane motioned to Sanchez to remain outside. 'I have matters to discuss with the duke, colonel. I shall announce you shortly.'

Keane entered and found Wellington standing with Grant and George Scovell, staring down at a map of Portugal. As he entered the duke looked up.

'Keane? Major Grant told me to expect you. Your travels were successful?'

'Sir.'

'And now you return at last. What news do you bring? Good, I hope. I hear that Marshal Massena has left Almeida and is advancing apace towards us.'

'I'm not sure that I would say "apace", sir. In fact I hope quite the opposite. He is, though, making his way towards us.'

'Major Grant tells me that you have managed to persuade him to come by the northern route, and as we are aware, that road goes directly to the Serra do Bussaco.'

'Yes, sir.'

'It is as good as I might have hoped. A splendid piece of work, Keane. But tell me, how did you manage it? To have the marshal, one of my most able enemies, believe the absolute opposite of what was the case. Your method must have been something quite radical.'

Keane paused. 'I gave him the code book, sir.'

'You gave him what? The code book?'

'Yes, sir, Colonel Folque's code book, I passed it to the French. Well, to their spy, Macnab. Had him believe that he had managed to acquire it. Then I transmitted regular messages in code which gave him the misinformation.'

Wellington said nothing for a few moments, then he turned to Keane. 'Allow me to collect my thoughts. My head is reeling. You did what? You gave the French our confidential code book? Grant, were you aware of this?'

'No, sir, in fact I was not. Keane, what were you thinking?'

'Yes, Keane, what the devil were you thinking? You may have successfully persuaded Massena to march to ground of my choosing, but you have seriously compromised the safety of our entire army. Explain yourself.'

Keane smiled and instantly realized that he should not have. 'In fact, sir, it's really fine. My man Archer, quite a brilliant fellow, medical student and mathematician, has devised a brand-new code. It's a great deal more secure than Colonel Folque's cipher. I have a copy here.'

He took a small black book from his pocket, containing the code on which Archer had been working for a fortnight, while the Ordenanza had been busy destroying mills.

He handed it to the duke, who without looking at it immediately passed it to Grant.

Wellington spoke quietly, but his face was incandescent. 'I see. It is being copied?'

'I have a team of clerks, ready to make copies, sir.'

Wellington nodded and then turned on him suddenly. 'That's beside the point, man. By God, I've a damned good mind to have you cashiered. I should have you shot.'

Keane said nothing. Grant, who had been thumbing through Archer's code book, spoke. 'You know, sir, this is actually not half bad. In fact, it's damned good. I think Keane's right. It is more secure than the old book.'

Wellington shook his head. 'I don't believe it.' He looked at Grant. 'Do you really think so, Colquhoun? Really?'

Grant nodded his head. 'Yes, sir, I do. In fact, I would go so far as to say that it's brilliant.'

Wellington stared at Keane. 'I don't know how you've pulled all this off, Keane. But you seem to have done so. You should thank Major Grant here. He is the only reason why you are not under arrest.'

'Thank you, sir. I am most grateful. I honestly believe that codes such as this will win this war.'

Wellington took back the code book and began to leaf through it while still continuing to talk to Keane. 'You're convinced that this is the way Massena will come?'

'Yes, sir.'

'And what if you're wrong? What then?'

Keane shook his head. 'I'm not wrong, sir.'

'How can you be so certain? I need positive proof.'

The time had come for Keane to play his masterstroke. He reached into his waistcoat pocket and drew out a piece of paper, which he handed to Grant. The major opened it and gasped. He read it, reread it and passed it to Wellington.

'Well, Grant, what is it?'

Keane spoke up. 'It's a note, sir, an order in Marshal Massena's hand, written to Marshal Ney, ordering him to advance by way of the top road, to Bussaco.' He did not mention that he had copied it from the original.

Wellington read the note. 'How the devil did you get this, Keane?'

'I have my means, sir. I retrieved it from the marshal's writing desk.'

'You were in Marshal Massena's headquarters?'

Keane nodded. 'Yes, sir, I also acquired this. I wondered if you might like it.'

He delved into his saddlebags, which he had carried into the palace, and brought out the silver snuffbox, which he presented to Wellington. The duke looked at the monogram and shook his head. 'Tell me, Keane that this is what I suppose it to be?'

'It is Marshal Massena's own, Your Grace.'

Wellington handed the box to Grant. 'Look, look at this. He gives the code book to the enemy and hands me this, Grant.'

Keane spoke again. 'Sir, I have also brought someone with me. Someone who is most keen to make your acquaintance.'

'Who's that, Keane? Don't tell me it's the marshal?'

Grant laughed and Wellington smiled at his own joke.

'No, sir, it is Don Julian Sanchez. He is waiting in the ante-room.'

'Well, bring him in then. Be quick about it.'

Keane motioned to the ADC, who opened the door and admitted Sanchez.

Wellington smiled and bowed. 'Colonel Sanchez. Delighted to meet you. Captain Keane here has been describing your exploits to us. You are, sir, a most invaluable aid to our mission here.'

Sanchez bowed in turn. 'Sir, Lord Wellington. Your fame is well known. I am honoured to fight on your side.'

His eye alighted on the snuffbox, lying on the table. He pointed to it. 'I see you have acquired some fresh booty. It looks a splendid piece. Very handsome.'

Wellington smiled at him. 'Yes, isn't it? In fact I've just been presented with it by Captain Keane. It belonged to Marshal Massena.'

Sanchez grinned and nodded. 'Yes, of course. Captain Keane has been very busy. I am fortunate to have acquired the marshal's own horse. A real beauty.'

Wellington looked puzzled but soon led Sanchez away to study the map and discuss the role of his company in the coming battle.

It heartened Keane to know that that Don Sanchez, mounted on Massena's horse, would go into battle on Wellington's side. He left the colonel deep in conversation with Wellington and was about to make his way from the headquarters building, when Grant called him back.

'I can see how you might have got hold of the snuffbox, but God knows how you got the horse. You're a rogue, Keane. Quite brilliant, but a rogue all the same.'

He took him by the arm and moving out of the anteroom with its flurry of scarlet-coated aides ushered him into a darkly cool colonnade. 'James, there is one more thing. A somewhat delicate matter.'

Keane wondered what it could be. Surely they had not found out about the loot from Viseu? Or might it be his fight with Foote? 'It's Captain Morris.'

'He's not dead, sir?'

Grant shook his head. 'No, no. Not at all. It's about Miss Blackwood. Kitty Blackwood. It seems that she and Morris have been seeing a good deal of one another these past few weeks while you've been away and apparently it began some months ago. Well, I'll be blunt with you. They are engaged to be married.'

Keane thought for a moment that he might have misheard. 'Sir?'

'Captain Morris and Miss Blackwood. They are betrothed, James. I am sorry.'

Keane said nothing for a moment, then, 'Oh, I see. Thank

you, sir.'

He walked away from Grant, unable to absorb the situation, and just as he was about to reach the double doors of the main entrance he felt a heavy hand on his left shoulder.

Turning, he saw Major Cavanagh. But his face was not that of the smiling friend he had been on their last encounter. Cavanagh was red with rage and his expression betrayed his anger.

'Captain Keane, a word if I may.'

He withdrew his hand, as Keane replied, 'Not now, sir, please. Now is not the moment.'

'No, so it would seem. Nor any other. The moment was lost on you, was it not? I have friends here, Keane and they tell me that you have been playing me for a fool. You assured me that you would do your utmost to confound Wellington's plans and press for a battle. And it would seem that you have been doing quite the opposite.'

Keane, his usual tact confounded by the news of Morris's deceit, turned on Cavanagh. 'You shall have your battle, sir. The duke has plans.'

'Take care, young man, and calm yourself. Certainly the duke has plans, but they are not those of my patron nor of my friends at court.'

'We will fight a battle, sir. The French are coming.'

'Yes, Keane, the French are coming. But we will not fight it on terms of my choosing. D'you see, Keane? Do you comprehend at all what you have done? You have alienated a man who might have done you a great deal of good.'

Keane shook his head. 'I do not need your favour, sir.'

Cavanagh, shaking his head in turn, smiled, knowingly. 'No, Keane, not me, you fool. You may be a spy, sir, but take care not to deceive the throne. By your lies you have gained the enmity of the prince regent.'

15

Keane was in a very dark place. His mind had been there for some time, but the days no longer seemed to have any relevance.

Grant's news had not entirely surprised him. For Foote to have made such an accusation had nagged at him with the possibility that it contained a degree of truth. The reality of it was altogether different. This was utterly unlike the earlier doubts he had entertained with regard to Morris. He had known that his old friend was not in truth suited to the intelligencers. He was no spy. Morris longed for the field. For his beloved cannon and his artillerymen.

Keane had known that he had been drifting away and had realized that it was bad enough that he would leave their company. But this? He wondered what drove a man to such betrayal. They had come through much together. He had seen them almost as brothers. Family certainly. He shook his head again and tried to search somewhere inside his soul for the explanation.

Perhaps, he thought, it is all my fault. I made him change. I made him play the spy and that is what has altered his character. He had known nothing of deceit before this. Now he is an arch-deceiver. He thought too that perhaps this was some terrible revenge. A moral judgement wrought upon him for killing Kitty's brother. The only consolation was that he supposed that Kitty must be happy.

It had been four days since the conversation with Grant. He thought too of the exchange with Cavanagh. The man was a fool. Keane had nailed his colours to Wellington's path and Cavanagh could go to Hell. Besides, the French were coming. News had come, from Martin, that Massena was on the move, his entire army it seemed marching towards Bussaco, as Wellington had wanted. Walking into the trap. But although Keane had understood, it had meant little to him. He had felt strangely numb. For the last few days he had gone through the actions of his duties but without any real engagement. He was detached, and everyone was aware of the change.

Sergeant Ross had brought him food and wine in his tent, where he had retired early every evening, rather than sharing a song or a few words before turning in.

Ross had tried to coax him out of his depression. 'I know what it's like, sir. I was the same when my woman ran off. Course you're not like that, not like me, and you wouldn't be so mad as I was, nor do what I did, neither.'

Keane looked at him. 'Thank you, sarn't.'

But Ross went away with a heavy heart and knew that it would take something more than sympathy to make his officer see sense.

On the fifth day, just as Keane was preparing to write another report on the quantity of ration required for Sanchez's lancers which would have to come out of their allowance, he was aware of a commotion outside his tent. Martin seemed, along with Silver, to be attempting to prevent someone from entering. And their actions did not surprise Keane when he saw who that person was.

Tom Morris pushed past the tent flap. 'James. This is nonsense. Major Grant has been to see me, alerted by your sergeant. This is folly.'

'Well, it's no folly of my making, Tom.'

'You must understand, James. We did not do it to deliberately spite you.'

'Why then? Why on earth would you even contemplate doing it?'

'I cannot explain. I only know that she is the dearest thing to me.'

'As she was to me.' He turned away, unable to look at Morris. 'I should call you out.'

'James, you and I both know that would solve nothing. Surely we can be sensible about this?'

'Were you sensible with her?'

'That's stupid. You've lost your reason.'

'Perhaps I have. I have lost my oldest friend and I have lost the woman I love. Did you not think of loyalty? To a friend? You might at least have told me first and not let me know of it from Major Grant.'

'James. I cannot undo what has been done. It is too late.'

Keane shook his head. 'Come back and join us. It can be as it was, Tom.'

Now it was Morris's turn to refuse. 'No, James. It can never be as it was, and you know that. I intend to rejoin my regiment. I yearn for the battlefield. Staff work and any amount of spying are not for me, James.'

Keane smiled to himself. 'Of course I know that. I knew it the moment that I signed you up.' He paused and said nothing for some time but seemed to stare into emptiness. Then he turned to Morris. 'If Kitty wants you, then so be it. Take her with my blessing. I'm old enough to know that when a woman's mind is made up there is no moving it.'

Morris smiled and clapped Keane on the shoulder. 'Thank you, dear friend. I cannot tell you how happy that makes me. I have been troubled by this since I first saw her and since she declared her love for me. You may be certain of one thing too: I shall never reveal to her who it was killed her brother.'

'Thank you.'

Morris spoke again. 'There is one more thing, though, James. In fact, I would have come to tell you of it even if Grant had not persuaded me.'

'What is it? Tell me.'

'It's Pritchard, James. He's alive. I've seen him.'

'You have? Alive?'

'As alive as you or I. I could not get word to you. You are elusive, James.'

'That is the nature of my position.'

'He goes by another name.'

Keane sighed. 'Macnab.'

'You knew? How?'

'How stupid I am. How very obvious. Of course. Pritchard is Macnab.'

'He has died his hair a frightful shade of ginger and adopted spectacles. But it is Pritchard. Of that I have no doubt. In fact, he's neither Pritchard nor Macnab. He's as Irish as you, James. His real name's O'Callaghan.'

At this, Sergeant Ross, who had been standing guard at the tent flap, peered inside.

'Sorry, sir, but did I hear you mention O'Callaghan?'

'If you did, Sarn't Ross, then you ought not to have done. But what of it?'

'If it's the same O'Callaghan I knew, he's a proper bastard, sir. Fought for Boney in Egypt. That's where I came across him. He led a company of free Irishmen, and what they did doesn't bear speaking of.'

'Nevertheless, Ross, do so.'

'Hate the English, sir, and worse still any good Scots Presbyterian. Jourdan took some of our lads prisoner after Acre and they fell into O'Callaghan's hands.' He paused.

'Go on.'

'Terrible cruel, sir, he is. General Jourdan had them ready for release back to our lines. Exchange for the same number of Frenchies. O'Callaghan released them all right. Minus their tongues, all of them. Cut them out. Poor buggers.' He turned to Morris. 'What's he look like, sir?'

'He's tall, though not as tall as the captain, and he has most distinctive hair. Curly. A great mane.' He smiled. 'Of course. He has a scar. You remember, James. Did you ever see him? Running across his cheek. Here.' He pointed to his own right cheek.

Ross nodded. 'That's him, sir. I'd swear it.'

'What else do you know of him, Ross?'

'Only that his family is Irish and loyal to the Stuarts. His grandfather served France in what they call the Wild Geese. The Irish brigade. He had family butchered in the rebellion. Back in ninety-eight.'

Keane nodded. 'Well, if that's the case, I can see how he might be cruel.' His own suspicions, it seemed, had been confirmed. 'Thank you, sarn't. That's most useful. Now we know our man.'

Ross left.

'Well done, Tom. You should reconsider staying with the intelligencers.'

Morris shook his head. 'I told you, James. I have no future
but with the guns.'

'Well, we must inform Grant of O'Connell's true identity at
once, and the duke of course.'

They left the tent, and as they did so heard a long drum roll.
It was close on 6 a.m. Reveille had come and gone and Keane
looked about him. The mist had come in thick through the night
and lay heavy all around Coimbra and up the road to Bussaco.
And in the haze the area of the camp where the guides had
made their bivouac, where the ordnance had their park, was
in commotion, with orders being shouted from all directions
and tents being dropped and stowed. But Keane had the tune
now. The drummers were beating 'to arms'.

'Sarn't Ross, what's this? Where is the army?'

'That's what I've been trying to say to you these past two
days, sir. The army's gone, sir. Gone up to that ridge to meet
the French.'

'This is it.' Keane turned to Morris. 'Too late to inform on
Pritchard now. Come on.'

'But where to, James? We have no fighting unit to join.'

'Maybe not, but we can still fight, can't we? I am a soldier.
What else can I do when the drums call? We'll find Craufurd.'

The Ordenanza had gone, led by Pereira and under orders
from General Beresford to join a battalion of Portuguese regulars. Von Krokenburgh too had ridden off with his men, to attach
the hussars to the 16th Light Dragoons.

So it was merely his own company, his bunch of talented
ne'er-do-wells, that Keane assembled now, as the camp disintegrated around them. He set off, on horseback, with Morris at

his side, through the mist, back the way they had only recently come. To Wellington's chosen ground at Bussaco.

It did not take them long to reach the ridge, but by the time they did the mist was clearing. They climbed from the village of Cacemas and soon found themselves on Wellington's new road running along the reverse slope of the ridge. Keane wondered where Craufurd might be and then, glimpsing a body of green-jacketed troops away to the left flank, he waved the men across behind him.

Entering the little village of Sula they saw a party of staff officers gathered around windmill and Keane trotted over, followed by the others.

Craufurd had seen him coming. 'Ah, Captain Keane, welcome. I had thought that your work was done for the moment. Should you not be off "exploring" with your friend Colonel Sanchez, over to the south?' There was a chortle from some of the officers, but Craufurd glared at them. His joke, though dry, had not been intended as a mockery.

Keane shook his head. 'No, sir. We intend to fight here, sir. Exploring can wait for a day.'

'Where will you go? You have no regiment.'

'I was rather hoping that we might be able to join you, sir.'

'I'm sorry, Keane, I have no place here for scouts. Try the cavalry. Good day to you.'

Keane nodded and turned away. Where, he wondered, could they find a position on the battlefield? How were they to play a part in what was sure to be a decisive battle? A decisive victory.

They turned and began to climb their horses steadily to the top of the ridge. The surface was covered with gorse bushes, rocks and boulders. It was perfect defensive terrain.

Keane looked east over the valley and saw nothing but haze. But as it slowly disappeared objects were beginning to come into view, like ghostly ships sailing out of a sea fog. He gasped. For there, where there had been fields and farms, were thousands upon thousands of men. The dust clouds said it all. Together with the glinting steel of fifty thousand bayonets catching the morning sun. It was clear that, while Keane had been sunk in his dark mood, the allied army had been making its way gradually up to the ridge for some days and the crest was topped in both directions by an irregular line of human figures in red, blue, green and brown.

He supposed that he might, on Craufurd's advice, join von Krokenburgh with the 16th, but Keane had no wish to fight alongside Blackwood's old regiment.

Better to be among the guerrillas.

Then, struck by sudden inspiration, he turned to Morris. 'That's it. We'll attach ourselves to Sanchez.'

'Can we do that, d'you suppose, James? I mean, have a proper scrap?'

'Not strictly speaking. It's not our role. But if you look at the men on this battlefield, it's not exactly what you might call a regular army, is it?' He was right. Wellington's army was a hodgepodge of nations and calibres of men.

The Guards – 3rd and Coldstream – were there along with some thirty battalions of British redcoats, four from the KGL, sixteen companies of greenjackets, kilted Highlanders and the Portuguese in their thousands. Wellington had cleverly mixed them in with each other so that in one division there would be a brigade of Portuguese and an element of riflemen. It was not a pretty arrangement and the sticklers among the staff had

tut-tutted at it, but in the field Keane knew it would be effective, the stronger, battle-hardened troops stiffening the resolve
of the greenshanks to stand their ground under cannon fire as
their comrades were blown to shreds beside them.

As Craufurd had told him, Sanchez and his guerrillas had
originally been positioned in the south, lest the French should
make another attack to flank the army. But, impatient for a
proper battle, he had led his cavalry up to the allied right wing,
close to the Portuguese, where the duke had been unable to
place any horse, and it was here that Keane, having ridden the
length of the allied line, finally found them.

Sanchez looked resplendent. Mounted on Massena's pale grey
mare, badges and buckles polished to a sheen, he was a parody
of a French officer and the perfect statement of the Spanish
contempt for their oppressors.

'Captain Keane, have you come to join us?'

'If we may, colonel. It's a good day for a fight. Wouldn't want
to miss out on this one.'

'I am pleased to have you. It has been a pleaseure to command
your lancers. And we shall meet the French together, just as we
promised we would.'

Scanning Keane and his men as he always did, he noticed
instantly that it was Martin and not Keane who was carrying
the much prized gun. 'Your boy has your gun, captain. How
is this?'

'It's of better use to us in his hands. As you have seen for
yourself, colonel.'

'But on the second shot he missed, captain.'

'There's a first time for everything, colonel.'

Sanchez laughed and rode across to his men, in their gloriously various uniforms, for the most part stripped from the bodies of dead Frenchmen.

Drums and bugle calls filled the valley below them now. The French were preparing to attack and the pop of musketry told him that the enemy skirmishers had engaged their own. They came up the hill out of the last strands of the mist, towards the centre of the allied line.

The French laboured up the steep hillside, knocking their feet against boulders, dropping muskets, bent double with the effort. And all the time the allied artillery, sixty guns, tore at them with ball, scything down the ranks. But still they came until at last they were at the top. The columns came to a halt and as best they could, across the rocks and gorse, sergeants moved the ranks to form line.

But most of them never competed the manoeuvre. For as they stopped, as Keane watched with pride, the muskets of two brigades were ordered to the present and opened up on them. Smoke blurred the view and then, within seconds, the blue mass had turned tail and was fleeing pell-mell back down the slope.

And as they watched, a single red-coated battalion, led by their colonel, and judging by their colours the 88th, charged with bayonets fixed, downhill into the rear of the French column, turning defeat into disaster.

It was the finest example Keane had ever seen of the use of the tactics taught to the British infantry. The classic method of seeing off an attack by the French. And he had seen enough of them in twenty years. He cheered and the men took it up. And soon the whole field around him rang with cheers as Boney's bluecoats legged it down the hill and back to their lines.

But, as any general will admit, though a victory might be yours on one part of a battlefield, the battle itself is often very far from won.

The allied guns on the far left wing had opened up now, and looking across the valley Keane saw another mass of men advancing from the French lines towards the ridge. He turned to Morris. 'Christ, they're trying another attack. That was only a diversion. Come on, let's take a look.'

They began to move to the north with the rest of the men and Sanchez's cavalry behind him. And as they did so, a figure in blue on a dark bay horse galloped past them all fast along the ridge towards the new attack, pursued by a horde of mounted red-coated officers.

Silver spoke up. 'That's Nosey, sir. Look. He's off to direct them hisself. You can bet old Massena won't do that.'

Sanchez rode up to them. 'Come on. What are you waiting for? That's your General Wellington, isn't it? Don't you want to join the action?'

He pulled away, hot in pursuit of the duke, his men pouring after him, and Keane spurred on and followed as if he was out on a field day in the old country, his horse leaping the bushes as she would any hedge or fence.

Galloping along the ridge behind the line of infantry, they skirted what remained of the action in the centre and dropped down to the new road before pushing up so that they were now level with the convent at Barca. The tall bell tower, with its gaping arches, towered above them against the morning sky. Riding along the side of the huge plantation which had once been the convent garden, they emerged to find themselves among scores of greenjackets moving steadily backwards up the forward slope, stopping to let off a round at a cloud of French skirmishers. Keane had been right; this was the main assault, for behind the skirmishers came six huge columns of blue-coated infantry. For a moment he thought that all must be lost. Martin summed up their fears. 'Where are our lads? Who's going to stop them?'

But Keane had spotted something. A single, solitary figure of a British officer was sitting on his horse up at the edge of the convent wood. Black Bob seemed to be alone, but looking more carefully they all began to see what Keane had caught sight of, for there, to Crawford's left, hundreds of men were lying down as if asleep.

Keane called to Morris, 'They're Craufurd's Light Bobs – the 52nd and the 43rd.'

The riflemen continued to retreat up the hill followed by the French, and then, just as the blue-coated columns reached the crest and threatened to swamp the allied line, Keane saw Craufurd remove his bicorne hat and wave it three times in the air. In an instant the recumbent redcoats were up and, their muskets already loaded and primed, within seconds had formed their line. The command was given and, with a precision that was nothing less than beautiful, they emptied their barrels into the face of the French.

Eighteen hundred muskets fired at close range and to Keane's eyes the French column actually seemed to shake, as if some great Titan had moved the earth and smitten it with an unseen force. He had never seen the like. Then, with their officers shouting huzzahs, the two British battalions pushed forward into the French with their bayonets and for the second time that morning, with the seventeen-inch steel shafts jabbing and stabbing death into their backs, the enemy gave way and scattered down the hill.

Keane turned to Morris. 'It is a complete victory, Tom. He's done it. Wellington's done it. He's beaten the best of them.'

He had hardly finished when Archer trotted up. 'Sir, have you seen? Down there.'

He pointed off to their right, not far from where the French were streaming down the hill. Across the valley floor, out of the village of Moura, Keane could see another column advancing towards them. Then another and another. Looking towards the ridge he saw immediately the troops waiting to receive this new attack. And they were wearing blue coats.

'Portuguese. They're bloody Portuguese.'

By some miracle the French had directed their *masse de décision*, the critical, powerful column that might decide the entire battle, against Wellington's blind spot, the only brigade on the field made up entirely of raw Portuguese levies and now outnumbered by more than two to one.

'They'll be slaughtered.'

Keane watched the horror unfold before him, slowly, almost dreamlike. He looked around for the familiar blue-coated figure. The bay mare. Surely Wellington's commanding presence was needed here now, if anywhere. As he looked, cannon fire from the Portuguese and British guns began to open up on the advancing French column.

Keane shouted over the cacophony. 'We need to get word to Wellington. The Portos need him. Before the French reach them.'

He began to turn, getting ready to ride himself to wherever the duke might be, but Morris had beaten him to it. Always the better horseman, he wheeled round and dug his spurs into his horse's flanks.

He smiled at Keane. 'Too slow, James. As ever. I'll do it. It is my turn, I think.'

Keane watched as Morris increased his pace and cantered along the ridge. He had spotted the general now, in conversation with Craufurd, and Keane noticed Wellington turn, drawn to the sound of the guns. Morris was nearing him when from the opposite side of the valley the French cannon began to reply. A ball came across and scudded past to their left, sucking in the air. Others fell among the infantry to their front and more began to land among the Portuguese as the French continued their approach march.

A rain of black roundshot fell to Keane's left, close to where the duke's party were standing, and he prayed that none would hit the general. Of course the odds were against it, but as he watched one of the cannonballs smashed into a figure on a horse who had been careering along the ridge, and with an obscene spray of blood sliced his torso in two, like a knife cutting through butter. Keane felt suddenly as if his own breath had been knocked from him and sat unsteady in the saddle. For the horseman had been Tom Morris.

He was conscious of Archer beside him. 'Sir, that was Captain Morris, wasn't it?'

Keane said nothing.

Ross was speaking. 'Captain Keane, sir, Captain Morris is dead, sir. He's dead. Shall I ride to the duke, sir. Shall I tell him, sir? The Portuguese.'

Keane collected his wits. Tried to obliterate the horror he had just witnessed. 'No, sarn't. I'll go.' He urged his horse into action and moved fast towards Wellington, coursing the ridge and in doing so riding over the bloody mess that had been Tom Morris.

'Sir. Your Grace.'

Wellington turned and saw him. 'Keane?'

'The Portuguese, sir. Over there.' Keane pulled up and, turning, pointed back the way he had come, towards where the four French columns were about to reach the top of the ridge. Wellington, instantly aware of the situation, tipped his hat to Keane and took off, followed by the cloud of staff.

Keane joined them, taking care not to look down at Morris's ruined corpse as he passed, and was almost back with his men when, looking towards the Portuguese brigade, his attention was taken by one of their officers. The man was sitting astride his horse at the rear of the second battalion, giving orders to a subordinate. But what most struck Keane about him was that the man wore a pair of round-rimmed spectacles and his face was topped by a shock of wavy orange hair.

Keane froze for a moment, then moved quickly, urging his horse past the staff officers and his own men towards the Portuguese. He could hear Wellington's voice as he passed. A loud voice, short and precise. 'Stand firm. Steady there. Stand and you will beat them. Make ready.' The commander-in-chief of the allied armies, giving the command as if he were a subaltern again.

Keane did not take his eyes from the red-haired man. Pritchard-Macnab-O'Callaghan, was talking now to another officer, and Keane recognized that man too, at precisely the same moment that Captain Aeneas Foote saw him. Keane turned back to his men. 'Silver, Garland, Heredia, sarn't Ross. To me.'

The three men came fast and Keane turned to move again, but Foote had left Pritchard and ridden to meet him.

'Keane, you're not looking for me?'

'No, it's him I want to talk to.' He indicated O'Callaghan, who nodded politely.

Ross spoke. 'Sir? Your orders?'

Keane pointed to the man who had been Pritchard. 'Get him. He's a French spy.'

Foote laughed. 'You're mad, Keane. Stark raving mad. That's Colonel Sir John Macnab. He's a British officer.'

Keane ignored him and spoke again to Ross. 'Get on, sarn't, get him.'

Ross turned and led the others off, towards O'Callaghan, at the rear of the Portuguese, but O'Callaghan had seen them too and before they reached him had pushed his horse through the two ranks of Portuguese and out beyond them towards the advancing French. The four men began to follow, but the infantry were closing ranks again and they had to struggle to get through, striking with the flats of their swords. O'Callaghan knew he had only one chance and he intended to make use of it. He stooped and then, with a quick movement, unbuttoned his tunic and pulled it off, throwing it to the ground to reveal the dark blue and gold waistcoat of a colonel of the Grenadiers of the French Imperial Guard.

Then he looked towards Keane and Foote, and with a last smile and a nod of acknowledgment turned his horse and rode hard into the French lines.

Foote stared after him. 'Well, I'm blowed. What the devil . . . ? Do you mean he was a spy?'

'A spy, Foote. Quite right, and thanks to you, he got away. You bloody fool.'

'Hang on, old man. There's no call for that.'

Keane stared at him. 'No, I suppose not. And there's probably no call for this either.'

Still holding his sword, he swung his right arm and smashed

the fist, metal hilt and all into Foote's head, knocking him from the saddle to the ground.

He looked swiftly across to where Wellington was rallying the forward battalions and saw to his relief that the duke could not have seen him.

The Portuguese appeared to have rallied and were pouring fire into the head of the French column nearest them. Another of the attack columns, though, had veered off at an angle and was bearing down upon a ragged battalion of Portuguese cacadores who, having been beaten up the hill earlier, had steadied themselves and reformed to the front of the convent complex.

Keane called to the four troopers, who had only just managed to extricate themselves from the Portuguese reserve. 'To me. All of you. Form on the convent.'

Dismounting, and not caring to see what had become of Foote, Keane drew his carbine from its holster and ran towards the entrance to the convent, a curious roofed triple archway with barley-twist pillars, decorated with pebbles and stones embedded in the masonry. The others ran to join him and together they stood in the arches, guns at the ready. The Portuguese in front of them were pulling back now in the face of the French advance.

Martin turned to him. 'Don't they ever bloody stop, sir?'

'No, Will, they don't bloody stop, unless we stop them. But we can do that, can't we?'

Martin smiled.

Keane called out, 'Form up. We'll give them a volley.' The Portuguese were on either side of them now in the arches and the cloisters. He glimpsed Pereira among them, trying to keep order. 'Lieutenant. Lieutenant Pereira.'

The lieutenant had seen him. 'Sir. We can hold them here, can't we?'

'We can and we damned well will. Form up. Two ranks. We'll give them a volley they won't forget.'

Pereira called a command in Portuguese and the blue-and-brown-coated troops shuffled into close order. Keane took command, watching all the time the French column as it began to deploy into a deadly line of muskets. 'Make ready. Present.'

Three hundred guns, muskets, carbines and an old and much loved gun from Ireland, which had seen better days but had never been better used, came up to three hundred tired shoulders.

'Fire.'

The guns spat smoke and flame and the French stopped.

'Reload. Make ready. Present.'

And through the white smoke French officers shouted commands and sergeants pushed and shoved their men into file, desperate to get a shot off before the second volley came in. But they were too late, and they knew it.

'Fire!' Keane screamed the word and again the guns gave voice. And this time it was enough. He could not see it through the smoke, but Keane knew that the French were breaking. He could hear it. A murmur of panic that grew by the second. Now was their time. 'Draw sabres. Fix bayonets.'

He heard Pereira shout the second command again, in Portuguese this time, and then the rattle and clank as just under three hundred triangular socket bayonets snapped on to muskets and the swish of metal on metal as his own men drew their long, curved swords. There was only one more command to give now. The last command of the day. He drew breath and bellowed, 'Charge.'

With a single movement they swept out from the convent and hit the French hard, steel piercing flesh and scraping on bone with a force doubled by the sheer weight of the men advancing behind it. Pushing the French down the hillside. He was aware that they were not alone. That to their right and left other battalions were doing the same, like a huge wave, released at last to dash upon the blue cliffs and crumble them to dust. And the French ran before them, tripping and tumbling as they went. And Keane's men went after them, pursuing them until they could run no more and so at last they stopped, at the foot of the great ridge. Wellington's ridge. The ridge of Bussaco.

Around him the men were catching their breath, doubled over, hands and weapons stained red with the blood of their enemies.

Archer looked up at him. 'We did it, sir. You did it.'

Keane shook his head and he looked along the valley and watched the French run.

'No, Archer, we all did it. And now all we've got to do is to do it again and again and again. Until we force those blue bastards out of this bloody country. And then we can all go home and sleep easy in our beds.'

HISTORICAL NOTE

The campaign in which James Keane plays a central role in *Keane's Challenge* focuses on the construction of the Lines of Torres Vedras and the defence of Portugal. It was to be one of Wellington's most audacious and most successful.

From June to September 1810 he played a game of cat and mouse with Massena, and nowhere was he more in need of his intelligence service than here.

The new field telegraph too came into its own and, quite apart from Wellington's tactical brilliance, it was through a combination of superior communications, engineering and intelligence that he was able to outwit the marshal and eventually bring him to battle on his own terms.

I am indebted, as before, to Julia Page's revealing and compelling publication of the letters and diaries of Major the Hon. Edward Charles Cocks (or Somers Cocks) for detailed information on the campaign and the life of an intelligence officer, although any suggestion of a resemblance of character between Cocks and Keane is not intended.

General Robert Craufurd was one of Wellington's most charis-

matic commanders of the war and was held in great affection
by his men. The son of a Scottish baronet, he had fought the
French over some thirty-one years, everywhere from India and
the Netherlands to South America, and in 1809 was given command of the nascent Light Division, which he made his own.
He had also held a staff post during the Irish rebellion of 1798.
Craufurd earned the nickname 'Black Bob', partly it is said on
account of his mood swings and partly from the heavy stubble
on his face.

Craufurd always led from the front and is the epitome of the
modern precept of the British army officer who will not allow
his men to attempt anything he himself cannot undertake.

Following the fall of Ciudad Rodrigo, Craufurd, commanding
the British rearguard, blew up Fort Concepcion and withdrew
across the border into Portugal, attempting to hold a line east
of the Côa river, protecting Almeida, with only 3,500 infantry
and 1,200 cavalry.

In the early hours of 24 July, Ney moved his force of 24,000
men against Craufurd, but the initial attack was stopped by
heavy musket and rifle fire. Undaunted, the French 3rd Hussars
attacked and devastated the left flank of Craufurd's line, wiping
out a company of the Rifles. Seeing that his line was in danger
of being rolled up, Craufurd ordered a retreat to the bridge
over the Côa. Although, in truth, Craufurd lacked the assistance
of Keane and his men, with gallant help from the Portuguese
cacadores his three British battalions, the 52nd, 43rd and 95th,
attempted to hold back the French while falling back from the
left. Seeing that the 52nd were in danger of being cut off by the
French troops occupying the knoll, Major Charles Macleod of
the 43rd and Lieutenant-Colonel Thomas Beckwith of the 95th
led a charge to retake it. Under heavy fire from French infantry,

the 43rd and 95th took the knoll and held it long enough for the 52nd to escape.

Ney then ordered the bridge to be stormed. The French moved forward but, under musket and cannon fire, failed to get further than halfway across. A second light-infantry attack pushed hard over the bridge until it was blocked by the bodies of the French killed and the wounded and the enemy were unable to advance any further. Craufurd's audacious defence had bought vital time and enabled him to rejoin the army.

Wellington's sacrifice of Ciudad and Almeida have long been sources of controversy. But as usual his logic was unshakeable.

The brilliance of his plan to retire behind defensive positions and play a waiting game was not universally acknowledged and a number of officers disagreed with him, including Craufurd, who favoured withdrawing completely. Others, including those in the prince regent's camp, demanded an immediate victory. That did not come until Bussaco, but it was this battle that made the French, including Marshal Ney, learn to forever fear Wellington's name.

His scorched-earth policy has also had its critics, but it was undeniably effective. Living off the land was, in the early years of Napoleon's wars, one of the great advantages of the French, allowing them to rely less on their supply chains and rendering them more manoeuvrable than and capable of running rings around their enemies. Wellington, however, spotted its great disadvantage and in denying the French the essentials of an army, which as his great adversary remarked 'marches on its stomach', dealt them a mortal blow.

Naturally, the ruination of the land did have an effect upon the Portuguese and there are reports of British and allied troops being attacked by farmers.

Edward Charles Cocks recounts how on 1 August 1810 two of his patrols in two villages were attacked by the peasantry and two men badly wounded. One was tied to a tree for a day, the other stoned and shot in the chest. Cocks seized inhabitants from each village and sent them back to Guarda for punishment.

Apart from the scorched earth, and the shock defeat of Bussaco, there were other notable reasons for the marshal's lack of success, for Massena, while being one of Napoleon's most brilliant generals, was also notorious for his addiction to booty and to the pleasures of the flesh. He was completely infatuated with his mistress, the young Henriette Lebreton, demanding that she be allowed to accompany him on his Peninsular campaign. She went along disguised as a cornet of dragoons, an extra ADC, in a scandalously cut, specially designed uniform. Rumour has always had it that Massena was two hours late joining his sub-commanders at the battle of Bussaco because he was otherwise occupied with her and that an ADC had to shout details of Ney's initial report through his locked bedroom door.

Massena was later to admit that his infatuation had in part led to the failure of his campaign and the end of his military career.

Henriette Lebreton (née Renique), was just eighteen and had been a ballet dancer with the Paris Opéra when she met Massena. She was the sister of one of his aides-de-camp, Captain Eugène Renique. By the time she and Massena met she was married to one of his former adjutants, Jacques-Denis-Louis Lebreton, a captain of dragoons, whom she abandoned to follow the marshal.

While Henriette appears to have been loyal to Massena and we can only assume that she was an astute career woman, her counterpart in the book is clearly less enamoured with her lover.

Her liaison with Keane and the affair of the copied orders are the stuff of invention, although clearly there were eyes and ears in the French camp, and who can say whether Henriette might not have been involved. Whatever her true nature, she remains one of the mysteries of the war, as her whereabouts after the battle of Bussaco are unknown.

As Wellington gradually began to beat the French in the Peninsula, the work of intelligence officers such as Keane became slightly more respected by the other, more traditional arms of the British army.

Grant's efforts and the work of the Corps of Guides and the exploring officers ensured that Wellington would continue to be far better informed than his enemy, giving him a vital advantage when faced by such superior numbers.

But it was by no means easy going. The work of the 'intelligencers' was arduous, challenging and always extremely dangerous.

Keane and his men will need to summon all their guile, courage and endurance when they face their toughest challenge yet, in the next book.